ALLIANCES

ALLIANCES

THE RAZIA SERIES
BOOK 2

S. USHER EVANS

Sun's Golden Ray
Publishing
Pensacola, FL

Sun's Golden Ray Publishing
Pensacola, FL
www.sgr-pub.com

For ordering information, please visit
www.sgr-pub.com/orders

THE RAZIA SERIES

Double Life
Alliances
Conviction
Fusion

Beginnings, a Razia Novella
The Razia Short Story Collection

DEDICATION

To Valerie
For always checking my eyebrows
For keeping my head above the water
And for being the sister I never had

CHAPTER ONE

The room was dark, with a single, dingy lamp hanging over a table where three men sat, each holding a hand of cards. They said little, except for the occasional grunt or movement to tap their grungy mini-computers to up their ante. The first sighed and rubbed the scruff around his chin. He reached into his pocket and pulled out a cigarette and a lighter.

"You hear that Llendo is running for re-election?" he said, cigarette dangling from his mouth.

"What else is new?" The short, squatty man and whose toes barely brushed the floor, threw a few chips into the virtual pile using his mini-computer. "The guy's a puppet. There ain't nothin' that comes out of his mouth that ain't been sent through the ringer about a million times."

The other two men chuckled and shuffled around their cards. The third man, with a long face and sallow complexion, pulled two more cards for his own hand and shuffled them together and apart again.

"But who else is there to vote for?" he asked, counting his cards and stacking them together again.

"That general? You know that buffoon Peate works for him. He ain't getting my vote until I know he's gonna play along."

The second shrugged and said, "Nobody'd vote for him in a million years."

"You and your millions." The third rolled his eyes. "Everything you say has been done a million times."

"Bah, can it," the first barked. "And hurry up and make your move."

"I'm taking my time. Don't want to get fleeced again," the third said. "You're all a bunch of crooks."

"Takes one to know one." The second man peered at his cards through a pair of thick glasses, hunched over.

"I am retired," the first man said, sitting back and taking a long drag of his cigarette. "None of that piracy crap for me anymore. Getting too dangerous for me."

"Gonna break a nail?" the second snorted. "Bad enough you got that girl. Whatsherface."

"I hear she's doing all right," the third said. "Kidnapped Jukin Peate's brother and held him for ransom last year."

"And what's she done since then?" the second said.

"More than you've done."

"I'm just saying, it's unnatural to have a woman out with the men," the first said. He paused for a moment and began to smile. "Although I can't say I hate seeing her scamper around '882."

"Shame she doesn't wear tighter pants," the second said. "I seen pictures. She wears these baggy things. I bet if she wore something that made her look like a girl, she wouldn't even have to fight nobody."

"She could come capture me any day of the week. I don't care what she looks like," the third said. "I'd lay down and let her do whatever she wanted to me."

"Care to test that theory?"

The three glanced up sharply at the sound of a distinctly female voice in the doorway.

"Hey, hey," the first man said, standing up. "We don't want no trouble. We're retired here, lady."

"You are," Razia said, stepping into the light with a smirk on her face. She turned her eyes on the third man in the room. "He isn't."

***

Razia kicked open the door and dusty light flooded the back hall. Her bounty was strapped to her trusty floating canvas, an angry scowl on his sallow face. With a proud smile, she drug him out into the open bar, already filled with pirates and other patrons with their attentions on their mini-computers. They didn't bother to look up at her, even as she paraded her hard-earned bounty by three of them.

They had ignored her when she walked into the bar as well, ignored her when she tried to wheedle information from the bartender about the back-room poker game.

"Thanks a lot," she said to him, as if he had been an integral part of her bounty capture. He grumbled something and busied himself. Razia glared at him before sulking into the dusty air of the desert planet D-882, headed towards the bounty office.

Razia, otherwise known as Lyssa Peate, was twenty-two years old, and a member of one of the four pirate crime syndicates, known as webs. While some pirates hijacked transporters and lifted antiques from rich houses, Razia's primary focus was capturing pirates in rival webs as a bounty hunter. Piracy was a game; thanks to hefty payments to the Universal Police and other political forces, a captured pirate would spend just one night in jail, returning to the streets with a zeroed out bounty. As a bounty hunter, Razia's bounty was primarily funded by other pirates who wished to see her off the streets—a sign of respect.

But eight months after gaining her full-fledged membership in Dissident's web, she was still considered something of a joke and her bounty hadn't moved a single credit. To be honest, the more people knew her name, the worse it had become.

But at the end of the day, she was still bounty hunting the universe's most wanted pirates, so she couldn't complain too much.

She picked her conquests strategically, only hunting the trickiest and most elusive pirates, ones that took more time and effort than other bounty hunters were willing to put in. She felt it made her stand out from the rest of the bounty hunters and pirates, and hoped it would draw more attention to her talents instead of her gender.

Her recent capture was no different. Guido Tedesco stole some very expensive material and suddenly found himself the fifteenth most wanted person in the universe. Once he realized his mistake, he went into hiding and hadn't been seen for a few weeks, waiting for his bounty to drop down to a reasonable number.

Well, now he wasn't even on the most wanted list, she mused as she walked out of the bounty office about an hour later. Tedesco had netted a cool thirteen million credits to her Razia bank account, now at a healthy size. It was a far cry from when she was struggling to make ends meet, dashing across the universe to excavate planets as a Deep Space Exploration scientist and then hunt the universe's least wanted pirates on D-882. Now, things were finally settling between the two halves of her life.

Her mini-computer buzzed at her hip, and she eagerly pulled it out. It was just a marketing message. Out of habit, she checked her missed calls and other messages, just to see if she'd missed anything in the few minutes since she last looked at it.

She hoped the buzzing was a message from her little brother Vel, her former intern who had returned to school full time over a universal month ago since his new semester started. He was excited to go, as he had spent seven months following her around on bounty captures and the occasional planet excavation. He said he missed his friends, and his normal life as a student.

She wondered if he missed her, too.

To distract herself from that very annoying thought, she turned to the pirate news:

	12) Fried, Max Wanted in connection with theft of antiques from estate on R-3633. Estimated cost of stolen property: 1,000,000C
	4) Bodhi, Gunnar Wanted in connection with transporter hijacking. Estimated cost of stolen materials: 16,000,000C
	15) Teon, Sage Wanted in connection with transporter hijacking. Estimated cost of stolen materials: 1,950,000C

She rolled her eyes. Sage had changed the photo on his wanted poster. For the fifteenth time this month, it seemed. Now he was just showing off.

Like clockwork, her mini-computer lit up with Teon's face. He was a year or so older than she, with shaggy blond hair and lively green eyes. With an annoyed sigh, she answered the call.

"You got him, right?" he asked.

"Yep," she nodded. "Just turned him in."

"That's good, because I was just calling to tell you that I—"

"Yeah, yeah, I saw it," Razia said with a smirk. "Still even."

They'd been playing this game for weeks. Not even an hour after she'd dropped Vel off at the Academy, Sage had called and goaded her into this silly competition: could he hijack a ship faster than she could catch a pirate named Costa Enoch. Of course, Razia found her bounty first, but the next week, Sage bet her that he could hijack another ship before she found another bounty, and thus ensued almost six straight universal weeks of friendly competition. She wasn't really sure why she still engaged with him, but it was nice to have someone to talk to— even if it was Sage.

"Have you registered to vote yet?" Sage asked, leaning back. "Fulfill your civic duty?"

"I believe my mother usually votes for me," Razia said. "Not as if there's much to vote for in this election."

"Great Creator in Leveman's Vortex, you're such a pessimist," he laughed.

"What?" she said, lazily strolling down the street talking to him on her mini-computer. "Nobody cares about politics."

"Hey now, some of us do," he interrupted. "I happen to be a registered member of the Conservative party."

"Conservative party?" She snorted. "What kind of...you...conservative?"

"I happen to agree with most of what they stand for," he scoffed. "I only suppose *you're* a liberal."

She rolled her eyes. "You don't know the first thing about politics."

"I don't understand how you can *possibly* want to re-elect President

Llendo," he muttered.

"Yeah, he's a moron who still has his assistants tie his shoes," she retorted, "but have you heard of some of the things that General State wants to do with the Universal Council?"

"General State wants to give the president's office more power to get more things done, and he wants to crack down on those who perpetrate violent crimes."

"Yeah, and Jukin works for him, so you know he's going to give him the go-ahead to round up all the pirates."

"State presided over Jukin's disciplinary hearing," Sage reminded her. Not as if she needed reminding of that terrible episode. "He knows piracy isn't that big of a deal. There are more important things to throw people in jail for."

"We don't need any more idiots like Jukin running around," Razia mumbled, glancing up at the ivory tower of the Universal Police headquarters on D-882. It was glinting rather pretentiously in the early morning sun, as if daring the desert planet to sully the pristine surface.

"So how's your other brother doing?"

"I dunno," Razia said, her eyes still on the large tower.

"Aww," Sage cooed annoyingly. "Do you miss your little buddy?"

"Shut up," Razia snapped, reminded, yet again, that her "little buddy" hadn't called nor messaged in over a week. Maybe he didn't miss her the way she was definitely *not* missing him.

"What's wrong?"

"Nothing."

"It's no use lying to me," Sage pressed. "I can tell when something is—"

She abruptly ended the call, pleased with the silence instead of Sage's incessant condescension. She paused, looking around the empty streets covered in the familiar orange tint from the dusty, desert planet. She supposed she could start hunting another bounty, since she was here, and maybe grab another couple thousand credits. But the idea seemed unappealing to her at the moment.

Her eyes swept up to the U-POL tower again, and her thoughts drifted to her eldest brother. She wondered if he was up there in his ivory tower, already hard at work in a futile attempt to arrest every last pirate in the city below him.

It probably drove him insane.

She stuffed her hands in her pockets and began walking to the nearest shuttle station, her mind shifting to a faraway planet that she thought she might excavate. She had to sell a minimum of three a quarter anyway, so she felt it was probably time to don her lab coat and glasses.

And it had nothing to do with wanting to see Vel again.

***

A few days later, Dr. Lyssa Peate walked through the sterile hallways of the Planetary and System Science Academy. Her hair was pulled back into her signature bun, and her black, thick-rimmed glasses were perched on her nose. Her lab coat billowed behind her, seemingly out of place in the hallway filled with students ranging from tiny pre-teens slouching under the weight of their books to burly eighteen- and nineteen-year-olds, many of whom eyed the young kids with mischievous smiles.

Lyssa had spent some part of ages eleven through eighteen here, when Tauron, her pirate mentor, forced her to attend lessons. For as much as she hated it here at the time, she felt a twinge of nostalgia at the hall of classrooms. She paused by one room, spying a rather obnoxious professor who taught a class in ethics. He'd never let her skip, no matter how much she protested that "certain famous scientists" needed her, which was her regular excuse to get out of attending boring classes. He didn't seem to recognize her, but it wasn't as if she wanted to talk to him anyway. She recalled a rather lengthy discussion on the ethics of using Leveman's Vortex as a dumping ground for unwanted space junk and was in no mood to continue it some six years later.

She continued walking down the hallway, turned a corner and spied a large screen on the wall displaying announcements for clubs, reselling text books, and advertising study groups. Her mind wandered to the last time she'd been in a hall like this, when the announcements abruptly stopped, displaying a newscaster.

"Pirate Tauron Ball was captured today by Captain Jukin Peate's Special Forces in a surprise move. We are hearing that the execution is

imminent. Now going to the live feed on D-882..."

A line of men stood on a platform, a corresponding noose behind them. She recognized the form of every man: Wade Baarda, who showed her how to throw a punch and took pleasure in showing her how terrible she was at it. Oskari Attenburg, who taught her to code applications and helped her rebuild her father's instruments. Stephanus Boveri, who complained about her laundry and cooking skills, but beat the crap out of a barfly who dared make a sexist comment about her. Elias Bohmer, Fredric Tivoli, Sigsteinn Aita— new hires on the crew, who had taken to picking on her like she was their annoying little sister.

And Tauron Ball—the man who took her in when no one else wanted her, who gave her a home when she had no where else to go. The man who had promised her that when she finished her last class, he would call Dissident and get her into the pirate web, so she could be the kind of bounty hunter that he'd always made her feel she could be. The only person who believed in her. The only person who ever made her feel she was worth something.

"And now they've placed the hood on the first pirate now."

"Oy, move it!"

Someone roughly bumped into her, snapping her from her memory. The short blonde hair would have been enough to recognize his lineage, but the sneering scowl definitively placed him as one of her twenty-four Peate siblings.

"Hey whatever-your-name-is," she said, feeling no shame that she had no idea what his name was. "Where's Vel?"

"I don't know," he said, his voice dripping with sarcasm. "Now gerroff!"

"What's the magic word?" Lyssa smiled, and, unable to resist digging the knife in a little deeper, added, "I know your nanny taught you some manners."

"Yeah, it's just a shame that you never learned how to be a lady," her brother snarled back, ripping his arm out of her hand. Lyssa let him walk away, as a lady was never something she aspired to be in the first place.

She headed down to the dormitories, found in the very lowest levels of the Academy space station. They always reminded Lyssa of a prison, long rows of barren doors leading to boxed rooms of the same size and shape, holding two DSE candidates. Luckily for Lyssa, students were housed together based on year, and each door held a placard with the names of the occupants. It took her some time to find the right level, but finally she stood in front of the door labeled *V. Peate.*

She knocked on the door and waited, amused at her own excitement to see him again. He'd really grown on her, it would seem (not that she'd ever admit that to him).

When he didn't answer, she knocked harder and waited, wondering if he was asleep. When he didn't answer a second time, she decided he wasn't in. Never one to be deterred by locked doors, she pulled a universal key out of her pocket and jammed it into the door. As a bounty hunter, she rarely needed to break into anything, but having some pirate skills was useful. The key molded itself into the lock, and she twisted and turned it until it softly clicked open.

The room was empty, as she expected. One side of the room was covered in posters of rock groups and naked women, and the other was devoid of personality. A bunk bed was pushed against the far wall, both beds a mess, but the upper bunk had the familiar Peate-provided bedding that she had been sent to the Academy with; one of the *only* things she'd been sent with.

She sauntered over to the bunk beds, climbed the metal ladder, and lay down on Vel's hard mattress. He'd tried to make it more palatable with blankets and padding, but it was still hard as a rock. Lyssa had heard once that the Academy provided the most uncomfortable beds to DSE candidates to prepare them for a life of sleeping on the ground on uninhabited planets. After deciding that the ground was softer, she dismissed that notion.

The door began to jiggle and then swung open. Vel walked into the room, hair combed and neat, his Academy uniform immaculate. She hadn't seen him in a few weeks and couldn't believe how much older he looked. He had filled out from the wide-eyed innocent kid that Pymus had shoved on her last year. Now, she noticed how tired he seemed accentuated by the purple bags under his smart silver-framed glasses.

"You look like death," Lyssa announced.

Vel screamed and jumped three feet, his bag falling to the ground.

"God in Leveman's Vortex, Lyss!" he panted, placing his hand to his heart. "You scared me!"

"I'm sorry," she said unapologetically, swinging her legs off the side of the bed.

"What are you doing here?"

"What do you mean 'what am I doing here?' I haven't heard from you in ages!" Lyssa slid off the bed. "Why don't you come hang out with me this weekend?"

"Man, Lyss, I'd love to but I…I can't." He looked genuinely sorry.

She tried not to look as hurt as she was. "Why not?"

"I've been pulling all-nighters all week," Vel said. "Lots of homework, reading, lab reports. I wanted to catch up on sleep, too—"

"You mean you wanna *sleep* instead of bounty hunt?" she asked, as if the concept was anathema to her.

"I know you came all the way out here to get me, but…I really…I can't…" He trailed off hopelessly.

"No, it's fine," she said hollowly. "I mean…I had a planet I was selling anyways…just thought maybe…"

She trailed off and tried to look as pitiful as she could. It seemed to work; after a moment, Vel sighed loudly.

"Fine," he acquiesced. "I'm starving. I was going to the cafeteria anyways. Want to join me?"

"Is that all I'm going to get out of you?" Lyssa scowled. "Dinner?"

"Take it or leave it."

***

The cafeteria was as crowded as always, but Lyssa didn't mind it as much as she used to. She was just happy to be back with Vel, laughing and ribbing him. She'd forgotten how much she enjoyed his company, the way they just bounced off each other's quips, how he kept pace with her train of thought. He, too, seemed to relax as he returned to the young kid she'd dropped off a few weeks ago. She could see how the strain of the term weighed on him, especially as he dug into his food even before they sat down.

"I didn't have time for lunch," he shrugged, inhaling one of two sandwiches in two bites.

"Is the new term that bad?" Lyssa asked. "They won't even let you eat lunch?"

"My term?" he said, confused for a second. "Oh yeah. Yeah it is." Without elaborating further, he took a huge bite out of his hard piece of bread.

"You know, I don't remember being that busy." Lyssa eyed him curiously. "And I was out with Tauron most of the time."

"Well, that's it, isn't it?" Vel said, a hint of seriousness in his voice. "You didn't want to be here. I do."

"Why?"

"Because my friends are here, my life is here." Vel looked around the cafeteria. "I'm happy here."

"I thought we had a good time together," Lyssa said, her face falling.

"We did!" Vel reached over to take her hand. "But…I'm not going to be a pirate, Lyss. It's not something…I mean, I'm in school to become a Deep Space Explorer…"

She frowned. It wasn't about being a pirate over being a scientist. It was about spending time with *her* versus not. But before she could tell him that, a highly displeased voice interrupted their conversation.

"I see you're back, Lyssandra."

Her second eldest brother Dorst stood above them, glaring at her with the same look of horrid disappointment and disapproval so common to the Peate family when it came to the family pariah.

"You are such a perceptive supervisor," Lyssa drawled, tossing a smirk to Vel, who did not return it.

"Please don't make me write you up again for insubordination," Dorst breathed, as if asking the Great Creator for more patience. "That will be twice in the past month. You've only been my employee for three weeks."

"Then, stop writing me up," Lyssa smiled, finally looking up at him. "What do you want?"

"Have you received any of my messages?" She snorted and he sighed audibly. "Of course not, because if you had, you would have answered them."

"Yep." Lyssa began scrolling through her mini-computer, hoping Dorst would take the hint.

"Lyssa, seriously," Vel said with a reprimanding tone. "Can you please?"

"Fine," she growled to Vel and turned to Dorst. "What?"

"You need to renew all of your licenses—your hypermile license and your first aid certification to name but a few, and you are significantly overdue on your booster vaccines," Dorst exclaimed. "I don't know how they're letting you even set *foot* on this station without putting you into quarantine!"

Lyssa shrugged. "You should figure that out. I'm obviously a danger to society."

"Lyssa," Vel warned, which she returned with an annoyed look. What in Leveman's was his problem and why was he taking Dorst's side?

"I'm scheduling you to get all of these completed this week," Dorst said. "And I want you to schedule an *hour* with me to go over your career plan. I don't know what Opal was doing with you, but obviously he failed to provide you any guidance or mentorship. You don't even have a professional development plan on record!"

"Oh, I don't know," Lyssa drawled slyly. "Pymus and I had a really good spiritual chat before he disappeared. Made me feel a lot more at peace with my life choices."

Vel rolled his eyes at her, but Dorst was unaware of their adventures in Leveman's Vortex the year before.

"Lyssa, I am serious," Dorst implored her, sitting down at the table. "I'm your supervisor, and I want you to succeed."

"I am succeeding just fine," Lyssa replied, scooting her chair farther away from him.

"Succeeding at what then?" Dorst asked. "Obviously, it's not excavating planets, because you rarely do that."

"I bring in the minimum number of planets required to stay in good standing in the Academy." Lyssa smirked, daring him to ask any more questions. "And what I do with my free time is my business."

"Vel?" Dorst said, turning to him helplessly.

"Sorry, Dorst." Vel shrugged. "That I can't budge her on."

Lyssa looked between the two of them, and her glare settled on Vel. "What in Leveman's is this? Are you two *in collusion*?"

"Well, he's the only one, it seems, who can get through to you," Dorst said. "I know we haven't had the best history together—"

"*Hah!*"

"But, I want you to know that I'm trying."

"To what?" Lyssa smiled. "Annoy me? Because I want you to know that *you* are succeeding…"

"Stop being such a brat," Vel snapped at her when Dorst gave him a pleading look.

Lyssa nearly smacked him. "Why are you on *his* side?"

"Ignore her," Vel said to Dorst's astonished face. "She's just acting out because I told her I didn't want to go with her this weekend."

Lyssa's astonishment melted into an angry scowl.

"Get *sucked*," she seethed to Vel, before turning on Dorst. "And I'm not an idiot. This little 'good supervisor' charade is nothing more than you trying to find out where Father has disappeared to."

"Lyssa, that's not it at all, I—" Dorst said, but Lyssa was already storming away from the table in true dramatic fashion.

***

Even with Lyssa's little angry tirade, Dorst had still been kind enough to put her in the line-up that day and schedule an appointment for her to meet with him *immediately* following (which she was definitely *not* going to attend). She accomplished her presentation without incident. The data was even mostly factual.

She waited in the buyers' room, a smaller holding area that was off the side of the presentation theater. Although she presented her planet excavation data in the larger theater, this small, musty-smelling room was where the buyers bid on her planet.

Chairs were haphazardly arranged in front of the small table where she was currently sitting, waiting for the buyers to trickle in and bid for her planet. The door opened and a few people walked into the room. A few she recognized, but one she didn't.

Because she was sure she would have remembered someone that handsome.

He wore a sharp suit, but even if he were wearing a potato sack, he was *gorgeous*. Dark brown hair, smoldering brown eyes, perfect skin. Lyssa found herself wondering if he smelled as good as he looked, and flushed bright red when he caught her staring at him.

She cleared her throat and did her best to actively ignore the man as she focused on the other, less attractive planet buyers.

"We'll start it at seventy-five." There were a few surprised looks from the sellers, but she didn't flinch. Once she stopped avoiding the Academy, she realized that a little effort in planet selling would let her sit on a big chunk of untraceable money while she bounty hunted. She watched some of the other, more successful scientists, and realized that the ones who made the most money charged three, sometimes four, times as much money as she did. So a few months ago, she started the biddings higher and was surprised when buyers went along with it.

"Eighty!"

"Ninety!"

"Ninety-five!"

"Ninety-six!"

"Ninety-seven!"

"Oh, come off it and just go with a full hundred grand," Lyssa muttered to herself.

"Hundred!" Her new handsome friend finally spoke up, not bothering to look up from his computer.

"Sold!" she said, ignoring the short, balding man who was about to bid more money. The bidders grumbled, their chairs scraping against the floor as they rose to their feet and filed out. Lyssa was left all alone with the handsome buyer. He leisurely stood up and walked up to her, and she wondered if he could hear how fast her heart was beating. She tried to talk herself off the ledge. He was just handsome, and there was no reason to be so stupid about it.

"Hi," Lyssa said awkwardly.

"Here." He shoved his C-card in her face. She took it, a small part of her excited that she was going to learn his name, so she could stalk him like a pirate.

Another voice quickly expressed horror that the first voice even had that thought.

She completed the planet transaction, doing her best not to stare at his smooth skin or pay attention to his musky cologne.

His company popped up on her mini-computer as she continued the transaction. She recalled it was the same one that another buyer had worked for—a smartly-dressed woman who had swindled Lyssa out of a huge planet selling deal the year before. And yet, she also offered Lyssa a job after she and Vel tag-teamed her to raise the price on a different planet a few weeks later. The memory made her smile, until she remembered she was angry at Vel.

"Are you done yet?" The handsome man was obviously impatient. Lyssa noted the shiny gold ring on his finger and quickly handed his card back.

"So what happened to the other girl?" Lyssa asked, trying to be conversational. She realized that she never bothered to learn the other woman's name.

"Who?" the man said, uninterested.

"There used to be a woman who worked for your company," Lyssa said lamely. "She was…she wore heels…and was…mean—"

"Oh, Antica," he said, watching his mini-computer. "She got promoted to vice president at a new company out on S-6642. Wedekind Planetary or something like that."

"Oh, good for her," Lyssa said, secretly grateful that she'd never have to go toe-to-toe with her again. "So—"

The man briskly walked out of the room, leaving Lyssa to berate herself for being so easily persuaded by a pretty face.

CHAPTER TWO

	17) (No last name listed), Razia
Wanted for	Engagement in piracy, bounty hunting, kidnapping, aggravated assault, resisting arrest
Reward	15,000,000C
Known Alias	None
Known Accomplices	Tauron Ball, Sage Teon
Pirate Web Affiliation	Dissident

Razia growled, turning to the search function for the latest records of pirate transactions.

	30) (No last name listed), Razia Wanted in connection with kidnapping of Vellexore Peate

	30) (No last name listed), Razia Wanted in connection with aggravated assault on U-POL officers

	30) (No last name listed), Razia Wanted for resisting arrest by U-POL Special Forces. Considered armed and dangerous

"Damn it." She refreshed her bounty profile two or three more times out of frustration. She found herself checking daily to see if maybe, just maybe, something had changed and she'd be surprised with a new bounty on her own head. Bounties did not last forever, and the five hundred dollars Tauron put up for her before he died had expired a few months ago. Pymus' fifteen million would expire in time as well, and if other pirates didn't start adding money soon, she'd be worth exactly zero credits.

At this point, she'd take just a few thousand.

Anything to show she wasn't doing all this work for nothing.

She couldn't help this feeling that she wasn't *doing* enough, that if she did more, she would see more results. Then again, she'd captured nearly twenty top pirates in the past six months. It was frustrating to watch other bounty hunters, even new ones, get more notoriety while she continued to bust her ass and remain stagnant.

She leaned forward and searched for the pirate she had just captured.

	N/A) Tedesco, Guido
Wanted for	N/A
Reward	N/A
Known Alias	None
Known Accomplices	None
Pirate Web Affiliation	Protestor

"So his bounty is null now," she muttered to herself. "Let's see if his capture has been announced."

```
SEARCH: TEDESCO, GUIDO
          15) Tedesco, Guido
          Wanted in connection with hijacking. Estimated
          cost of stolen material 25,000,000C

-END OF RESULTS-
```

She couldn't hold in a frustrated growl as she stared at the search results, or lack thereof. Guido Tedesco was a high priority, highly visible pirate and there wasn't *even an announcement* of his capture?

There wasn't an announcement when she captured Santos Journot, but that was because he was the son of one of the runners and it would be embarrassing.

There wasn't an announcement when she captured Olvire Gongago, though he was the third most wanted pirate, or when she captured Silas Brendler, who had been giving bounty hunters the slip for weeks. The excuse then was that Gongago wasn't really that important and Brendler was bound to be caught eventually.

And now there wasn't an announcement for her capture of Guido Tedesco. She wondered what the excuse was going to be this time.

With a low snarl, she smashed the numbers on the dial pad on her dashboard to call her pirate web runner.

"What do you want?" Dissident growled. He looked, if anything, even more grotesque than usual with a cigarette hanging from his yellow mouth. Their interactions had been few and far between these past few months, as she no longer had a need to call him to ask for a new bounty to capture, and he was happier pretending she didn't exist.

"Were you aware that I captured Guido Tedesco?" Razia asked, knowing the answer.

Dissident grunted.

"So why's there no announcement in the intraweb?" Razia watched his finger as it drifted closer to the end call button.

"I guess it got lost in the process." He didn't sound very sorry at all. "These things happen, you know—"

"Oh, give me a break," Razia growled. "You announce to the

Great Creator every time Sage Teon takes a *shit,* but I don't see a single record for me!"

"Maybe because Sage Teon taking a shit is more interesting than you are," Dissident snapped back.

Razia's eyes narrowed at Dissident, and she found herself itching to get her hands around his grubby little neck.

"Fine, you win," Razia said. "What do you want from me?"

In response, Dissident ended the call.

Razia fought the urge to call him back and threaten him again. It wouldn't do any good anyway. Her threat of bodily harm was only enough to allow him to keep her in the web—no more, no less. Besides, he was still getting what he wanted out of her. Top pirates in rival webs were being captured. What did it matter to him if she didn't get the credit? It's not as if any other runner would take her. Even as good as she was, she was still a woman.

She leaned back into her chair and tried to calm herself down before she did anything stupid. Vel always said that when she ran off on an angry whim, she usually regretted it. He was right, of course, but she'd never tell him that.

After all, he chose to go back to the stupid Academy instead of spending time with her.

What kind of a—

She took another deep breath. She was getting angry again.

"Calm down kiddo. With that temper, you're going to have a stroke at twenty."

She smiled as the memory of Tauron's voice came rushing back to her. She closed her eyes, remembering the way he looked. He was tall with light brown curly hair that he kept short (except for one brief period where he lost a bet and it pooled out like a frizzy ball). He had a smile that could—and did—melt any female heart that crossed his path.

When he tossed it her way, it felt like home.

The happiness quickly turned to an aching pain in her chest.

Before her mind dwelled on the inevitable conclusion to that train of thought, she opened her eyes to return to the issue at hand. Tauron had warned her repeatedly that being a woman in this business wasn't going to be easy. Most pirates were idiots, he'd said, because if they had half a brain, they'd be doing something other than piracy. Their experience with women was limited to the whores and the waitresses in the locations they frequented, not necessarily the best places to learn respect for women.

Still, she supposed she'd been carrying this optimistic notion that everything would just fall into place, that she'd be celebrated the way Tauron used to be, and afforded every opportunity and support from her runner.

Here she was, nine months in the top twenty, and she was still seen as nothing more than a chocolate-fetching joke.

A completely alone chocolate-fetching joke.

"Screw them," she said to herself. "I'm going to make them respect me whether they like it or not."

Nodding to herself supportively, she turned back to the pirate web, intent on finding someone to hunt that would be more interesting than Sage Teon's bowel movements.

As luck would have it, it didn't take Razia very long to find an interesting pirate that wouldn't be too risky to capture. Cree Hardrict, one of Contestant's top pirates, had been a regular member of the five most wanted pirates for over a year now. Between the valuable hijackings and his strategic captures of other pirates, he was on nearly everyone's hit list. But he was a good pirate, and when he was seen on D-882, he was surrounded by a hoard of Dal Jamus-sized bodyguards, an unfortunate habit picked up by most of Contestant's pirates, thanks to Royden Relleck starting the practice last year when he was the most wanted in the universe.

Still, no one had seen Hardrict on D-882 in over a month, and with no hijackings or bounty captures to speak of in the pirate intraweb, his number had slipped out of the top five. Razia had discovered four secret aliases, but in the past month, he had been using only one of them:

Kayden, Bobby		
Time of Transaction	Location	Amount
UT20015-04-06-23:98	Belvoir Supplies and Sundries A-539	30C

UT20015-04-06-15:76	McNair Diner B-725425	30C
UT20015-04-06-04:25	Belvoir Supplies and Sundries A-539	50C
UT20015-04-05-90:15	Transport Station G-279	20,0000C
UT20015-04-05-79:45	Andrews Diner B-725425	50C
UT20015-04-05-61:34	Belvoir Supplies and Sundries A-539	50C
UT20015-04-05-49:86	McNair Diner B-725425	45C
UT20015-04-05-34:01	Belvoir Supplies and Sundries A-539	40C
UT20015-04-05-19:29	Hill Cafe B-725425	50C
UT20015-04-05-05:05	Belvoir Supplies and Sundries A-539	50C

The three planets he had been frequenting were located in a system not too far from S-864. The system itself was the location for one of the few inter-system transport hubs, a central meeting place for transporters of people and materials. Pirates didn't often hijack from transport hubs. They were too populated and pirates preferred the flair of boarding a ship in space. So Razia couldn't quite figure out why Hardrict had spent the better part of the past month out here.

Besides the transport hub, he seemed to be flitting back and forth between A-539, an all-water planet owned by the military, and a newly settled planet, B-725425. The latter planet was discovered and categorized decades before, but thanks to the advent of atmosphere-producing machines, it had been re-sold in the last few years and was slowly becoming a thriving processing planet for the nearby ore-mining planet of G-279.

Although A-539 was owned by the military, she was sure it was barely used. The military was basically a jobs program in the Universal Being Union (or UBU). It was a large force that quelled any skirmishes between cultures before they got out of hand. Since there were rarely any issues, the military spent most of its time in training and exercises. The Universal Police was an arm of the military, and all branches reported to the commander of the Universal Forces. As with the U-

POL, the military cared not for pirates—as long as the leadership continued to receive their payments.

And speaking of, Razia noted with a growl, she needed to send Dissident a couple thousand credits for her monthly dues.

Turning back to Hardrict, she analyzed his transaction history again. He was going back and forth between the military planet and the processing planet, with only sporadic stops on the ore planet. As well, he was frequenting different cities at every stop, almost as if he was being hunted by someone and had to move to a new location.

Moving around was one way to avoid capture—a pretty boring way, in Razia's opinion—but in this case, it was effective. There weren't many cities on either planet from what she could tell. B-725425 had only six processing plants on the entire planet, and Hardrict didn't seem to be visiting them in any particular pattern. If she were going to capture him, she'd have to be waiting for him on the right one.

The military planet was, as expected, limited access, meaning once a ship broached the atmosphere, it would be detected and would have to provide reason and identification, or else it would probably be shot out of the sky. She had no idea how Hardrict was able to get onto that planet, but decided against attempting to enter a heavily guarded military planet. The only other stop, an infrequent re-fuel at the transport hub, was a non-starter as well. He'd filled up the day before and he wouldn't be needing to stop again anytime soon.

Her only option was to capture him on B-725425, which left her wondering how she was going to read the mind of a pirate jumping between six different cities.

She suddenly wanted to talk to Vel.

Collapsing all of her bounty hunting notes on the screen in front of her, she dialed Vel's number and waited.

No answer.

She called again, her nose scrunched in a pout.

No answer.

"Son of a—" Razia blew air out of her mouth. Maybe he was still mad at her for yelling at him, or maybe he was in the middle of class and unable to talk.

"But…I'm not going to be a pirate, Lyss. It's not something…I mean, my dream is to become a Deep Space Explorer…"

He said he was happy at the Academy, and maybe he was. It was clear that whatever ire Dorst had towards him for calling out their mother last year had dissipated. She supposed they were best friends now, two normal Peate siblings having a good time learning how to be Deep Space Explorers just like the rest of the stupid family.

How boring.

She didn't need him anyways, she told herself. She was fine without him before and she'd be fine without him now. She had Razia and she had Lyssa, the two halves of herself and that was enough for her. Who needed a third wheel anyway?

She glanced down at B-725425—the dull gray planet beneath with dots of bright lights in one of the cities as she orbited above. It was night down below, but the processing plants seemed to run non-stop.

That was one of the problems with planet excavations, she mused as she lazily slipped into her DSE mindset, always bound by the light of the local star to provide enough daylight to complete an excavation (or a long run)…

She bolted upright as a thought came to her.

She opened an application that she rarely used. It was a Deep Space Exploration application that calculated the day and night time on a planet, so a DSE could decide where to land to maximize daylight. She plugged in B-725425 and dropped markers on the different coordinates of the six processing plants. The application calculated the rotation speed of the planet, showing her what side would be facing the local star and where it would be night.

She quickly swiped backwards on the touchpad, and the planet and universal time sped backwards as well. She stopped when she reached the time when Hardrict had been on the planet last, noting the angle of the star and the angle of A-539.

She performed the same action on the planet A-539, placing a pin on the planet and noting the angles to the star and to B-725425.

With A-539 rotated to the time that he left, and B-725425 rotated to the time that he arrived, it was almost a perfect straight line between the two planets.

Which meant, based on his last transaction dated only half an hour ago, she could most likely calculate where he was going to be based on where he left.

She cackled and rubbed her hands together.

***

Razia was extremely pleased with herself as she waltzed down towards the only bar in this small town near the ore processing plant. The air was filled with rust and odor and that particular ozone smell from the atmosphere-producing machines that hummed nearby. Smells aside, nothing was going to bring her down. A few moments after she arrived on B-725425, Hardrict made a purchase in a small cafe in this city—just as she'd predicted, using both her Razia bounty hunting instincts, as well as Lyssa Peate's knowledge of planetary movement calculations.

Take *that*, Vel.

Although she couldn't really call this place a town; most of the "buildings" were giant shipping containers stacked one on top of the other. In fact—she paused to look around—there were only four or five actual buildings, including the diner.

She shrugged it off; it seemed a bit strange to her to see all of these boxes just waiting here, but she had no idea how ore processing companies worked, so perhaps it was normal. She also didn't understand why Hardrict would be transporting cargo from the military planet to this processing planet and not from the ore planet itself, but that was a mystery that she was not interested in solving. She came here for one thing: capturing Cree Hardrict.

She popped into the cafe and sat down, scanning the bar for any sign of her quarry. His purchase was very recent; from the cost, probably a sandwich. She spied such a sandwich in front of an empty chair, but no sign of Hardrict. She caught eyes with the bartender, who motioned over to the bathroom.

She tipped her head to him and flashed him a smile before sitting down at the bar and waiting. This was her favorite part, waiting for the pirate to realize that he was trapped in the bar, laughing at his futile attempt to escape, and then confidently entrapping him while tossing out a few choice lines. Perhaps she'd taunt him for his lack of goons now, or maybe she'd just make fun of Contestant, or maybe—

All of Razia's thoughts came to a screeching halt. A taller woman in a dark suit with a mane of curly light brown hair walked through the door, sat down at the bar, and ordered a drink. She pulled out a small and stylish mini-computer and began playing with it, scrolling through what was obviously the pirate intraweb.

Razia stared, open-mouthed.

Who did this woman think she was?

Razia was the only female bounty hunter!

Feeling a need to stake her claim, Razia sauntered over to the woman and folded her arms over her chest.

"And just who in Leveman's Great Vortex do you think you are?"

"None of your business," the woman replied back, without looking up.

Razia gaped at her. "I'm sorry, but I don't think you know who I am."

"Should I?" the woman said, tossing back her quite lovely hair. Up close, Razia could see the underlying strands of deep brown that clumped together in perfectly curling tendrils, the smooth skin that adorned her cheeks. Leveman's, she looked like she worked for that uppity planet-selling company!

"Yes!" Razia said, trying to not be envious of her hair and complexion. "And what makes you think that any runner would allow you into his web—"

"What are you talking about?" the woman replied. "I'm not a pirate."

"Then what are you doing here?" Razia asked, spying a pirate's face peering back up at her from the woman's mini-computer.

"Just leave me alone. You're bringing too much attention to me," she whispered, hunching over her shoulders.

"You're bringing the attention to yourself," Razia pointed out, not bothering to lower her voice whatsoever.

"And how am I doing that?" The woman rolled her eyes.

"As I said before, *I'm* the only woman pirate."

"And as I said before, I'm *not* a pirate," the woman snapped back with equal vigor.

"Yes, but you're looking at the pirate intraweb," Razia drawled, waving her arms around for effect.

"Really?" The woman put her mini-computer down and twirled around in her seat to face Razia. "I'm looking at the pirate intraweb? I couldn't tell. I thought that I was looking at the universe's ugliest sons of bitches."

"Good, then you can leave," Razia folded her arms over her chest.

"I was being sarcastic."

"I couldn't tell."

The woman made a face. "If I pay you, will you leave me alone?"

"The only way I'll leave you alone is if you leave this bar and don't set foot in any pirate bars ever again," Razia said with a menacing glare, "because you are *definitely* not going to capture the guy that I'm here to get today."

The woman was about to retort when the bathroom door opened and Cree Hardrict walked out. Satisfaction rushed over Razia and she forgot all about the horrible woman she was arguing with. She'd outsmarted another bounty and now it was time to—

"Cree Hardrict," the woman said, standing up and brandishing a badge. "I am Lizbeth Carter with the Universal Beings Union Intelligence Agency, Major Crimes Directorate, Insurance Fraud Division, Piracy Branch, and I need you to answer a few questions."

"God in Leveman's Vortex, lady," Hardrict said, rolling his eyes. "*Leave me alone!* I ain't answering any of your questions no more!"

"Hold up," Razia blinked. "First of all—government?" She snorted. The government was about as big of a joke as the U-POL. "And second of all, you can arrest Hardrict *after* I've turned him into the bounty office."

"You ain't turning me in nowhere, stupid bitch," Hardrict spat at Razia.

"I'll show you *stupid bitch*," Razia snarled, advancing towards Hardrict. Before she got two steps, a small hand had latched onto her jacket arm.

"Lady, you are interfering with government business, and if you continue to do so, I'm going to have to arrest you," the other woman said, fire in her eyes. "I suggest that you—"

"And I suggest that you let me get my bounty before I pin you to the wall with that shiny badge of yours." Razia ripped her arm out of the woman's grasp. "I can drop your ass so fast, it'll make those pretty curls of yours go straight."

"I would love to see you try," the woman taunted, getting up in Razia's face.

"I feel so wrong hitting a girl though," Razia replied, her voice low and dangerous. "Especially one that can't hit back."

"Do you think you're the first bitch I've had to put back in her place?"

"Make your move," Razia snapped, ready to to rip this woman's hair out.

She saw Cree Hardrict sneaking out the door.

"And where do you think you're going?" Razia said, not taking her eyes away from the other woman's.

With that, Hardrict sprinted out the door. Razia pushed the woman back and dashed out after him. Unlucky for the bounty and for the other woman, Razia was the better runner, and training with Vel on planets had even increased her speed. It was really only a matter of seconds before she was able to grab Hardrict by the back of the shirt and yank him to the ground.

With one good punch to the face, he was out.

"By the order of the Universal Beings Union and President Llendo, I order you to hand over that pirate!" The woman came running up behind her. Razia was shocked at how fast the woman could run in those velvet pumps.

"So who's ordering me?" Razia said, smirking and tying up her bounty on top of her trusty floating canvas. "You, the government, or the President, who, by the way, I think is a big fat idiot..."

"I...am," the woman panted, bending over.

"When you can fight me for him, I'll think about it," Razia laughed, grabbing the ropes attached to her floating canvas. "Until then, go get some water and take a breather."

Out of the corner of her eye, Razia saw the woman stand upright and then charge.

Naturally, Razia side-stepped her and the woman teetered to the ground. Razia rolled the bounty on the canvas and stood back up just as the woman was coming around to punch her. Razia rolled her eyes and caught the woman's fist, twisting it around her back.

The other woman cried out and sank to her knees, while Razia leaned in to whisper in her ear. "I've been playing with the big boys for too long for that to work. Try again when you've had a little more experience."

And with that, Razia pushed the other woman to the ground and took her bounty back to her ship.

CHAPTER THREE

"And then some government woman tried to take my bounty!" Lyssa said, lounging on her bed. She had delivered Cree Hardrict to the bounty office about an hour ago, proudly standing in line with her accomplishment as other pirates leered nearby. She even made sure to waltz by Linro Lee, one of Hardrict's fellow pirates in Contestant's web, who was also turning in a bounty. To her chagrin, he said nothing about the sixth most wanted pirate at her feet, preferring to comment on how she would be prettier if she smiled more.

That, coupled with maintenance on the notoriously defunct shuttle on D-882, which caused her to sit for over an hour in a stifling station with the universe's most awful-smelling men, put her in a foul mood indeed. By the time she finally reached her ship parked in the only docking station that would take Lyssa Peate's credits, she was tired and hungry, and wanted someone else to know it.

To her annoyance, it had taken nearly four tries for the stupid kid to answer, and even now he was *barely* paying attention to her!

"Mm-hmm," he murmured. "Nice bounty catch, then?"

Lyssa peered through her mini-computer, hoping that he could feel her anger from all the way at the Academy. He was switching back and forth between a thick textbook, and scribbling down notes every so often, oblivious to the steely gaze traveling through the universe's interconnected network of communication satellites.

"And then I grew a second head. Then Jukin and I made up."

"That's nice."

"God in Leveman's Vortex, Vel," Lyssa whined. "Pay attention to me!"

"Oh what?" Vel smiled and again, she was struck with how much older he looked with those glasses. "You don't have anyone else to talk to?"

She glared at him.

"Why don't you call Sage? He's always up for listening to you complain…"

"I would rather make up with Jukin!" Lyssa huffed, folding her arms over her chest.

"Speaking of making up with brothers, I really think you should give Dorst a chance. He's trying to make friends with you."

"Oh, right, sure. Then we'll go reminisce about how much fun he had locking me in the closet for three days when I was eight," Lyssa snapped, recalling the only vivid memory of her second oldest brother. "Sostas was pissed. *At me.*"

Vel made no notice of the memory, nor the mention of their father. "Why don't you just hear him out?" he asked, pulling off his glasses and using that calming voice she hated. "What could it hurt?"

"I'm sorry, but did you forget what happened the last time I tried to make amends with someone in the family?" Lyssa wouldn't forget it as long as she lived. Standing in the Great Hall, and the words her mother said. She tried to shake them off, but they still swum around in her brain.

"That's partially why Dorst is so keen on making things right with you. Everyone was pretty shocked at what Mother said to you. I wouldn't be surprised if Sera—"

"I'm not talking about that anymore," Lyssa snapped, unwilling to relive one of the worst memories in that house. And that was saying a lot. "And I don't think Dorst wants to make up. He just wants to spy on me like Pymus did."

"Has he asked you anything about Father?"

"...No," Lyssa responded after a few minutes. "Not in the past few weeks, I mean. But he has in the past."

"People change, Lyss. You've even changed...a little."

She rolled her eyes and knew the question that was coming next.

"So, are you ready to tell me what you saw in Leveman's Vortex?"

"I told you already," Lyssa mumbled. "Bunch of stuff. Sera at Harms' bar. Sage at the Academy. Telling me things I should know."

"Then there's that bit you won't tell me about."

She couldn't look at him, but scowled. How in Leveman's did he expect her to explain something like that? The way it felt to see herself in the river—that sad, defeated abandoned person. Knowing that she, Lyssa, had been the worst offender, the way she thought of herself, the way she let others treat her. And how she came to realize that Lyssa was her strength. The pain she felt drove her to become the person she was today. The peace in her soul, understanding that she could be Lyssa and Razia, and the two halves of her could live in harmony.

Vel wouldn't understand any of that; Lyssa didn't understand half of it herself. But saying it out loud? The thought of it made her skin crawl.

"Well?" Vel pressed.

"Well, it's none of your business!"

"Fine," Vel said, turning back to his homework.

"I shouldn't have to tell you in order for you to pay attention to me," Lyssa snapped angrily, her chest aflutter. "That's not fair!"

"No, but you should want to tell me, because I'm your brother and your friend. That's what friends do, you know. And siblings. They're honest with each other about things that are bothering them. I mean, you won't even admit to me that you're still excavating planets as an excuse to spend time with me."

"I'm not excavating planets to spend time with *you*," she sputtered.

"Oh yeah?" Vel smiled. "So then, Razia, if you're one of the most wanted pirates now, and you are definitely not wanting for money, why are you still parading around as Lyssa Peate every few weeks?"

"I'm ...this..." she stammered, struggling to find a reason that wasn't the truth. "I'm still a...I'm still doing this DSE stuff....because it's not...bounty hunting isn't enough money yet!"

"Oh?" Vel said, looking very much like he didn't believe her.

"Yes, in fact, and selling planets is good, untraceable money," Lyssa replied, glad that she had come up with a better reason than the real one. "I'd prefer to have a lot of money saved before I give it up completely."

"Shame you wasted your inheritance then."

"What?" Lyssa blinked.

"Your inheritance," Vel replied, as if it was old news. "You know, the one we all get when we..." He trailed off when he caught sight of her face.

"And how much, little brother, is this inheritance?" she whispered dangerously.

"Five?" Vel squeaked.

She relaxed a little."Five million? I mean, that's a lot, but that's not —"

"No." Vel winced. "Billion."

Her face dropped as she thought about how many years she could bounty hunt on that kind of money. Five *billion* credits was a lot of money, even in pirate terms. That would be enough money to cover gas for...and parking for...and she could buy a bigger ship—one with a *jail* and...

"Oh that stupid *bitch!*" Lyssa screamed, all of her anger directed towards the woman who gave birth to her. "*How dare she keep my money from me!*"

"Calm down, Lyss," Vel said, doing damage control. "I'm sure your money is still there.

Lyssa gave him a knowing look.

"Seriously," Vel said. "Mother doesn't control that account. It's handled by a trust at the Universal Bank."

"So why don't I have mine?"

"Well," Vel trailed off, looking a bit nervous.

"Well *what?*"

"Well, normally the boys get theirs when they graduate the Academy, but the girls...the girls get theirs when they get married."

Vel winced at the impending explosion.

"I swear to God in Leveman's Vortex," Lyssa grumbled through clenched teeth. "This stupid family and their stupid patriarchy! I get enough of this bullshit from the pirates. I don't want to—"

"Why don't you go to the bank and see where your money is," Vel offered, cutting her off before she really got going on a rant, "*before* you go kill my mother."

Lyssa gave him a dangerous look. "If I have to get married to get that money…"

"You could ask Sage." Vel grinned devilishly.

"Get sucked," she hissed at him before abruptly ending the call.

***

The headquarters for the Universal Bank was located on the third planet in the capital system, named S-864. It had taken Lyssa nearly six hours of sitting in dead standstill traffic to even get onto the planet, then another two or three hours of scouring for a parking spot. As usual, the only thing she could find was a shuttle's ride away, although this planet had a slightly more reliable transit system than D-882.

From the moment she stepped off of her ship, she was surrounded by people. Every single size, shape, color, smell—all mixed together in some weird soup of different species. Even on the train, she weaved this way and that way through the throngs of people trying to find a seat for the hour-long ride into the government district.

The city was grungy from too many people, and the white tiled wall was covered in posters for the upcoming election. Pictures of good-natured-yet-stupid Llendo and the stern General State stared down at Lyssa from almost every angle. She stuck her hands in her jacket, one hand firmly on her mini-computer, and carefully walked up the gum-covered steps, trying to avoid the trash, discarded food, and other garbage.

Once out of the transport system tunnels, she was greeted by a blue sky with puffy clouds visible between the tops of the giant metal skyscrapers that filled this city. Her stop was the Presidential Square, the last remaining vestige of the planet's original civilization. The old stone was out of place surrounded by the towering skyscrapers, but then again, the presidency almost seemed like an afterthought in the

Universal Beings Union. Thick stone walls surrounded the square between the Presidential Palace and the Universal Bank, on the other side. Next to the palace was a stone clock tower, still working after all these thousands of years but displaying a twelve-hour time span. The clock was only right once every few years per Universal time and there was often a big celebration commemorating when the two times did line up.

The image of the clock tower and the palace was the official seal of the presidency, the proud statement of the history of S-864. Lyssa spotted movement on the wall and saw two gray-uniformed soldiers walking the length. She wondered who in Leveman's would ever try to hurt the president? People only remembered the office existed during elections anyway.

She dragged her eyes away from the two guards and settled on the beautiful stone and glass building across from the presidential palace. The Universal Bank—central to the security and the stability of the Universal Beings Union—was constructed next to the palace probably in the same century, though it had seen significant upgrades in the years since first constructed, most likely paid for with a fraction of the centillion credits that passed through the bank every second. The columns—beautiful ivory pillars that supported a carved overhang— were either more recent than the original structure or they were meticulously preserved. From all the way down here, Lyssa couldn't make out what the overhang inscription said, but it was probably something about money.

She began climbing the twenty or so steps to reach the top level and couldn't help but notice there were two or three doors at ground level, each guarded by a man with much bigger guns than the military's. Lyssa mused that at one point the basement of the Universal Bank may have held a veritable mountain of gold and silver, which used to be the guiding currency before everything became electronic. Now, she supposed those rooms were filled with computer servers and databases, although probably just as heavily fortified. Every transaction that occurred in the entire Universal Beings Union was routed through this building. If there were even the slightest doubt about the Universal Bank's integrity, it could upend the entire system of government.

She pushed open the impeccable glass doors and entered a room that was highly air conditioned and almost deathly quiet. Her shoes tapped against the beautiful tile mosaic floor as her eyes swept the room nervously. She looked up to see a giant chandelier covered in gold and shimmering like diamonds.

Well, they had to have a place to put all of that unused gold and jewels.

Tellers lined the wall, but there didn't seem to be any customers to serve. Lyssa noted most of them seemed to be lazily watching their monitors or even their tablets, sliding a finger over the screen as if reading a book.

Lyssa chuckled, resisting the urge to roll her eyes. Her taxes at work. She strolled up to the first window along the wall, and reminded herself to be pleasant.

"Yes, can I help you?" the teller drawled, her green hair curled in a frizzy ball around her head. She lazily placed her tablet down, and Lyssa could see it was showing a television series. And from the looks of it, a scandalous one about a woman and a horse farm.

"My name is Lyssandra Peate," she said, as the teller quickly switched off the passionate love scene on the tablet. "Apparently, my family has an account with a couple trillion credits in it, and some of that is mine."

The woman was unimpressed.

"Anyway," Lyssa cleared her throat. "I think there was some mix up about my inheritance, and I'd like to clear it up."

"ID, please."

Lyssa pulled out her Lyssa Peate C-card and slid it over. She took an extra few seconds to make sure it was the right one this time. She didn't want to have another "incident."

"Your account balance is—"

"I know what's in my account," Lyssa said, getting annoyed. "But there's some other account that my family has, some inheritance. Peate is the last name. Or even Serann."

The woman began typing furiously in her computer. She glanced at Lyssa again before turning back to her computer. Then she furrowed her brow and typed some more.

When the teller went to pick up her phone, Lyssa's blood ran cold. She again checked at her Razia C-card, just to make sure that she didn't accidentally give the woman the wrong one. No, her Razia card was safe in her pocket.

"Miss Peate," said a male voice behind her.

"Doctor, actually," Lyssa said, hiding her C-card back in her pocket. He must have been a manager, as he was wearing a tie and a forced smile. Even though he had addressed her correctly, she still couldn't shake the paranoia that something bad was about to happen.

"Doctor, excuse me," he nodded. "Step into my office?"

"Is there a problem?" Lyssa asked, her eyes subconsciously panning the room for U-POL officers.

"Ah, well," he hedged. "Can you step into my office?"

Her guard up, she followed him to the end of the cavernous room, down a series of halls and offices that reminded her of the Academy. The familiarity of the hallways put her even more on alert, and she half expected Jukin and his lieutenant to jump out of a room any second. The manager stopped in front of a door and held it open for her.

"Please, Dr. Peate," he offered. As she passed, she could see a light sheen of sweat on his head. She kept an eye on the door as she sat down, trying to look at ease, but staying ready for a fight.

"Dr. Peate, first of all, let me thank you for taking the time to—"

"Save it," she snapped, on edge from his odd behavior and being trapped in this office. "Where's my money?"

"U-unfortunately," he swallowed. "I can't tell you where your money is."

She stared at him, her eyes wide. "Why?"

"The funds in question were seized as part of a U-POL investigation a few years ago." He nervously clasped his hands in front of him.

Her heartbeat quickened. Why was the U-POL digging in Lyssa Peate's inheritance?

"Is there something I did wrong?" she said, forcing her voice to sound normal.

"Oh Great Creator, no, no," the manager stammered. "I believe that there was some kind of…issue with the fidelity of the account, and the entire account was seized for investigation."

"Were they looking at any of my other transactions?" she asked, still not convinced that he was telling her the truth. If the U-POL checked even a week's worth of transactions from Lyssa Peate, they would see a bunch of transactions that placed her in pirate bars and parking garages on D-882.

If that were the case, then someone out there, someone in the Universal Police, knew that Lyssa Peate was really Razia.

She wasn't ready to give up being Lyssa Peate yet. She'd just now come to terms with being both people. She couldn't go back and give up—

"Of course not, ma'am," the manager said, mistaking her nerves for annoyance at the invasion of her privacy. "We received an official request, and we complied with providing only the time period in question—right around three years ago. We in the Universal Bank pride ourselves on protecting the privacy of our customers, even in the face of Universal Police requests."

She let out the breath she was holding, letting him ramble on about their privacy laws and policies. Her secret was still safe.

"So where did the money go?" Lyssa asked, her heart calming down long enough for her to take a breath.

"Unfortunately…I can't tell you."

"Yes, you can." Lyssa laughed. "This bank keeps sterling records of all transactions in the universe. U-POL or not, you can tell me where that money is right now."

"…I'm afraid the record and transaction histories were…expunged from our data servers."

"Ex…expunged?" Lyssa gaped at him. "How? You're not allowed to delete data! You're the Universal Bank!"

He withered under her stare. "Under extremely special circumstances, we may remove files from our electronic databases. Unfortunately, when the U-POL tell us to do something, we can't argue with them." He laughed nervously. "But…there is a paper copy of the records, or should be." He paused to look at something on his computer. "On B-583. I believe your family's entire archive is there, what with all of your cousins and second cousins!" He laughed nervously.

"Good. So go get it," Lyssa snapped.

"I'm afraid it will take ten to twelve weeks to retrieve the information," he stammered, nervously. "That is, after we receive approval. I'm afraid the case was never closed, and in order to release the files, we'll have to check with the U-POL officer who was leading the investigation"

"And who is that?"

"The captain of the U-POL Special Forces."

***

Razia normally gave the ivory tower of the U-POL office on D-882 very little notice, maybe a glare from time to time when she was angry about something. She remembered when they were constructing it. Tauron had said that the U-POL were compensating for many different things by building a white ivory tower in the middle of a pirate-infested city. General State had called it "a beacon of hope in a dark city." Then he stuck his precious Special Forces captain on the top floor and never returned again. There were at least a hundred floors, but rarely anybody came or left except for the Special Forces who performed their rounds on D-882, in their valiantly futile effort to find a pirate not affiliated with a web.

Today, however, one very irate Deep Space Exploration scientist stormed up those ivory stairs and marched her way right into the front lobby.

Even though Razia could waltz right up to Jukin and slap him in the face without consequence, this was no time to hide behind her pirate self. No, this fight was Lyssa's, and it had been a long time coming.

Of course, *of course* Jukin had stolen her money for some U-POL garbage operation. He couldn't even stand the sight of her once Sostas had chosen her to be his assistant. Jukin had already spent a couple of years at the Planetary and System Science Academy, but dropped out completely after Sostas decided to skip over him and eleven of their siblings to settle on Lyssa. Lyssa was young, but she remembered the fuss and the fights between her parents—her mother begging Sostas to change his mind or else her "baby" was going to get hurt.

In the police academy, of course.

"You were born."

The memory of last year's dinner was fresh in her mind, the way her mother had announced to everyone in the room that she didn't care if her daughter lived or died. That stupid bitch probably signed off on Jukin taking her money. She figured Lyssa would never notice, or maybe she'd just roll over and accept the fact that her money was gone.

Maybe Lyssa would have rolled over before, maybe when she thought Lyssa Peate deserved to be treated like everyone's whipping dog.

But not now, she thought as the lift continued dinging as it drew higher in the sky, Now she was ready to fight for what she deserved. Now she knew that she was worthy of *respect*.

The lift dinged on the highest level in the building, and she found herself in an ornate room with stylings similar to the Manor. There was a pair of double doors on the end of the room carved from the finest, dark wood. A middle-aged woman sat at a desk, typing musically at a keyboard. Her eyes swept to the unexpected visitor and she plastered on the nicest, most pleasant face she could.

"Can I help you?" she asked, giving Lyssa the once over.

Lyssa ignored her completely as she barreled past, willing to knock out Jukin's secretary if needed.

"Excuse me, you can't just—"

Lyssa flung open the mahogany doors, anger pulsing in her ears.

"Where in Leveman's Vortex is my inheritance?" she bellowed, her voice echoing off the marble walls.

A man wearing the U-POL uniform stood up from the beautiful conference table, and Lyssa realized she hadn't actually been in the same room with Jukin Peate since she was a little girl.

The image of him was unsettling; he was definitely of the Serann lineage, with short, combed blonde hair, much like Vel when she first met him.

But his face reminded her of a young Sostas Peate.

"What is the meaning of this?" Jukin's voice brought her back into the room, and to the reason for this unwelcome family reunion.

"You took my inheritance," Lyssa snapped. "Give it back."

"It's not your inheritance if you've been disowned," Jukin replied icily.

"I'm sorry, but it doesn't work like that," she snarled. "You *stole* from me."

"Well, why don't you go crying to Father? I'm sure he'll happily baby you."

"Baby me?" She laughed. "Baby me? Leaving me on planets for days at a time was babying me?"

He scoffed and rolled his eyes. "God in Leveman's Vortex, you are so melodramatic."

"I'm melodramatic?" she sneered. "Thirty-five years old and you're still pissed off that Sostas spared you from his *unique* brand of parenting? So pissed off that you stole five *billion* credits from me? You win the *prize* for melodrama, Jukin."

"I needed that money for an investigation," he said, his face unreadable.

"What, the pirates don't give you any money, so you just stole from me?" Lyssa smiled, her voice dropping lower. She knew she was walking on thin ice now. If she ventured too close to talking about Razia, he might recognize her.

She was surprised when a voice deep down wished he would.

"Watch your mouth, Lyssandra," Jukin seethed. She obviously struck a nerve. "Sister or no, I can and will throw you in jail."

"I would love to see you try." Lyssa smiled, her fingers itching to grab her Razia C-card. She wanted to throw it in his face, to tell him and everyone in this building that she was really Razia the bounty hunter.

It wouldn't just ruin his career, it would be the scandal of the century. Jukin Peate, famous for his unending quest to eradicate the universe from all pirates, and his own sister was one of them. The thought made her burn happily inside, knowing that she could make him feel the same way she did all those years ago, when she begged him to save her life on Tauron's ship and he *left* her.

She wanted to make him hurt as bad as she hurt when Tauron died.

She wanted to make him hurt as bad as she did right now, knowing that her own brother didn't care enough about her to recognize her.

Jukin had continued his assault while she had been lost in her own mind. "You've always been a spoiled little brat. A night in jail would do wonders for you."

"Be sure you throw me in that pirate jail. I hear they've got a great breakfast," Lyssa replied without missing a beat. She was in his face now, as much as she could be with the height difference between them. He didn't cower, continuing to snarl at her as ferociously as she was to him. She was almost daring him to recognize her, as her secret was precariously perched on the tip of her tongue.

Jukin, however, blinked first.

"Get. Out."

"Fine," Lyssa said, straightening up. "But know this: I'm going to get my money back if I have to break into the Universal Bank and steal it from your account myself."

And with that, she turned around and marched out of his office, so wrapped up in her own anger that she barely noticed Lizbeth Carter seated on the other end of the table, a perplexed look on her face.

CHAPTER FOUR

"You look awfully sneaky," Harms said, eyeing Razia curiously. "I don't like it when you look at me like that."

She had marched directly here from Jukin's office, barely remembering to stop off in a restaurant to quickly change into her black tank top and cargo pants. It wouldn't do for Harms, or any of the other pirates, to see her in a lab coat and glasses on this planet. But Harms, the pirate informant and Razia's sounding board, would be able to help her get back at her stupid older brother. Even if he didn't know he was.

"Tell me how the Universal Bank works," Razia said, leaning across the table.

"Why." It was more a statement than a question.

She shrugged. "Curious."

"Whenever you're curious, I get heart palpitations," Harms said with a hint of accusation in his voice. "What are you after?"

"I…want to know if there's a way to transfer funds from one account to another," Razia asked, barely able to contain a smile. How delicious it would be to transfer Jukin's entire life savings into her

Razia account. She didn't even care if she left a paper trail. There would be nothing he could do, no charges he could bring against her.

"Yes, of course. Just call the bank. Although there will be a record of it, so I suggest that you don't transfer into that damned secret alias you have—"

"How about a transaction, but one party doesn't know about it?" she said, swirling her orange-tinted water in her hands. "As in taking money from one account and putting it in mine..."

"So, stealing money?" Harms asked, eyebrows raised. "That doesn't sound like you."

"Let's just say, this person has it coming." Oh, and they would all know soon enough whom she was going to target.

"Warranted or not, you can't do that." Harms' voice snapped her from her reverie. "Stealing money is not included in the pirates' agreement with the Universal Bank."

Razia was ready for that answer. "So, how about if I covered my tracks? I know there's a way to completely erase transaction histories."

"Darling, darling, darling," Harms' tone was forceful. "You are toeing a very thin line. You can't tamper with bank accounts."

"Why not?"

"Because that undermines the very purpose of bounty hunting." Harms sighed. "Imagine if everyone had the ability to erase transaction histories—you'd never be able to find another pirate again."

"What if someone was doing it anyways?" Razia's face grew more serious.

"Then they'd be in a heap of trouble, and not just from pirates. The Universal Bank is the reason why we have a stable system of government. If everyone were to lose faith in the integrity of their record keeping..." Harms said, watching her. "So don't even *think* about—"

"I'm not..." Razia sighed, trailing off. She wanted him to understand—but how was she to explain that Jukin Peate stole five billion credits from her? Jukin Peate had no more quarrel with Razia than any other pirate; she'd have to tell Harms about her other life. She didn't quite trust him enough to keep that secret, not when his line of work was selling pirate information to other pirates.

"What are you thinking there, missy?" Harms smiled at her silence. "I hope you aren't going to get mad at me again."

She smiled sheepishly. It had taken her almost three weeks to work up the courage to come back to his table after their nasty fight. She sat in his booth for five silent minutes, trying to figure out the words to tell him that she was sorry, she valued his guidance, and that he was right. But, happily, Harms simply took her hand and told her that she could apologize by never ignoring his advice again.

"Come on, Raz. I thought you were done with this attention-seeking stuff, huh? You're a top pirate now, one of the best bounty hunters."

"Yeah, except I don't know if you've noticed, but there hasn't been a single announcement put out about any pirate I've captured." Razia sighed, effectively distracted from thinking about Jukin's bank account. "Dissident isn't posting them."

"Now why would he do that?" Harms asked. "You captured Cree Hardrict last week, didn't you?"

"Did you see an announcement about it?" Razia asked, hopefully.

"Well, no. Sage told me, but—"

"See?" Razia huffed. "And nobody's put any more money on me since I kidnapped V—Jukin Peate's brother."

"So? You've still got fifteen million on your bounty?" Harms smiled. "Still in the top twenty?"

"For another year or so, then it'll expire," Razia mumbled, biting her lip. "I'm just worried. I don't want to go back to being in the six hundreds again…or worse."

"You've got a whole year to plan for that, and that *doesn't* mean going out and doing something stupid," Harms said, squeezing her hand. "Aren't you going to this meeting tonight?"

Her head snapped up. "What meeting?"

"Didn't Dissident tell you?" Harms said, although he probably very well knew that Razia had no idea what he was talking about. "Some guy asked all of the runners to gather their top pirates tonight to discuss something secret."

"No, he didn't tell me," she growled, her blood beginning to boil as she let loose another rant. "I don't understand why, after all of this time, he still continues to think that I am unworthy of being included with the rest of his pirates!"

"You know I can't reason with you when you're like this," Harms said, sounding quite like he was more amused than annoyed. He tapped something into his tablet and sent a message over to her.

"What?" Razia said, looking down at her mini-computer

"That's the name and number of one of the waitresses in the bar where the meeting is to be held. She's the one who told me about it, and she's one of my best informers." He smiled. "Tell her I sent you. If she can get you in, she will."

"Really?" Razia blinked at him. "And you aren't going to tell me why it's a bad idea, or how Dissident would be pissed, or anything like that? Just giving me the name of your informant and sending me on my merry way?"

"Breaking into a secret pirate meeting is less dangerous than breaking into the Universal Bank," Harms replied simply. "Lesser of two evils."

"Are you trying to…" Razia said, her hackles raising. She stopped mid-sentence as he gave her a knowing look. After taking a deep breath, she simply smiled, thanked him, and left to find his informant.

***

Harms' informant Ina was probably once very beautiful, but years of smoke, stress, and working in a bar had aged her prematurely. That, however, was not the reason for queasy feeling in Razia's stomach as they stood in the alley behind the bar where the meeting was to take place.

Ina was waving around one of the most grotesque outfits that Razia had ever seen. The black skirt was barely a few inches long with a chiffon underskirt that puffed it out even shorter. The top wasn't much better, a black, stretchy material that seemed about four sizes too small. If Ina's outfit were any indication, Razia would barely be covered.

"If you want in, that's what you have to wear," Ina said, shoving the clothes at Razia.

Gingerly, Razia took the hanger and couldn't hide the disgusted look on her face. The outfit smelled like smoke and booze and shame.

"And you're sure nobody will recognize me?"

"Nobody will be looking at your face," she said frankly, tossing a blonde wig at Razia and walking back inside the bar.

Razia stared at the ensemble, sickness rising in her throat. She had prided herself in never, *never,* debasing herself to get information or to capture a bounty. She had never worn anything other than her tank top and baggy pants. She had never even…

But there was a *meeting.*

And it was going on *without her.*

With a final glance to the ratty blonde wig, she swallowed her pride and the contents of her stomach. She put on the clothes behind the garbage bin, and balled up her long hair and pulled the wig over it. She used the camera on her mini-computer to make sure none of her brown hair was visible under the yellow strands. When she caught sight of herself, the device nearly fell out of her hand.

Wearing the wig and the sneer of disgust from her outfit, she looked exactly like her eldest sister Sera.

Shivering, she swore to herself to never die her hair blonde.

"Are you coming?" Ina barked at her from the other side of the door. Razia adjusted her bust and pulled down her skirt as low as it would go, and then confidently walked into the kitchen.

Ina thrust a dull silver platter in her hands and commanded her to follow. "You'll be serving drinks, it's the easiest." There were women on the other side, pouring a bevy of colored drinks into differently shaped glasses. "Just fill up with whatever the barman gives you and walk around the room. When you've got an empty platter, go back and get some more."

"Sounds easy enough," Razia said to herself. Two young women walked out of a swinging door, dressed the same as Razia and holding the same sort of dull silver platter. They threw their platters on top of a window, and someone behind the counter began putting different drinks on them. Razia adjusted her skirt and queued up behind them, and, once they left, pushed her platter up where theirs had been. After hers was filled, she took it with one hand. Struggling for a few minutes, she got the hang of the balance and walked through the swinging door.

In contrast to the bright kitchen, this room was very dimly lit—

only one low light over a dirty table in the middle of the room. She couldn't resist the smile that grew on her face.

It truly was a bounty hunter's paradise.

Jeam Bullock, Eli Stenson, Flynn Sloan and a couple of Dissident's favorite pirates. Max Fried, Olvire Gongago, Jarvis Loeb—Protestor's best pirates—all seated together at another table with…

She had to hold in a gasp as she passed by the table.

The runners were *there*.

Her eyes swept back to the table where Stenson and Sloan sat and, sure enough, there was Dissident. All of five feet of him. He was hunched over the table, his yellow skin sagging off his bones. He looked most unhappy to be there, too.

She spotted two older men at other tables that she didn't recognize, and assumed they were Protestor and Contestant. Although, she did remember Insurgent, and she averted her gaze when she passed by his table. He had been the mastermind behind a pirate shakedown the year before, his son VJ undercover as Santos Journot. Razia had been the only one to see through the ruse, and turn him in. Though she didn't see the younger man; but he'd been awful quiet since she'd exposed his little charade last year.

Instead, she saw two other men she didn't recognize. They were also dressed in nice suits, unlike the rest of the pirates who wore raggedy and stained shirts covered in dust from the planet. The two men were deep in conversation, ignorant of the rest of the room. Razia strained her ears to hear their conversation.

"From the lists that the runners gave us, we're only missing one or two pirates," the bald one said. Razia could make him out the easiest, because the scant light in the room reflected off of his hairless head.

"One or two pirates I can deal with," said the other, a shorter man with black hair. "We'll give them a few more minutes, but after that, I want you to tell Sam to close off the doors."

"Is the ship ready?" the bald one asked with a furtive glance around the room. "I don't want any delay after the meeting is over."

"Everything is set," the dark haired man replied quietly. "The kitchen is adequately monitored, and we've placed several guards at the door."

Razia slowly walked away, before they noticed that she was listening to them. If the front doors were barricaded and the kitchen was guarded heavily, she would have problems sneaking out if she were caught.

Dropping the rest of her drinks in the trash can, she walked back into the kitchen, on the hunt for an exit strategy, should she need one.

Her eyes fell on the bar, the tables in the center, the heavy iron pans hung up on the wall. She walked over to the door she had come in and cracked it open.

"Where're you goin'?" a gruff voice said behind her.

"Nowhere!" Razia squeaked, jumping around to see a giant guard-like man peering down at her. "Smoke break?"

"Ain't nobody's leaving until this meeting's over," he said, roughly pushing Razia out of the way and walking out the door, presumably to stand guard in alley.

"Shit," Razia cursed. She spotted a half-open door on the other side of the kitchen. As she approached it, hoping it would lead to another exit, she heard a hurried whisper.

"Both Harman and Alfr Jos are here."

Razia blinked and leaned in closer. She recognized that voice.

"The meeting is set to start any moment now, more details—"

Razia swung open the door and put her hands on her hips. Hunched in the small food cupboard wearing a dark brown wig was Lizbeth Carter, the annoying government worker, talking into her mini-computer to record her words.

"I was...looking for some more glasses," she fumbled, getting to her feet and putting her mini-computer behind her back.

"Never mind that. I thought I told you to stay away from pirate activities?" Razia raised her eyebrow.

"What are you doing here?" Lizbeth said, recognizing her.

"I asked you first."

"You asked a rhetorical question," she snapped back. "Shut the door if you're going to stand there."

"Why should I?"

"I would leave if I were you," Lizbeth said, slipping her mini-computer between her breasts. "This isn't something that a bounty hunter needs to get involved in."

"And some government investigator who can barely hold her own in a fight should?" Razia asked, looking her up and down.

Both jumped when a voice spoke behind them.

"The meeting is starting, if you'd like to listen in," Ina said quietly, leaving the door open behind her.

***

Razia slipped quietly back into the dark room, blending in with the wall as much as possible. Lizbeth had come out before her, carrying drinks, but there was no movement in the room, so she assumed that Lizbeth had planted herself against the wall much as she had. The low light in the room had become, if at all possible, even lower, hanging over the giant circular table in the room. The hands and faces of some of the more important pirates and the runners were visible, as were the two gentlemen that Razia had heard talking earlier.

"Well now, we're all comfortable? We've all got a drink to keep us company?" The bald one was speaking loud enough to be heard, and yet at the same time very softly. He had stood up, so only the gray uniform was visible in the low light.

The man with the black hair cleared his throat and unfolded his hands. "Gentlemen, before we begin, I must stress the severity of our original request that this meeting remain known only to those of us in this room." Razia realized with a jolt that more giant, Dal-Jamus-sized guards were stationed all around the dark bar. "Our association with a high ranking government official necessitates this secrecy, and we do hope you'll honor it."

She shifted uncomfortably.

"As most of you know, there is an election coming up—"

"You don't say!" someone piped up from the side of the room.

"An election?" That was Costa Enoch, Razia had captured him not even a month ago.

"No kidding?" Jeam Bullock guffawed from the table where Dissident sat.

"Quiet!" Dissident snapped, smacking Bullock from across the table. Razia couldn't help but smile. Dissident did know how to keep his pirates in line.

"And we're here to inform you that the current administration is about to change, and we would like your assistance."

"We can't just go cutting checks to political parties." Insurgent leaned back in his chair. "We have to know there's something in it for us."

"What's your stance on that numbskull Peate?" Protestor asked. "The current administration has been very easy to work with. We might not give you our vote if we feel you don't have our best interests at heart."

"Gentlemen, gentlemen," the bald man interrupted. "Let's put politics aside for a moment. This is more about money. We have a very lucrative deal that we'd like to cut you in on."

This had the entire room, including Razia, quiet.

"You see, we know how…adept you gentlemen are at rerouting materials while in transit," the bald one said. "We simply ask that you, perhaps, focus a little more on government transports."

"Why?" Waslow Needler asked from the corner.

"The government pays very handsomely for the materials that you will be stealing," the second man said. "So when they are stolen, we can file a claim with the insurance company and be repaid for the material that remains in our possession. We will then deliver the supposedly stolen material to the government, allowing us to be paid for the material twice. Of course, we would be more than happy to provide a healthy cut to our partners."

Razia looked around. The pirates didn't seem too impressed. "You want us to steal some stuff?" That was Max Fried.

"How much we talkin' here?" asked Conboy Conrad, his boots on the table and a cigarette in his mouth.

"Depending on the shipment, you may receive upwards of fifty million per ship," the bald man said.

A murmur arose from the group as they seemed to be on-board. No one was going to say no to fifty million free credits.

"We've provided your runners with a list of ships and their expected routes," the black haired man said. "I trust the four runners will divvy it up fairly."

Dissident and Contestant glared at each other, but nodded.

Somehow Razia knew that Insurgent and Protestor weren't going to get even half of the ships.

"Oh, and one last thing, of course." The bald man laughed. "We welcome your support to General State's campaign."

Razia chuckled to herself. They wouldn't have to twist Sage's arm to give his support—

Just as the thought crossed her mind, a cold hand snaked its way up her thigh. She turned to hit the Leveman's out of whoever it was, but her fist was caught in mid-punch.

"You know," Sage whispered into her ear, "I wondered if I was going to see you."

She should have known. One hand was caught in his grip and the other squeezed his wrist down at her thigh. She whispered into his ear, "I will *end* you."

Sage released her and leaned back against the wall and chuckled happily. "You aren't supposed to be here."

"You wouldn't *dare*."

"You're right. I don't want to imagine what you'd do to me later...or maybe I do." He winked at her. "Where'd you find this little get up?"

"Get sucked."

"You got an exit plan?"

"Of course I do," she lied.

"Might want to use it," he whispered, looking forward.

Razia turned her eyes back to the center of the room and saw that the two men were conferring with one of the waitresses.

They stood up slowly, looking around the room. "It appears as though we have an uninvited guest," the bald man said, motioning to the guards around the room. Razia dipped her head down and shuffled towards the door, when the low-hanging light over the table shone to the side of the room, to where Lizbeth was standing.

Blessing this golden opportunity, Razia began scooting towards the door, although half of her wanted to stick around and watch Lizbeth try and dig herself out of this one. So far, she was stuttering and looking about wildly. Razia snorted; Lizbeth didn't have an exit strategy either.

Razia put her hand on the door, but it swung open towards her. She stepped back to get out of the way, but she found herself face-to-face with a belt buckle. She lifted her head up and met the eyes of a giant guard glaring down at her. Then, she felt the warm light shine on her.

"And what do we have here?" the bald one said. "Two?"

Her wig took that as a cue to slide off of her tilted head and her dark brown hair fell down her back.

For a brief, glorious moment, she hoped perhaps no one would recognize her.

Then, the catcalls began.

"Well, well, well, look who it is…"

"Nice legs there, cutie..."

"Why weren't you wearing that when you captured me last month? I would have gone willingly."

Well, better to face it than slink away in shame. She turned around and folded her arms over her chest. The guard who was blocking her way out pushed her forward so that she was farther away from the door.

"All right, you caught me," she said, fixing her glare around the room at the leering pirates. "I just thought it was odd that you invited Loeb over there who, by the way, *I* turned in last month. Yet I,"—she pointed to herself—"have been in the top twenty for the past six months and I have to sneak in. Funny how that works, isn't it?"

"You mean...this is a pirate?" The bald man asked Dissident who shifted, a bad taste in his mouth.

"In a manner of speaking," he grumbled. "She wasn't invited either way, so feel free to kick her out."

"Thanks," Razia said sarcastically.

"You heard the runner," the black-haired man said to his giant guards stationed around the room.

"Oh come on," Razia whined. "I'm in a mini-skirt."

That got the attention of all of the men in the room, who leaned forward to catch a glimpse.

"*You can all get sucked into Leveman's Vortex!*" Razia hissed, looking around at the wall of beefy men who were slowly closing in on her.

They weren't too smart, probably, based on their size. She could slip by them without much trouble. But with so many pirates in the room, all of whom were hostile to her, even if she were to fend off these giants, there was no telling if she'd be able to get to the door without five or six pirates grabbing her. She needed a distraction, she needed something to…

Out of the corner of her eye, she saw Sage motioning to her, his hand on the light switch. Her eyes swept to the kitchen door, taking a mental picture of the obstacles between her and her exit, and then she nodded to him.

The room was bathed in darkness and she slipped between two of the men, who grunted loudly as they ran into each other, trying to grab her. She swung open the door to the kitchen, the bright light blinding the inhabitants of the dark room before it shut behind her.

She found Lizbeth, struggling in the vice grip of the kitchen guard.

"Seriously, I wasn't trying to leave," Lizbeth whimpered, tugging at his grip.

"Oi, idiot," Razia said, hoisting one of the cast iron skillets from the wall and swinging it around with all her might. It hit the man's arm with a loud bang and he released Lizbeth. Howling, he gripped at his arm as Lizbeth gave her a thankful look.

The door on the other side of the kitchen burst open and three more guards spilled out, snarling at them.

"*Get them!*"

"Exit?" Lizbeth offered to the open door.

"By all means."

CHAPTER FIVE

Razia and Lizbeth burst out into the dark street, running as fast as their legs would carry them, and not stopping until they were a good ten blocks away. With no sign of anyone following them, Lizbeth fell to her knees, wheezing and gasping for air, while Razia simply watched her superiorly with an eye on direction they'd come from. She was more winded from the panic of nearly being massacred, but wasn't going to let Lizbeth know that.

"Are you gonna survive?" Razia asked, as sarcastically as she could muster. "Shall I call you a doctor?"

"Get sucked," Lizbeth spat.

"You're welcome, by the way, for saving your ass back there." Razia sniffed, folding her arms across her chest.

"Yeah, thanks. I only wish my knight in shining armor wasn't such a complete bitch about saving me." Lizbeth paused, giving Razia a serious look. "But thank you. I wasn't quite sure how I was going to get out of that one."

"Let that be a lesson to you, then," Razia said, peering around the corner for anyone who might be trailing them. "Stay out of pirate business."

"Can't," Lizbeth said with a pleased smile. "I have a job to do."

Razia couldn't believe it. "What in Leveman's Vortex does the government want with pirates? That's the U-POL's job."

"It became our business when we got wind of possible kickbacks and insurance fraud. That's my area. You'd be surprised how many people fake pirate hijackings."

"Well, you heard them," Razia said, looking back towards the direction of the bar. "They want pirates to hijack government transports so they can resell them. Go tell your bosses and stop meddling in pirate business."

"There's more to it than that," Lizbeth replied. "Contestant's pirates have been hitting government ships for months. Why now include all the other pirates? Besides, did you not notice that there were pirates from every runner *except* Contestant?"

Razia was about to answer with a sassy remark, but instead realized Lizbeth was telling the truth. She hadn't seen Relleck, or Cree Hardrict, or any of Contestant's favorite pirates. And if this woman was right, and his pirates had been hijacking government ships for months…

"Contestant would never willingly share that kind of lucrative deal," Razia finished aloud. "Fifty million per ship?"

"Which means that there's something more going on than just what they talked about tonight." Lizbeth paused as an oddly curious, yet smug expression formed on her face. "I looked you up, you know. Razia 'no name listed.' Hear you're a pretty good bounty hunter."

"I'm a *damned* good bounty hunter."

"Indeed. From what I've heard, you're a master at tracking pirates through their money transactions." Lizbeth said, a smug smile on her face that Razia did *not* think boded well for her.

"Yeah, so?" Lizbeth wiggled her eyebrows, and Razia began shaking her head, laughing at the ridiculousness of the idea. "No way. I'm not helping you."

"Oh, come on. I saw the way your brain was working there with Contestant! I need someone who knows all about these pirates to help me figure out when something isn't right!"

"No way. I'm too busy."

"Doing what? Excavating planets?" Lizbeth said with a sly smile.

"No, I don't need to excavate…." Razia's face melted into a shocked scowl as the words sank in.

Not again.

"Son of a bitch," she swore. "How did you find out?"

"It was pretty hard to miss you storming into your older brother's office the other day," Lizbeth noted, casually looking at her nails. "At first I thought, wow, what balls on this woman to march into the offices of the man who is trying to kill her and her friends. Then he called you 'Lyssandra' and I looked you up and…well…" Lizbeth motioned to Razia's outfit. "It's a pretty shitty disguise. You aren't even bothering with a wig? Though blonde really doesn't suit you."

Razia said nothing, but glared icy daggers at the offending woman.

"So, I take it you're going to help me now?" Lizbeth smiled. "We'll have to go on your ship, of course. I don't have one."

Razia grunted as she stormed down the street.

"I've got to stop by my hotel too!" Lizbeth called after her. "Don't worry. I can find you!"

Razia responded with a middle finger.

***

"Nice ship," Lizbeth said, standing in the lower level of Razia's ship with a set of matching luggage that appeared brand new. She had changed from her maid outfit to a smart business suit, her curly hair perfect with nary a wisp out of place. She had reapplied some makeup, it appeared, as her lips shone with gloss.

"Took you long enough," Razia muttered, annoyed at the thought of this woman making her wait around for hours just so she could look pretty or something.

"Sorry, but you did park way out in the middle of nowhere," Lizbeth said, rolling her luggage onto the ship. "Where should I put these?"

With considerable effort, Razia stuck her thumb towards the back, where her bedroom door lay open.

"Where am I going to sleep?" Lizbeth asked, standing in the doorway.

"Why do you think you're going to sleep here?"

"Because I don't think you want to let your mother know you're really a pirate. Might break her heart."

"If I'm lucky," Razia grumbled. "Just put your crap in there and meet me upstairs. I doubt this is going to take very long."

"Sure of yourself, are you?" Lizbeth emerged from the bedroom rolling an impeccable black leather bag.

"Yeah, pretty damn sure," Razia said, hoisting herself up the ladder.

"Um," Lizbeth said, looking up. "How am I supposed to get my bag up there?"

"Figure it out," Razia snapped, marching over to her big squishy chair on her bridge. She wasn't going to be helpful; she was being blackmailed after all. She heard sounds of struggle, emphasized for effect, and then finally the sound of the bag rolling on her metal floors.

Unfortunately, the woman appeared no less the same perfectly put together when she sat down in the jump seat Vel normally occupied and crossed her ankles daintily.

"Well, you're here," Razia barked. "What do you want from me?"

"As I said, these hijackings of government ships, they've been going on for months. Mostly with Contestant's pirates, which was why I was hunting Cree Hardrict before you…" She pursed her lips, giving Razia a look.

"You can still go question him," Razia said with a smirk. "You know he only spent a night in jail. I'm sure he's out there somewhere."

"Yes, well I doubt he's still doing the same thing he was doing before, thanks to you," Lizbeth snapped. "Which means that all the work that I put into tracking his movements is now moot."

"Sorry," Razia said, not sounding sorry at all.

"Which means that you get to help me find someone else," Lizbeth said. "I was able to track Cree Hardrict and the other pirates until he hijacked the cargo and then…" She sighed, pulling out a stack of papers and handing them to Razia. "Then I lose track."

"Of course you do," Razia said, scanning the documents quickly.

"This is going to go a lot easier if you cut out the sass," Lizbeth replied sweetly. "I need you to help me locate where the cargo is going, or who it's being sold to. After I get that...then... I have concrete proof of the insurance fraud and can begin making arrests."

"Fine, who are you looking for next?"

"Arpad Bernal?"

"It's your lucky day." Razia smirked and opened her hit list.

Hit List	
Max Fried	Lino Abbracciabeni, Andrej Connolly, Kam Kaur, Jarl Daley
Arpad Bernal	Sacha Amjad, Justus Jansens, Michael Aleshite, Pinchas Akerman
Jarvis Loeb	Eadmund Sowards, Sulaiman Matthewson, Izidor Bencivenni
Royden Relleck	Paul Robert, Zachery Passerini, Thomas Strand, Dimitri MacIntyre

"Impressive list," Lizbeth noted.

Razia grunted, displaying the four aliases for Arpad Bernal, and the transaction history from the Universal Bank.

Amjad, Sacha		
Time of Transaction	Location	Amount
UT20015-04-06-56:92	Bisette Bistro D-882	50C
UT20015-04-04-46:75	Madam Guerri D-882	50C
UT20015-04-04-46:70	Madam Guerri D-882	50C

Jansens, Justus		
Time of Transaction	Location	Amount
UT20015-04-06-23:98	Driscoll Eatery D-882	50C
UT20015-04-05-54:84	Nol Stroud D-882	75C
UT20015-04-05-15:64	Valencia Diner D-882	50C

Aleshite, Michael		
Time of Transaction	Location	Amount
UT20015-04-06-99:13	Lefteris Bar D-882	25C
UT20015-04-06-50:54	Bisette Bistro D-882	50C
UT20015-04-04-46:65	Madam Guerri D-882	50C

Akerman, Pinchas		
Time of Transaction	Location	Amount

UT20015-04-05-23:98	Drechsler D-882	75C
UT20015-04-04-46:82	Madam Guerri D-882	45,000C
UT20015-04-04-46:73	Madam Guerri D-882	50C

"Wait a minute," Razia said, her eyes hopping from one table to the next. "He hasn't made a purchase in over two days."

"What does that mean?"

"It means he's got a different alias?" Bernal already had six aliases —any more and it was verging on paranoia.

"You look confused."

"Bernal is a good pirate, but there's no good reason why he'd create a new alias all of a sudden."

"Could it be something else?" Lizbeth offered. "Maybe somebody else paid for his meals for a few days? Or maybe he created a new alias to do this hijacking thing? Maybe he's getting hunted?"

Razia chewed on her thumb. Something didn't sound right. She turned to the intraweb and looked at his recent activity.

	5) Bernal, Arpad Wanted in connection with transporter hijacking. Estimated cost of stolen goods: 1,200,000C
	8) Bernal, Arpad Wanted in connection with transporter hijacking. Estimated cost of stolen goods: 4,200,000C
	9) Bernal, Arpad Wanted in connection with transporter hijacking. Estimated cost of stolen goods: 6,200,000C

"Well, whatever he's doing, he's not hijacking government ships," Razia noted, looking back at Lizbeth. "Not recently, anyways."

"He wasn't at the meeting either," Lizbeth said, shaking her head. "But I know he's been hijacking ships. I've seen him with stolen cargo."

"Where is the government material coming from?" Razia asked, starting to doubt the abilities of her new government colleague. "And what is it, exactly?"

"It's part of a big contract the government awarded two years ago. Mining ore from G-245, sending it through a processing plant, then transporting it to different military bases across the UBU," Lizbeth said. "It went to two large transport companies. They subbed out to other, smaller companies, who subbed out to other companies, and so on."

"Do you have the entire chain of companies?"

Lizbeth handed her the last thick stack of papers in her briefcase. "The full supply chain."

Razia's eyes poured through the list, the words and names not making any sense or catching her eye. She wondered if she was going to have to search through all of these. There were at least a hundred companies per page. It was going to take some time, and most of these were going to result in a dead end. The whole process was mind-numbing.

And then, on the sixth page, her eyes paused on one of the sub-, sub-, sub-, sub-contractors.

Benson Zephyr Transport, Inc.

"You….son of a bitch…" Razia shook her head. She never thought she'd see that name again.

"Who is it?" Lizbeth asked.

"Damned ass," Razia breathed, turning to her dashboard and searching for the data she had uncovered the year before.

	310) Delmur, Evet
Wanted for	Engagement in piracy, bounty hunting, kidnapping, theft, grand larceny
Reward	10,000C
Known Alias	Luka Arular, Merkaba Backus, Zowie Canales, Canet Conboy
Known Accomplices	Gunnar Cole, Frank Eigenberg
Pirate Web Affiliation	None

Razia could still see him tossing that infernal bag of chocolates at her. The way he gawked at her when she told him she was a bounty hunter.

But, she thought happily, she still had all of her research—all of his transaction histories, his aliases. With a gleam in her eye, she set to retrieving it from the bowels of her hard drive. Oh, she'd show him chocolate fetcher this time. Oh yes, indeed.

But to her annoyance, when she searched on the four aliases she'd found last year, none of them had been used since she'd discovered him.

"Catch me up, genius," Lizbeth said, having been sitting in complete silence for the past five minutes.

"Last year," Razia began, sitting back down, "Dissident had me hunt this guy. Turns out,—she snorted ruefully—"Dissident thought it would be funny to send me after some old guy and retrieve some candy for him."

"Is that a euphemism for—"

"No," Razia snapped, giving her an odd look. "Like chocolates or something. Anyway," she cleared her throat, "I found him at this diner, real out of the way place. He was shipping stuff between G-245 and S-6642, but never got hijacked. That's how I found him, actually, just looked for the transporters with the highest rating in the transport guild."

Lizbeth fumbled through her papers. "I don't have any records of shipments going to S-6642."

"But do you have J-646 on your list?" Razia asked, peering at the star map of nearby planets.

"J-646," Lizbeth said, scanning through her papers. Her eyes lit up and she grinned, "Yes! The military is building a few thousand warehouses there to store military equipment until it's needed."

"Yeah, and I bet they didn't notice that one trucker hadn't been delivering his cargo there," Razia smirked.

"Well done, Dr. Peate," Lizbeth said with a smile.

Razia frowned as she scanned S-6642 with another DSE application, looking for life, "Well that's odd."

"What?"

"There's lots of wildlife," Razia said, pointing to her DSE application, "but only one place on the entire planet where there's anything resembling human life." She pointed to a small spot in the middle of the planet. Without missing a beat, she opened a different application, this one more pirate-like, and used those same scanning satellites to check for radar signatures. The planet on the screen was then covered in small dots radiating concentric circles—radars. The entire planet was covered.

"We won't be able to get past the stratosphere without raising suspicion." Razia sighed, sitting back.

"Is that normal?"

"Not for a civilian planet." Razia shook her head. "But sometimes commercial companies get protective of their properties. So either we can perform a space jump—"

"Is that?"

"Put on a special suit, jump out of the ship high enough in the atmosphere so you aren't picked up by radar, and parachute in," Razia said, shuddering as she remembered the last time she'd done one of those. It was the first time Tauron realized she was petrified of heights. He made sure to rib her about it soundly when he found her five hours later, miles away from the target landing site, stuck in a tree.

"What's our other option?"

"Our other option is to have some legitimate excuse to get onto that planet," Razia said, biting her lip and searching for the buyer's information in the Planetary and System Science Academy record. Since it was recently settled, there might be a way she could use her Dr. Peate credentials to gain access, if she could see who sold them the planet to spur some ideas.

NAME	S-6642
DISCOVERED	20012-08-03
DISCOVERED BY	D. PEATE DSE2474786
SOLD	20012-08-27-10:50
SOLD TO	WEDEKIND PLANETARY SERVICES
AMOUNT	45,000C

"Well, I could always lie and say I was checking on my brother's purchase," Razia shrugged, pointing to the name. "Looks like Dorst sold it to them."

There were other notes—the biological and chemical signatures and other analyses—but she paid them no mind. She located the planets on her star maps. It was surrounded by mostly inhabitable planets, save J-646. She opened an internet window and searched for the company that bought the planet, one which seemed slightly familiar.

"Wedekind Planetary Services," Lizbeth read aloud. "What are you looking for?"

"I think I've heard of them before." Razia scanned their public internet site for anything of interest. Her eyes landed on a news story, a new Vice President of Operations for S-6642. It was the woman who had weaseled her out of eight thousand credits last year, the woman who wore pearls and a set of killer heels. Antica was her name—Antica Mikaelsson.

"Wow, she looks like a ball-buster," Lizbeth remarked.

"Yeah," Razia said. "She's swindled me out of my fair share of planets. But," she smiled at Lizbeth, "she also offered me a job last year."

"You-who? You-Lyssa or you-Razia?"

"Me…Lyssa," she said, shaking her head. "I could always see if she's still interested in hiring me?"

"That sounds a lot nicer than a space jump," Lizbeth said.

"With her? The space jumping might be safer."

***

As luck would have it, Ms. Mikaelsson *was* interested in having Dr. Lyssa Peate come in for an interview. It took some strong arguing on Lyssa's part to convince the secretary to hold the interview on S-6642 with Ms. Mikaelsson, who was trying to pawn her off on of the other executives, but in the end, Lyssa was able to secure a meeting with Mikaelsson the next day. S-6642 was less than ten hours' hypermiling time from D-882, but Lyssa decided to have a little fun with her passenger and demonstrate more expeditious methods of traveling long distances using a well-known religious icon.

"You are insane," Lizbeth seethed, her face shimmering with sweat and tinted green as she struggled against the stabilizing pressure. "I've never…I have to go to Temple now. I haven't been to Temple in *years*."

"Oh, the Great Creator doesn't mind me using His gravity for a bit of speed," Lyssa brushed her off with a wry smile.

In fact, the detour had been so out of the way that they only just arrived in the system with only an hour to spare before Lyssa's interview. She was wearing her normal "DSE-appropriate" attire, although she could practically feel Lizbeth judging her when she walked out of her closet.

"So you're going to an interview like that?" Lizbeth asked, unable to keep herself quiet at the wrinkled pants, and the lab coat with a coffee stain on the lapel.

"This is how I always look," Lyssa responded, adjusting her glasses.

"I mean…you could at least iron your shirt."

"I don't iron," Lyssa snapped, her annoyance growing at this conversation. "Besides, if I show up looking odd, she may think something is up."

"What, so putting yourself together is considered 'odd' for you?" Lizbeth asked, raising her eyebrow.

"*Yes*. God in Leveman's Vortex, you sound like my sister." She paused for emphasis. "I *hate* my sister."

When they arrived at the docking station on the planet, Lyssa was struck at how…empty it was, especially for such a newly settled planet with only *one* place to land a ship. This docking station should have been filled with ships bringing in supplies and people to continue work on the planet. It was definitely odd, but Lyssa wasn't sure how much she trusted Lizbeth's spying skills, so she was grateful for the lucky break.

"Try and stay out of sight, okay?" Lyssa said.

"Out of sight from whom?" Lizbeth wondered out loud, obviously noting the absence of any other living soul.

"Just…whatever," Lyssa sighed and stepped into the lift.

When she emerged a few moments later on the top floor, she found, yet again, that it was devoid of human life. The hallway smelled of fresh carpet and paint, as if it had just been installed recently. She peered into the empty offices that lined the hall, each one equipped with the same desk, computer monitor, chair, even the same framed printed picture.

She turned a corner and saw the very first person she'd seen on this planet—a mousy secretary who was typing away on her computer.

"Oh!" the secretary said with a sweet smile. "You must be Dr. Peate!"

"Yeah," Lyssa nodded, looking around to see if there was anyone else in the building.

"Ms. Mikaelsson is in a meeting, but she will see you shortly." The woman smiled again before returning to her computer.

Lyssa peered past her into the office where she could see Antica. She was sitting at her computer, alone, reading something on the screen. She made no move to talk to anyone, and Lyssa couldn't hear the sound of any phone conversations.

She repressed the urge to roll her eyes at the obvious lack of respect for her schedule and sat down. Eyeing the secretary, she pulled out her mini-computer and tapped out a message to Lizbeth: *Where are you*

A few moments later the message came in: *I'm down in the basement. There's nobody here*

Same up here. I'm waiting to go have my interview

Oh, be sure to talk about how super qualified you are with all your bounty hunting

Lyssa couldn't stop a snort and cleared her throat as the secretary gave her a puzzled look. She chewed on her lip, pondering where they could land the kind of huge transport ship she had seen Evet Delmur flying last year. The docking station itself was big, but not *that* big.

A new message came in from Lizbeth: *See if you can figure out what this planet is being used for*

Obviously.

Don't be sassy with me.

"Dr. Peate, Ms. Mikaelsson will see you now," the secretary said, interrupting the virtual argument.

Lyssa stood and slipped her mini-computer into her pocket, following the secretary into the expansive office. Lyssa appreciated the view of the expansive forest before she nodded to the only other occupant in the room.

"Dr. Peate," Antica said, wearing a smart suit and her signature killer pair of heels. Lyssa actually began to wish that she'd let Lizbeth offer her some clothes as she took a seat opposite the beautiful woman. "So nice of you to come out this way."

"I was out here anyway," Lyssa said, trying to sound casual.

"Oh?" Antica sat down at the table and crossed her legs superiorly. "I wasn't aware that there were any undiscovered planets out this way?"

"I thought I saw one when I was...*anyway*," Lyssa cleared her throat. "I'm glad you had the time to meet with me."

"Dr. Peate, I won't lie to you," Antica said. "When I first met you, I thought you were a weak pushover who barely cared enough about herself to get out of bed in the morning."

Lyssa's eyebrows shot upwards.

"But over the past few months, you seem to have recognized your potential and taken steps to achieve it."

"Thank you?" Lyssa said, wondering where this interview was really going.

"Wedekind isn't a company for people with low self-esteem. If you don't believe you are the best at what you do, you will be killed, do you understand?" the woman said, before pausing to smile. "Figuratively, of course."

"Of course." Lyssa had a mental image of Antica slipping off her stiletto and wielding it as a weapon.

"As a planet buyer, when you represent this company, there are certain expectations. We can't be spending thousands of credits on a planet that isn't worth our time."

Lyssa swallowed her retort about the time this woman took her for eight thousand credits and replied, "I was actually hoping to discuss a different line of work. I'm...rather bored working at the Academy. I wanted to see about moving to a planet. Fresh air and all that."

"Unfortunately, planet development is a slow-moving business," Antica said. "We only just completed this building and are in contract negotiations for another fifteen. I'm not sure someone with your skill set would be useful during this phase of work."

"You'd be surprised what my skill sets are." Lyssa said with a wry smile. She sensed an opportunity to steer the conversation into more productive waters. "I do have some experience with dodging pirates. Is that a big problem for you?"

Antica's face was unreadable. "Why would it be a problem?"

"I didn't see any processing facilities here. I assume you had all the materials to construct this building transported in versus made here on the planet. Pirates…well, they tend to hijack transporters…"

"That's right, I forgot your brother was Captain Jukin Peate." Antica nodded. "So you know all about pirates, do you?"

"I have overheard some conversations about them." Lyssa remarked with a half-shrug. "I know it's a big problem. A lot of government-owned ships are being stolen near here on their way to the arsenal nearby. Any of yours, too?"

"We've paid a lot of money to ensure our transporters are adequately protected from pirates," Antica said with a smile.

"Paid to whom?" Lyssa asked, not even bothering to sound innocent. It wasn't completely uncommon for corporations to pay the runners to leave their shipments alone, but something about this place gave Lyssa pause.

Antica narrowed her eyes for a moment and then smiled again. "You are quite perceptive, aren't you?"

"I pay attention," Lyssa replied before looking out into the unsettled forest that stretched for miles. "So, how much of this planet have you settled? Doesn't seem to be anyone else here. What are you guys even *doing* on this planet?"

"Dr. Peate," Antica cut her off quietly. "One thing you need to learn about Wedekind Planetary Services is that we keep our intellectual capital close. Our population strategy is one of our most closely held proprietary secrets. And we haven't yet finished our interview, so I can't be divulging our corporate secrets to an outsider." She paused and smiled. "Especially one with such interesting questions."

Cursing internally, Lyssa simply nodded. It was clear that Ms. Antica Mikaelsson wasn't going to give her any more information that would be helpful, and this was nothing but a dead end. She just hoped that Lizbeth was able to find out more. But when she checked her mini-computer, she found the following message from Lizbeth:

Well, this was pointless.

CHAPTER SIX

Lyssa sat cross-legged in her bed, trying to concentrate on the ugly faces staring up at her from her mini-computer. When she and Lizbeth returned to the ship, Lyssa re-checked her plotted star maps of Delmur's movements, and, as expected, the farthest out he had traversed was S-6642 before heading back to G-245. Either he was turning around, or he had switched to another alias she didn't know about after stopping at S-6642. She had nowhere to start either, since all of her leads had gone cold.

She supposed she could call Harms, as she was quite sure that the informant knew where to find Delmur, but didn't really feel like trying that hard. He had been charging her an arm and a leg when she came to him for information, possibly punishment for the way she had yelled at him, and she didn't want to spend a huge chunk of money on this Lizbeth woman.

That very woman was wandering back and forth between her pristine suitcase and the bathroom, each time grabbing some new lotion or a brush or a pair of tweezers, interrupting Lyssa's thoughts.

"Are you done yet?" Lyssa snapped, finally after Lizbeth's fifteenth trip.

Lizbeth continued her ministrations. "Is there a problem?"

"How much crap are you going to rub into your skin?"

Lizbeth squirted more into her hands and rubbed it into her arms. "Enough so my skin doesn't flake off. We can't all have perfect skin like you."

"I don't have…" Lyssa trailed off, nervously looking at her mini-computer again.

"So what's your deal?" Lizbeth asked, rubbing the lotion onto her face. She was sitting in the hideaway bed that Lyssa had installed for Vel, so he didn't have to sleep on the Academy air mattress the whole time he was here. It was strange to see Lizbeth's things where Vel's normally were.

It was strange to have another girl in her ship.

Especially one who seemed to just ooze sophistication and femininity. Her luggage was pristine, her clothes immaculately hung next to Lyssa's stained and wrinkled shirts. Lyssa began to feel a bit self-conscious in her ratty old shirt and shorts with coffee stains on them. Her hands, which were rough, seemed mannish, her legs pale, and her hair dry and brittle. She fought the urge to go brush it.

"Yo, Lyssa or Razia, are you listening to me?" Lizbeth said, placing the comb down. "What do I call you anyways?"

"Lyssa is fine," she said. "Except, you know, when we're with other pirates."

"Obviously. So what's your deal?"

"What do you want to know?" Lyssa asked, picking at her comforter. "You already know my dirty little secret."

"That's what's so curious to me," Lizbeth said, sitting back on her elbows. "You were the daughter of a well-known scientist, studied at the Planetary and System Science Academy. Got your degree." She chuckled. "And then decided to become a pirate?"

"When I was a kid, Tauron Ball plucked me off an Academy field trip. Threatened to kill me, in fact. And…" Lyssa sighed, remembering her mother's words. "My family just left me to die."

"What?" Lizbeth blinked in confusion. "Why?"

"Long story." Lyssa waved her off. "But Tauron took me in after that."

"But your brother killed him?"

Lyssa's eyes shot upwards before she could mask the hurt in them. Lizbeth had said it so casually, like it was just another fact.

"Sorry," Lizbeth said quietly.

"It's just…kind of raw, I suppose," Lyssa said, sitting back into her pillows. "It only happened two…"

Dear Great Creator in Leveman's Vortex, she realized with a jolt. Next month would be three years.

"Wanna talk about it?" Lizbeth said.

"Not much to say that you probably didn't hear in the news," Lyssa said, trying to sound normal. "Jukin captured him and—"

"One thing I could never figure out was why Jukin stopped with Tauron?" Lizbeth mused. "Why not hunt other pirates?"

"Well," Lyssa said hollowly. "Jukin paid a lot of money to some high ranking politico—nobody knows who it was, or how much money, but it was just enough for a small window of opportunity for him to…" She swallowed. "I guess he thought if he could catch one pirate, more money and supporters would follow. Unfortunately for him,"—she grinned—"the runners made damned sure that no one else supported him after that. He lost nearly all of his police force and was told he was no longer allowed to hunt pirates."

"*I* heard that when he captured Tauron, he had gone rogue. The entire operation was done in secret without the approval of any of his superiors. His reprimand went all the way up to General State. The fact that State was considering a run for president and didn't want to seem soft on piracy was the only reason Jukin didn't get canned."

Lyssa shook her head in amazement. "Politicians are stupid. To think, if State had been less focused on his career, we could have been rid of Jukin completely."

"Sorry," Lizbeth said. "Is it hard for you to talk about it? I mean, you've probably got some conflicted emotions."

"Not at all," Lyssa said, firmly. "As far as I'm concerned, my loyalties lie with Tauron."

"So if that's the case, why keep up the Lyssa Peate charade?"

"Good money," Lyssa said, without elaborating. If she wasn't comfortable telling Vel about what she saw in the river at Leveman's Vortex, she was damned sure not going to tell this stranger.

"You're an interesting individual," Lizbeth said, eyeing her.

"What about you?" Lyssa said, eager to shift the conversation. "What's your deal?"

"I'm just a girl who works for the government, working a case, trying to get a promotion." Lizbeth sighed. "Most of the guys in my office have laughed at me. They think I'm barking up the wrong tree."

"I know the feeling. I've been in the top twenty for seven months and I still can't get any respect from my own damned runner, let alone anyone else."

"But you're one of the most wanted people in the universe," Lizbeth said, sounding a bit surprised.

"My entire bounty was funded by my old Academy supervisor in an attempt to blackmail me." Lyssa glared at Lizbeth. "Seems to be a theme."

"Well, if you had a better disguise, maybe people wouldn't recognize you!" Lizbeth smiled back at her before pausing curiously. "Why *doesn't* Jukin recognize you?"

"He doesn't like to remember that Lyssa Peate exists." She recalled his snarling face in his office, the way he openly berated her.

"So he really doesn't recognize you?" Lizbeth said. "All that… anger is directed towards Lyssa Peate? Not to Razia?"

"Yep," Lyssa said. "There's a special level of hatred for me in the family."

"What did you do?"

"I did *nothing*," Lyssa snapped, her hackles raising.

"Wow, sorry." Lizbeth's eyes widened from the ferocity of the retort. "So what happened with your boss? Is he still blackmailing you?"

"I took care of him," Lyssa said, intentionally vague.

"I thought pirates didn't kill?"

"We don't, he just...." she trailed off, wondering how best to phrase it. Obviously, she couldn't tell Lizbeth that Pymus had fallen into Plethegon because the Great Creator deemed his soul unworthy to pass the Arch of Eron. "Let's just say he realized his mistake and backed off."

"But didn't cancel his bounty on your head?"

"No, thankfully," Lyssa said. If her bounty was cancelled, she'd be in serious trouble. "Still, I would much rather have other pirates ponying up some credits. His bounty won't last forever."

"They've got to come around soon," Lizbeth said with an optimistic smile. "I mean, you've made more progress in two days than I've made in four months."

"Yeah…" Lyssa sighed, annoyed that she hadn't gotten further.

"Well, I'm beat. Good night."

Lyssa grunted the same and flipped off the light next to her bed. She lay in the darkness, unable to sleep from the sound of someone else who was not Vel breathing nearby. Her mind ran through thoughts and memories of the day, coming to circle around the memory of Tauron's death. She didn't know the particulars of how Jukin got the money or whom he paid off, but the result was the same either way, so what did it matter?

She flipped over on her side, hoping the change of position would clear her mind. Her eyes fell on a speck in the distance. Lyssa's ship was orbiting around S-6642 until they could figure out their next steps, and she was sure they were the only extra-planetary vehicle out here. As the speck grew in the window, it began to take the shape of a giant woman with a vapid smile holding a serving tray. The image was somewhat familiar, a brand ingrained in her head from years of advertising exposure. In the depths of her half-asleep mind, she remembered the woman was selling alcohol.

The vapid woman's figure was large enough to fill the window, and that was when she noticed a small diner at the base of the giant plastic woman, and a docking station large enough to hold huge transport ships.

Lyssa's eyes suddenly snapped open and she was wide awake.

"Lizbeth."

"Mmph…"

"Wake up." Lyssa turned on the lights.

"What?" Lizbeth whined, her eyes blinking in the brightness.

"Look out there," Lyssa said, pointing out her window.

"It's Lorna Howell," Lizbeth muttered, rolling back over. "Do you want a drink or something?"

"She's got a diner at her feet," Lyssa said, annoyed that Lizbeth was doing something as stupid as sleeping when there was a new break in their investigation.

"So?" Lizbeth mumbled.

"So, there's also a docking station there," Lyssa smiled, kicking herself for not realizing it sooner. "And last year, I found Delmur at a diner not on S-6642!"

To her annoyance, Lizbeth said nothing, obviously asleep.

"So," Lyssa repeated louder. "That means that we can probably find out where Delmur's gone to now!"

"God in Leveman's Vortex," Lizbeth groaned. "That's fantastic, but can we take care of it…I don't know…tomorrow?"

"I wanna go now," Lyssa said, already halfway to her closet to throw on her pirate clothes.

"Machine. You're a damned machine," Lizbeth sighed before tossing the covers off.

***

Razia double and triple checked her Delmur notes, but this was a different diner than where she had found Delmur the year before. That one hadn't had another transaction since about a month after her encounter. Perhaps without Delmur's regular money, they were forced to close.

Much like the diner last year, this one was completely devoid of people or other ships in the docking station. The only difference was the giant statue of a girl that stood on either side of the diner and docking station, her vapid smile and blonde hair calling on patrons to buy a brand of alcohol.

But, Razia noted with a smile, it was definitely big enough to host multiple transport ships.

Grabbing the still half-asleep Lizbeth by the arm, Razia pulled her towards the diner. Through the big windows, Razia could see the walls were papered with all kinds of advertisements, some for the same alcohol that the woman above was selling, some for a brand of food, but most of them were for General State's presidential campaign. His stern face met them with an icy glare even before they set foot inside the diner.

"Do we have to go inside?" Lizbeth asked, yawning.

"Of course we do," Razia replied, pushing open the door. There were two people inside the diner: a snoozing cook whose apron looked as if he hadn't cooked in some time, and a waitress who was doing games in a game book. She couldn't remember if they were the same two from the other diner, but they surely looked similar.

"Well!" The waitress looked up and shoved the cook awake. "Look here, we got ourselves some guests!"

"Is it one of them?" the cook asked sleepily.

"No, no, it's these two pretty girls," the waitress adjusted the tie on her apron. "Have a seat where you like, at the bar or at a table."

"We'll sit over here," Razia said, dragging Lizbeth over to a table.

"What can we get you to drink, then?" the waitress said, holding her pad and pencil ready in her hand.

Razia was shocked. Waitresses in bars were one thing, but diners like these usually used computerized ordering systems. Normal pad and pencil waitresses had disappeared long ago.

"Oh, this thing?" the waitress said, noticing Razia's stare. "Steve likes to do things the old-fashioned way. No computers for us in this place!"

Razia gave Lizbeth a look, but Lizbeth was too busy trying to stay awake to notice.

"Coffee," Razia said.

"Coming right up!" The waitress scurried over to the counter to pour a cup.

"Wake up," Razia hissed at Lizbeth. "For someone who's gone through so much trouble to get this far, you are awfully uninterested in what's going on."

"Ugh, what?" Lizbeth snapped back at her.

"Look around," Razia hissed at her. "I found Evet Delmur in the same kind of place last year. There's advertising everywhere, but who in Leveman's Vortex would come all the way out here? The only customers they'd have would be Antica and her secretary, and I don't think Antica's much for diner food."

"So what?" Lizbeth yawned.

"*So* you told me to point out when things are weird. And this place…oh, thank you." Razia forced herself upright and smiled as a coffee was placed in front of her.

"You are quite welcome, darlin'!" The waitress grinned.

"General State, huh?" Razia asked, looking to the poster glaring down at them.

"Oh, that bozo?" The waitress sniffed, giving him the once over. "We only put up the posters we get. The advertising is just enough to cover the costs of running this place, you see."

"Don't get much business?" Razia asked as Lizbeth laid her head down on the table to go back to sleep.

"Oh goodness, no. Most folks don't even know that this little place is below Lorna."

"I see," Razia replied, kicking Lizbeth under the table to wake her up. "So how long have you been here?"

"'Bout a year," the waitress said, glancing back over to the cook who was snoozing again. "We used to be over near B-7926. We were about bankrupt when this gentlemen came in and asked us if we'd like to open up out here. He said that business was gonna pick up once S-6642 was better settled." The waitress shrugged.

"Oh?" Razia said, trying to seem innocent. "Really? Wasn't S-6642 bought just a few years ago? Seems a bit…soon to put you out here, doesn't it?"

The waitress gave her a curious look. "Yeah, well…so what brings you two out here?"

"We're looking for a man named Zephyr Benson, otherwise known as Evet Delmur," Lizbeth said with a yawn, much to Razia's consternation. "You seen him?"

"Oh y-no." The waitress cleared her throat and began absent-mindedly writing on her pad and paper. "I mean yes, but not for a few months, that is."

"Why'd he stop coming out here?" Lizbeth asked, ignorant of Razia's silent mouthing to knock it off.

"Well, I'm sure I don't know."

"What's on the menu?" Razia snapped before Lizbeth could ask any more questions.

"Soup and a special," the waitress said. Razia could hear the nerves in the waitress' voice.

"I think we'll try that special," Razia said quickly.

"Right away!" The waitress grinned, writing it down and trotting back over to the counter.

"Don't ask such direct questions," Razia hissed at Lizbeth

"I got tired of you dancing around the truth," Lizbeth growled. "Just ask the damned woman, what's the problem?"

"Look at this place," Razia hissed back. "You wouldn't even know it was here unless you were told it was here. It's covered in advertising, but doesn't get any customers? And I don't see a computer anywhere to take our C-cards."

"So what?"

"Not to mention all of these posters for General State," Razia said, pointing to the stern general. "Didn't those two guys say that they worked for him?"

"Yes, they did which is why I'm trying to get to the bottom of it. I don't understand why you're beating around the bush instead of just being direct—"

Razia saw the glinting metal out of the corner of her eye. But she didn't register what it was until a bullet hole appeared three inches from Lizbeth's head.

"*Shit!*" Razia screamed, diving under the table.

"*Are you crazy?*" Lizbeth screamed and dove under as well. Bullets ricocheted off the table and onto the windows. "You'll kill us all!"

"Sorry dear," the waitress said, her gun pointed at the bullet-riddled table. Razia could see the waitress' feet in front of them, and held her breath that she wouldn't dip under the table where they would be sitting ducks. "But you see, I got direct orders to kill anyone who stops by here who ain't part of what we're doing. And if you hadn't asked so many questions…"

"Go on, shoot back at her!" Lizbeth spat at Razia.

"*With what gun?*" Razia hissed, low enough that the woman wouldn't hear. But they had to do something fast, or else the woman would blast a hole clean through the table and actually hit them.

Razia spotted a broken shard of her coffee cup laying next to them and the woman's panty-hosed legs standing in front of the table.

"Sorry girls, I really hate to—"

Razia dug the cup fragment into the woman's leg, who screamed and dropped her gun to the ground. Razia leapt out from under the table and snatched it up. She fumbled for a few moments to hold the giant shotgun menacingly; she'd never actually held a gun before.

However, her ruse seemed to be working as the waitress began sobbing hysterically.

"No, no," the woman said, tears streaming down her face as she clutched at her bleeding leg. "Please don't! I was only following orders. Please…"

"I'm not going to kill you," Razia snapped, gripping the gun tighter. "But I still want to know who ordered you to kill us. And why?"

"MaryAnne…" The cook was also waving a shotgun, but lowered it when he saw Razia had the waitress cornered. "Don't go telling her nothin'."

"Please don't hurt us," the woman sobbed. "Please, I beg of you…"

"You two are under arrest!" Lizbeth stood up from under the table and yanked out her badge. "Assault on a Universal Government employee, using what I would wager to guess are illegally acquired guns."

"What in Leveman's Vortex are you doing?" Razia drawled.

"Arresting them," Lizbeth said plainly. "Also, the Universal Police are on their way."

"Oh great, they'll be back out on the street tomorrow," Razia shook her head.

"Not *those* police," Lizbeth sighed. "Now, you may be granted immunity if you provide a full confession." She sat down on a nearby chair with her fingers on her mini-computer. "What is this diner doing here? What is your connection to Krishna Harman? How are you connected to General State? What kind of cargo is being passed through here?"

The cook and the waitress, who was still quietly sobbing in pain, said nothing.

"Can you threaten them or something?" Lizbeth asked to Razia, exasperated.

"I've already got a gun pointed at them. What more do you want?" Razia snapped back.

"I don't know, say you'll shoot them or something."

"Why don't *you* threaten to shoot them?"

"Because I'd get fired; but you're a pirate."

"You can threaten us all you want," the cook said. "But we ain't gonna tell you *nothin'*."

"You heard the man," Razia said.

"Can you at least *tie them up* or something, *bounty hunter*?" Lizbeth threw her hands up.

Razia shoved the gun into Lizbeth's hands and marched back to her ship to retrieve some of her bounding material, muttering angrily about receiving orders from a helpless investigator.

***

Some three hours later, the Universal Police finally showed up. As expected, they weren't the Special Forces, but the regular police. They took no notice of Razia as she helped herself to yet another cup of coffee, her third since they had arrived at the diner. Razia had attempted to locate something that looked like food in the back room, but found it completely devoid of anything defrosted.

Even though she was hungry and over caffeinated, she was enjoying watching the scene in front of her: Lizbeth trying to retain control of the situation while the Universal Police, apparently the most inefficient three that they could send, were trying to take her statement.

"And I also have reason to suspect they've been supporting the transfer of stolen goods from pirates," Lizbeth said.

"Whoa," the officer said, holding up his hands. He was a portly man with a thick layer of unshaven scruff around his sweaty face. "Lady, we don't deal with pirates. Talk to Peate."

"You don't, but I do," Lizbeth said, exasperated. "I've talked to Peate. He's not interested in taking this case."

"Then why'd you drag us out here?" the officer asked lazily.

"Because they shot at me!" Lizbeth cried. "And I am an agent with the Intelligence Agency!"

"Well, looks like your friend stabbed her in the leg," a deputy mentioned.

"That was after they shot at us!"

"Yeah, I'm not sure we've got enough evidence to continue this investigation," the officer replied, closing his notepad. "If pirates are involved, we have to contact Peate's team, and then there's a sixty day waiting period until they can start their investigation."

Razia snorted in amusement.

Lizbeth, however, looked like she was about to wrap her hands around his meaty neck.

"So what are you going to do with these two?" she snapped. "I need you to arrest them so I can interview them!"

"Looks like little missy over there needs to get to a hospital." He motioned to the waitress being tended to by two other police officers. "She'd have half a mind to have me arrest your friend over there." His eyes drifted over to Razia, who smiled and sensed that she was about to pile onto Lizbeth.

"I'd like to see you try. I'm a pirate," she said.

"Aw shit," the officer cursed, giving Lizbeth an exasperated look. "And you want me to arrest these poor people? What did they do to you?"

"They shot at me!" Lizbeth screamed, finally losing her cool.

"All right, lady, I'm gonna ask you to calm down," the officer said. "We're gonna take these two to the nearest hospital, and we'll let you go with a warning."

"A war—are you serious?!" Lizbeth gaped as the two officers helped the crying waitress out of the diner, followed by her concerned cook.

"And you just be happy that it's only a warning, lady," the officer barked before he followed the other officers out the door.

Lizbeth stood, her eyes wide and her mouth hanging open as the police ship left the station.

"Well, I think that went well," Razia said, breaking the silence of the diner.

"Get sucked," Lizbeth seethed at her. "You think this is funny?"

"I'm just glad to see my pirate dues are being used effectively," Razia said, sliding off of the seat. "That was an incredible display of bureaucracy and stupidity."

"No matter," Lizbeth sniffed, seemingly trying to brush off this latest frustration. "We know we're onto something. The pirates are coming here to transfer illegal goods. The question is, where are they going?"

"And that is your mystery to solve," Razia smiled, folding her arms across her chest. "I'm out."

"Out?" Lizbeth gaped at her. "What do you mean, 'out'?"

"I'm *out*," Razia repeated. "I don't see anything going on here that's outside the normal business of piracy."

"What?" Lizbeth blinked at her. "But we've found something! This is obviously a lead! They *shot* at us!"

"Yeah, and I *don't* get shot at," Razia said firmly. "Go on and tell Jukin that I'm his sister; tell everyone. But from the looks of things, I don't think anyone's going to believe you."

"What?" Lizbeth breathed.

"Look at you," Razia laughed, motioning at the empty diner. "You've stooped so low as to employ a pirate to help you. You had to sneak into a pirate meeting. I don't see any back-up nor any team with you."

Lizbeth stood up straighter. "What are you saying, Lyssa?"

"I'm saying that I think you're barking up the wrong tree, and you should quit while you're ahead. Can't you take a hint?"

And with that, Razia left a stunned and speechless Lizbeth in the empty diner.

CHAPTER SEVEN

Razia wasn't upset in the least that she deserted Lizbeth. Fists, she could handle. Pirates operating on the same playing field, she could handle. But when firearms were involved—outside of the realm of the pirate laws, that's when she decided she was over it. If someone was willing to shoot her over insurance fraud, then they could keep their money for all she cared.

Besides, if Dissident approved of it, she wasn't going to poke the bear. It was bad enough that he could barely stand her; she shuttered to think what he'd do if she got in the way of him and a hefty payout.

Also, she was sure he was still pissed at her for breaking into that meeting. She hadn't heard from him, so she was just hoping he'd forget about the whole thing. And if he hadn't, she'd *make* him forget by capturing another high-visibility pirate.

Hit List	
Max Fried	Lino Abbracciabeni, Andrej Connolly, Kam Kaur, Jarl Daley
Arpad Bernal	Sacha Amjad, Justus Jansens, Michael Aleshite, Pinchas Akerman
Jarvis Loeb	Eadmund Sowards, Sulaiman Matthewson, Izidor Bencivenni

Royden Relleck	Paul Robert, Zachery Passerini, Thomas Strand, Dimitri MacIntyre

The last time she'd updated this list, these pirates were in the top ten most wanted, but that had been over a month ago. She hadn't even been paying attention to see if any of them had been caught, or even if they'd risen up the most wanted list.

She clicked on the name third pirate's name—Jarvis Loeb—linked to his latest activities in the pirate intraweb.

***

	7) Loeb, Jarvis Wanted for engagement in piracy (bounty hunting)
	8) Loeb, Jarvis Wanted for transporter hijacking. Estimated cost of stolen goods: 925,000C
	9) Loeb, Jarvis Wanted for transporter hijacking. Estimated cost of stolen goods: 1,400,000C

***

She frowned. His latest activity was from over three weeks ago.

She clicked on the aliases in her hit list, each one displaying the accompanying record in the Universal Bank.

Sowards, Eadmond		
Time of Transaction	Location	Amount
UT20015-04-04-83:55	Isidoros Bar and Grill D-882	100C
UT20015-04-02-72:05	Nogah Diner D-882	30C
UT20015-04-01-23:98	Josephe Clothiers D-882	5,000C

Matthewson, Sulaiman		
Time of Transaction	Location	Amount
UT20015-04-04-83:45	Isodoros Bar and Grill D-882	25C
UT20015-04-02-72:15	Nogah Diner D-882	15C

UT20015-04-02-72:09	Nogah Diner D-882	15C

Bencivenni, Izidor		
Time of Transaction	Location	Amount
UT20015-04-03-44:10	Titus D-882	40C
UT20015-04-03-44:03	Titus D-882	15C
UT20015-04-03-43:95	Titus D-882	15C

"Well that's odd," she muttered. Between the three aliases, she expected to see a transaction at least once a day, if not more often. But she was spying gaps as long as two days, and the last transaction on any account was over six days ago.

In fact, she cross-checked the previous history of Arpad Bernal, Max Fried, *and* Relleck to the same result. None of them had made any transactions or had any activities on the pirate web in a week, to include a record of capture, which might have explained why they'd been dormant.

She sat back, chewing on her lip as she pondered.

Loeb and Fried were both in Protester's web, while Bernal and Relleck were in Contestant's web. Contestant's pirates weren't at the pirate meeting, but Lizbeth had said they'd been hijacking government shipments for months.

She sniffed as she caught her train of thought venturing closer to Lizbeth's investigation. What did she care if they were hijacking government ships?

Well, she cared if she couldn't find any pirates to capture.

"Then I'll add a new pirate to my hit list," she answered, suddenly recognizing that she was talking to herself.

With a growl, she returned to the pirate intraweb, navigating to the front page, and looking to see if any pirate caught her attention:

	31) Wigmund, Gutermuth Wanted in connection with transporter hijacking. Estimated cost of stolen goods: 20,000C
	42) Zaki, Carroll Wanted in connection with piracy (bounty hunting)

	33) Lucio, Sargent Captured by Carroll Zaki
	54) Mladen, Kuang Wanted in connection with transporter hijacking. Estimated cost of stolen goods 4,000C

Razia furrowed her brow. There was an awful lot of activity from pirates outside of the top twenty on the latest pirate news. Sure, those pirates popped up every once in a while, but the major stories were always about the top guys. There was also no mention of any government ship hijackings, even from the lower ranking pirates. She was *sure* that over the past week, all of those pirates who attended the meeting had been hijacking as many ships as were available.

She searched on Jeam Bullock, a member of Dissident's web. He was most assuredly at the pirate meeting, and had voiced his support for the effort.

	10) Bullock, Jeam Wanted for engagement in piracy (bounty hunting)
	11) Bullock, Jeam Wanted for hijacking of Hernando Shipments, LLC. Estimated cost of stolen goods: 1,500,000C
	14) Bullock, Jeam Wanted for hijacking of Guto Transport, Inc. Estimated cost of stolen goods: 1,200,000C

Well, now she *was* curious.

There was no way that he'd wait over a week to hijack one of the ships. That bald man had made it clear that the deal was only good until the next election, when General State would presumably win, and that was only two weeks away.

She paused for a moment, wondering why General State's men even had connections in President Llendo's administration to engineer this whole operation. She then quickly dismissed the thought under the auspices of not caring.

Besides, there was a curious mystery afoot. Pirates were told to hijack government shipments, but there was no record of the crime? Not only that, but every pirate on her hit list had suddenly vanished from the Universal Bank.

She mulled over the possibilities. She knew from personal experience that the runners didn't post every transaction to the pirate web, but to not post any of their top pirates? That made no sense.

And for all of them to disappear from the Universal Bank, too?

She wondered for a brief moment if maybe Jukin had engineered a large-scale ambush of all of the pirates after she and Lizbeth had been kicked out of the meeting. After all, it would be a nice target—at least twenty of the top pirates and their runners all crammed into a single room. Jukin would salivate at the thought of—

A new transaction popped up on Loeb's alias, drawing her attention.

Sowards, Eadmond		
Time of Transaction	Location	Amount
UT20015-04-10-63:10	Eamon's D-882	50C

"Hmm…" She smiled. Maybe they hadn't vanished after all.

***

Eamon's had become, if possible, even more popular with the top pirates than when it was being used as a clever trap for the most wanted by the runner Insurgent. The runner had been allowed to keep his nightclub open, as long as he stopped trying to discover the aliases of pirates in other webs. He then upped the ante by hiring even more security and beautiful women to serve drinks and flirt. It was the place to be seen by anyone who could get through the heavily guarded front doors.

Razia hadn't frequented this place in a long time, as she didn't see the value in watching other pirates get laid.

Also, technically she was still banned since she busted Insurgent's pirate shake-down.

But tonight, she needed to get inside, and she wasn't going to take no for an answer. Lucky for her, she had made a new friend the year before who would be more than happy to help her out.

"*Lemme go*!" VJ whined, struggling against her as she twisted his arm behind his back. She had been waiting in the alley where they had first met and pounced on him when he walked outside for a smoke break.

"Get me inside," she ordered.

"Leveman's, Razia. You know I can't!" She twisted more, his black curls falling in front of his face. She began to realize why he was more at home running a bar than being a pirate.

"We can do this the easy way or the hard way," Razia whispered. "I would pick the one that doesn't result in a concussion."

"C'mon, don't get me in *trouble*," he moaned, pushing at her arm. "Man, I didn't hear the end of it last time—Pops was furious at me for getting caught. Leveman's, I'm *still* on probation—"

"Concussion it is."

"No, no, no!" He winced as she reared her fist went backwards. He quickly handed her a key card. "Here…Leveman's…take it…"

"Pleasure doing business with you," Razia said, releasing him to a heap on the ground.

With the influx of new business, the bar had been expanded to the surrounding buildings and now sported a dance floor for uncoordinated pirates to dry hump dancers paid to be there, a gambling room for pirates to give even more money to Insurgent, and a huge new bar space to accommodate the top pirates and their crews.

She spotted Eli Stenson, a fellow pirate in Dissident's web, who did his best to ignore her greeting. Same went for Jeam Bullock, who completely left his table when she walked over to chat with him about his recent activity. With nowhere else to go, she went to stand against the wall, scanning the faces of everyone in the bar for those she recognized.

"Where's your little maid outfit?"

"Baggy pants again? Come on girl, I wanna see your *ass*!"

She grimaced, spying Linro Lee and Gunnar Bodhi, two of Contestant's pirates, goading her from a nearby poker table. She tossed them a rude gesture and continued scanning the bar.

"See? That's why we all like your friend more than you."

"She's better to look at, too."

Razia's eyes widened. "*Friend?*"

Snarling, she marched over to the two pirates, who suddenly seemed much more concerned for their well-being than when she was on the other side of the room.

"Whoa, whoa, we were just kidding!" Lee babbled, sitting back.

"Y-you can't capture us in here!" Bodhi shook his head, his face paling.

"What friend?" Razia hissed.

"Y-your girlfriend over there," Lee said, pointing past Razia. She whirled on her heel, scanning the bar for-

Her eyes narrowed and her blood pressure spiked.

Lizbeth leaned across the bar and smiled at Zolet Obalone, whose young cheeks flushed bright red as two drinks appeared at his hand. Lizbeth winked at the kid, flirtatiously playing with her straw and very sexually sipping it. Obalone was babbling and rubbing the back of his head.

Razia was over to the bar in three strides. "*What in Leveman's Vortex are you doing here?*"

"Excuse us, honey," Lizbeth cooed at Obalone, who looked relieved to have an escape. When Lizbeth whirled on Razia, she was back to her normal, no-nonsense self. "What do you mean, *what am I doing here?* You may have ditched me, but I'm still investigating this insurance fraud."

"By coming to Eamon's?" Razia asked.

"Yes," Lizbeth replied, giving her a look. "What are you doing here?"

"I'm a pirate," Razia said defensively. "Of course I'd be here."

"I've been coming here every weekend for over a month and I've never seen you here," Lizbeth said with a stupidly satisfied smile on her face.

Razia's face reddened.

"I *knew* you couldn't stay away from this!" Lizbeth grinned knowingly. "I heard from a pirate that you're nothing if not up for a challenge."

"Oh yeah?" Razia drawled, looking around the bar. "And which of these idiots have you been talking about me to?"

"That handsome guy over there," Lizbeth said, pointing behind

Razia.

She turned around and immediately rolled her eyes. "Figures."

"Well, if it isn't my favorite curmudgeon!" Sage grinned, walking over to the two of them. "Look at you making friends. I'm so proud of you."

"Not quite," Lizbeth said, giving Razia a searing look. "She hasn't quite warmed up to me yet. Left me to figure out my own way back to civilization."

"Don't worry, she left her little brother alone on an undiscovered planet for three days last year," Sage snickered, his eyes not leaving Razia's snarling face.

"Go away," Razia huffed, cutting him off before he could say anything else.

"Oh, get sucked Lyssa, he's not here to talk to you," Lizbeth said, turning to Sage. "So, any new information for me today, Mr. Teon?"

"Only that my runner is pretty pissed that Little Missy over here ruined his party," Sage said, much to Razia's chagrin. "Other than that, nothing to report."

"Do you know if any pirates are hijacking ships?" Lizbeth pressed. "Or if anyone's getting paid?"

"Nobody's getting paid," Razia replied, feeling the need to show up Sage. "And nobody's been hijacking anything either, because it hasn't been showing up in the pirate intraweb."

"Oh-ho, Lyss," Sage winked at her. "You obviously missed Conrad Conboy boasting about the new ship he bought with his payments. And Bullock over there, he's just bought himself a new mansion on R-3633. Said he's gonna retire."

"What in the…?" Razia said, her mini-computer in her hands.

"It's not in there," Sage said, before she was halfway to searching on the first pirate. "Runners agreed that all government ship hijackings would be under the table."

"But if they're under the table, how are they getting money?" Razia asked, before she could stop herself. "The ship is reported stolen to the insurance company, the insurance company puts out a wanted notice, bounty goes up."

"And that's why nobody's moved in about a week," Sage replied, knowingly. "Or did you, in your infinite genius, miss that little tidbit?"

Razia waved her hand, feeling like she was on the edge of something important. "But if there's no insurance claim, there's no payment to the company, so how are they paying the pirates for their work?"

"Well, as you said you were *out*, I don't see how it's any of your concern?" Lizbeth smiled. "So why don't *you* go away while I continue my conversation with Sage here."

"No need to fight over me, ladies," Sage laughed. "Plenty of me to go around."

Razia gave him a stare so cold it could have frozen lava.

"Hot damn." Lizbeth licked her lips, interrupting Razia's death stare. "Who is *that*?"

Razia followed her gaze and felt sick. "Please don't."

"Girl." Lizbeth grinned madly, like a cat about to pounce. "Tell me right now if you're hitting that."

"Depends on your definition of hit," Razia mumbled as Sage's eyes were on her again.

"If it isn't my favorite pieces of garbage from Dissident's web." Royden Relleck smirked as he stood in front of them. He was handsome, with short buzzed hair and high cheekbones, so it was no wonder that Lizbeth had latched onto him.

Razia shifted uncomfortably as Relleck's eyes passed over her. She still hadn't forgotten the way he had propositioned her, nor the way that he and Dissident had conspired to capture her for Pymus. Then again, he hadn't told anyone what really happened between the two of them either—so perhaps he was worried that she'd tell everyone that she nearly captured him.

Lucky for her, his attention was directed immediately at Lizbeth, who was giving him the most obvious pair of come-hither eyes Razia had ever seen.

"And what's your name, sweetcheeks?" Relleck cooed.

Razia vomited a little in her mouth, but Lizbeth giggled and tossed a curl behind her shoulder. Razia finally noticed that she wore a *very* short skirt and a shirt that showed more than a little bit of cleavage. It was no wonder that Relleck and almost every other man here were acting like morons.

"Lizbeth," she said, girlishly sipping her drink. "What's your name, other than handsome?"

"Name's Relleck," he said, leaning against the bar. "I'm one of the best pirates out there."

"Oh?" Lizbeth said, playing with the straw on her drink and biting her lip. Razia couldn't see why Lizbeth didn't burst into laughing fits, as Razia was about to. "I didn't see you at that party last week. I thought that was for *top pirates*." She punctuated each word with a sultry glance.

"Heh," he laughed, touching her hand on the bar. "Well, you see, I'm too good for those idiots. I got my own deal worked out. Going tonight to make another run, in fact."

Razia's eyes bugged out of her head, and beside her, Sage's mouth fell open in surprise.

"Think I could distract you from that?" Lizbeth asked, letting him gently rub her hand.

"Baby, not even *you* could get me to miss this run tonight." Relleck grinned before licking his lips slowly. "Though, maybe…if you make it quick."

Lizbeth then laughed girlishly. "Slow down there, big boy. You gotta buy a girl a drink, first. So what's this big deal about, huh?"

"Baby, you're going to have to promise a lot more than a drink to get me to talk about that," Relleck said, his hand intertwining with hers. "Working with some big movers and shakers. Can't just spill my secrets over a drink…"

"Well, why don't you buy me that drink, and we can," she laughed and gave him another come-get-me glance, "*talk* in private."

"You got it, baby," he said, brushing his finger on her cheek as he turned to find a bartender.

"Well, that was interesting," Lizbeth said, dropping her sexy glance.

"Sickening is what that was." Razia made a disgusted face.

"Oh please, like you've never sweet talked your way into a bounty," Lizbeth said, before stopping to look Razia up and down. "On second thought, I don't know if you know *how* to be nice."

"I dunno. She did let him go last year," Sage mumbled.

Razia snapped her head around so fast it nearly cracked. "Ex-*cuse* me?"

"I'm just saying. First with VJ, and then all of a sudden—"

"Oh, do you think I just showed him my boobs and he let me go?" Razia seethed with anger.

"I didn't *show him my boobs*," Lizbeth said sounding offended, but she was obviously not a part of this conversation.

"I'm saying that you let him go," Sage retorted. "And there's no good reason why you should have done that, so I can only *assume*—"

"Assume what?" Razia's face heated up in anger and embarrassment.

Sage's face also turned red. "I'm just saying that you fight with him a *lot*."

"I also fight with you, asshole," Razia growled, pointing her finger at him. "I seem to be surrounded by people who piss me off!"

"So you're not…?" Sage sputtered.

"Not *what?*"

"Ugh, forget it!" He stormed off, leaving Razia completely confused.

"Where'd she go?" Relleck said, standing in front of them with two drinks in his hand. Razia looked around and realized Lizbeth had disappeared during her tête-à-tête with Sage.

Razia got a whiff of one of the drinks and coughed. "God in Leveman's Vortex, Relleck, why don't you just skip the alcohol and drug the poor girl?"

"Yeah, and maybe if you'd get drunk, you'd quit being such an annoying bi—*Oof!*" Relleck wasn't able to finish his taunt as her fist connected with his stomach.

***

Razia very quickly found herself lying face up in the street, having been unceremoniously dumped there by the two bouncers.

"Worth it," she smirked, pulling herself upright.

She dusted herself off and turned back to the club. She still had questions, such as why the runners weren't posting the announcements of the government ship hijackings and where the money was coming from. But at least she'd figured out why she hadn't seen any activity in the intraweb.

She stuffed her hands in her pockets and began the walk back to her ship when she heard a familiar voice.

"Yo," Lizbeth said, walking out of a dark alley with a grin on her face. "Have fun in there?"

"What are you still doing here?" Razia asked. "I thought you'd be long gone by now?"

"I'm waiting for Relleck to come out. I want to see what kind of 'special deal' he's got."

"So why don't you go wait at his ship?" Razia asked, unable to hide the disgust on her face.

"If I could find it, I would," Lizbeth said. "But since my bounty hunter quit on me…"

Razia sighed and unhooked her mini-computer, making a dramatic show of finding Relleck's last parking transaction. This was the *last* bit of help she was going to give this Lizbeth woman, especially if she was going to sleep her way to getting what she wanted.

"He's in a parking deck four blocks away. Under the name Owen King."

"Thanks," Lizbeth said, pushing off of the wall and walking down the street.

"Use a condom," Razia said, unable to stop herself.

"Excuse me?"

"I said, use a condom," Razia replied. "He sleeps around a lot."

"And you would know?"

"I've seen him with a different girl every night."

"Well *thank you* for that *astute* observation," Lizbeth said with a warning tone that Razia missed entirely. "I'm so *grateful* that you're looking out for a fellow female."

Razia rolled her eyes. "Yeah, right, just make it quick so you can quit slutting it up around pirate bars. The sooner you finish your stupid investigation, the better."

"Are you jealous of all the attention I'm getting?" Lizbeth asked sweetly.

"I'm not jealous, I'm disgusted," Razia replied, unable to hold back. "You walk in here with your tits and your ass hanging out, and you expect me to respect you in *any* way?"

"Wow," Lizbeth said, shocked. "Just because I *like* looking like a woman doesn't make me a slut. And just because you don't respect my methods doesn't mean you can't respect my results!"

"And what kind of result are you going to get by sleeping with Relleck?"

"God in Leveman's Vortex, I'm not going to *sleep* with him," Lizbeth exclaimed. "I'm going to *hide out on his ship*! So I can figure out *where he's going*!"

Razia opened her mouth and then closed it again.

"It's a miracle," Lizbeth gasped sarcastically. "You finally shut up."

"Hey, you can *get sucked*," Razia growled.

"You know, for a girl who spends a lot of time with men, you are awfully catty," Lizbeth said, squaring her shoulders and placing her manicured hands on her hips. "Did you have some bitchy sisters or something?"

Razia blinked at her, remembering with vivid clarity the Peate sisters. They were catty, and had nothing else to fill their days but gossip about each other and everyone else in the family. She remembered the way they circled her like feeding sharks when she was at the Manor last year, commenting on everything from her skin to her clothes to her apparent loneliness.

The thought that she was anything like them was enough to shame her into silence.

"And besides that," Lizbeth said, steeling her glare. "You, *of all people*, should appreciate what it feels like to be the only person on your own team. I know what the other pirates say about you."

Razia shifted uncomfortably.

"Funny enough, it was the exact same thing you said to me," Lizbeth continued humorlessly. "'Why doesn't she quit while she's ahead? Can't she take a hint?'" She paused to smile. "'Somebody just needs to bed her so she'll stop causing so much trouble.'"

Razia's eyes widened; she hadn't heard that last one.

"I've heard worse, trust me," Lizbeth said. "But you know what keeps me going? I know when I'm right, and I want to shove it in their sweaty faces when I show them all up. Because I know I'm better than all of them anyways."

Razia clenched her jaw, repentant but unsure of what to say.

"So I guess I'll be proving it alone," Lizbeth said, turning to walk away.

Razia couldn't let her walk away. "Lizbeth, wait. You can't sneak onto his ship by yourself."

"I can *handle* it—"

"No," Razia said, jogging after her. "Relleck rarely does anything alone, and he never plays fair. Trust me I…know from experience. He wouldn't hesitate to…well…" She remembered the way Sage berated her the year before. "It's never a good idea to go up against him without some kind of backup."

"So what, you want to come with me now?" Lizbeth asked.

Razia shrugged, adding, "I would feel kind of bad if something bad happened to you."

"Is that as close to an apology as I'm going to get from you?"

"Why in Leveman's would I apologize?"

CHAPTER EIGHT

Relleck's ship was a monstrosity, the biggest ship in the reserved docking station near Eamon's. And with all the other pirate ships nearby, that was saying something.

Razia and Lizbeth waited until one of Relleck's drunken crew members came stumbling out of another lift with a new female friend, offering them an opportunity to slip on behind him. They hid in the first open room they could find, an expansive gym with state-of-the-art weight equipment. Razia figured that it would be a safe place. None of Relleck's crew would be interested in working up a sweat in here after drinking heavily; though, based on the noises coming from upstairs, she was sure they were working up a sweat in other ways.

Razia did her best to ignore the sounds, as she was more interested in counting each of the inebriated members that stumbled back to the ship. She wasn't sure if Relleck was sporting eight or nine crew members now, but she'd counted six so far. Finally, after what seemed like ages, Relleck was shoving the last of the three crew members onto the ship, berating them for getting so drunk they could barely stand up. For spending so much time at Eamon's, Relleck seemed mostly sober, which was strange to Razia.

Soon after he arrived, the ship rumbled to life and D-882 disappeared out of the window.

"I'm sending you a bill for my parking fees," Razia muttered to Lizbeth. Razia was a bit nervous about being on Relleck's ship. Even though his crew was drunk, they wouldn't be drunk forever. And what if Relleck was bluffing about his "run" tonight?

"Do you think we'll be safe in here?" Lizbeth whispered.

"You should be more worried about how we're going to follow Relleck onto whatever ship he hijacks," Razia said, unwilling to let Lizbeth know she was nervous.

Lizbeth seemed wholly unconcerned. "I thought maybe we'd just slip in behind them onto the ship?"

"It'll be kind of hard to do that with all of Relleck's goons hanging around," Razia said, wondering if this was the worst idea she'd had in…well, ever. "I'm not even sure how long we're going to be on this ship. They looked pretty drunk."

"Relleck said he was leaving tonight," Lizbeth said. "Do you think he can hijack a ship without his crew?"

"I wouldn't think so." Razia again wondered if Relleck had been bluffing about his run that night to get in Lizbeth's pants, and began to feel even stupider for offering to help her.

"I thought you'd be an expert at this kind of thing," Lizbeth said.

"I haven't hijacked a ship in years. Not my cup of tea."

"Oh, do you have moral fiber or something?" Lizbeth teased. "Pirate?"

"Getting hijacked is considered an inevitability by most transporters, cost of doing business," Razia said, repeating what Tauron used to say to her. "It's not moral or immoral. Just happens."

Lizbeth was about to respond when they heard voices. Or one voice, in fact.

"Yeah, no, they're not coming. Stinking drunk, the whole crew. No, I don't need them. I'll have the stuff and be back before they even sober up."

As quietly as she could, Razia slid open the gym door and saw Relleck talking on his mini-computer with someone. He was stuffing some supplies into a bag and slinging it around his shoulder. The ship shuddered to a stop and the hatch opened, revealing a docking station.

"C'mon," Razia said, motioning to Lizbeth to creep closer to the open hatch. Relleck stood at the foot of the ship, engrossed in conversation with a man on the dock. Neither man noticed the two girls as they hurried off and hid behind some nearby shipping boxes. Razia strained her ears to hear what Relleck was saying.

"...just leave it here....it'll be okay..."

"...ain't got no business....need to get it approved..."

"...approvals....up your ass..."

After a few minutes of heated conversation, Relleck went to close up his ship, but stopped and glanced around curiously. He shrugged and shut the hatch, shouldering his bag. Razia and Lizbeth followed close behind.

The station was huge, and although Razia had no idea which planet they were close to or which system, this place was obviously heavily used by transporters. As they left the docks into another hallway, Razia realized that this station was also an inter-system shuttle hub—a place where those without ships could purchase tickets to ride to different systems. The UBU had established a system of shuttles between S-864 and the most inhabited systems for the rather large sub-section of the population without a means of transportation.

The open room smelled of body odor and old fuel and seemed much smaller with all the people packed into it. They bumped into each other as they moved about, headed for their ships or shuttles to other transport stations or planets.

It was difficult for Razia to keep an eye on Relleck, walking ahead of them. He strolled through the throngs of people, twisting and turning as he made a beeline for the main terminal area. Here, there were sundries and small restaurants selling everything from cups of soup to pillows for transporters to sit on during the long days traveling through space.

Relleck seemed to be in no hurry, stopping to grab a cup of coffee and chat with a cute girl at the sundries place. When Razia saw his C-card slide through the reader, she immediately searched her list of aliases for him. After a moment, she found what she was looking for:

Passerini, Zachery		
Time of Transaction	Location	Amount
UT20015-04-10-90:43	Transport Station G-279	15C
UT20015-04-10-85:06	Eamon's D-882	50C
UT20015-04-10-84:98	Eamon's D-882	50C

"We're on a transport station near G-279," Razia whispered. Relleck was still sitting at a table as if waiting for someone.

"So we're near G-245?" Lizbeth asked.

Razia rolled her eyes. "Leveman's, don't you know anything about how planets are named?"

"No," Lizbeth snapped at her. "It's not something you generally learn in school."

"They're not named for the system. They're named for the type of planet. G-2 planets have high concentrations of iron ore," Razia replied, as if it were obviously common knowledge. "So no, obviously, we're no where near G-245."

"There's no government contract with G-279 to my knowledge," Lizbeth said, watching Relleck stand up to greet a transporter. The other man was older, with a potbelly and a scruffy beard. Relleck offered his new friend a seat, and the man sat down with considerable effort. Razia smiled as the man ordered something from the pad at the table and slid his C-card through the reader.

Transport Station - G-279		
Time of Transaction	Account	Amount
UT20015-04—10-90:45	Moses, Angelino	15C
UT20015-04—10-90:45	Agertop, Esaw	20,000C
UT20015-04—10-90:44	Solokov, Cynesige	20C
UT20015-04—10-90:44	Eliphelet, Maier	50C
UT20015-04—10-90:43	Passerini, Zachery	15C

"Angelino Moses," Razia murmured. She searched on his name in the Universal Bank and pulled up his last transactions:

Moses, Angelino		
Time of Transaction	Location	Amount

UT20015-04-10-90:45	Transport Station G-279	15C
UT20015-04-10-90:40	Transport Station G-279	100,000C
UT20015-04-07-60:45	PAYCHECK SALAZAR SHIPPING	45,000C
UT20015-04-01-50:47	Universal Savings Grocery W-346267	4000C

"Looks like he works for Salazar Shipping," Razia said watching them continue to talk. "Is that one of the shipping companies on your little list?"

"Oh sure, because I've memorized all six hundred of them."

"What, you don't have a list of them already in your mini-computer?" Razia asked, eyebrow raised.

Lizbeth still didn't seem to understand. "Why would I do that?"

"Wow, you really do suck at this."

"Ssh!" Lizbeth said, as Relleck stood with the man's keys in his hand. Relleck said a few more words to him, and the two men laughed as Relleck strolled away, spinning the keys around his finger. The other man looked pleased with himself, if not ready to go on vacation, as he sipped on his coffee.

"I'm not an expert in pirate hijackings," Lizbeth noted, dryly. "But I don't think—"

"No, it wasn't normal," Razia said. "At least, when Tauron used to do them, the guys were a little bit surprised—if not annoyed. It was never…expected like this?"

"Let's see where he goes," Lizbeth said.

***

Razia shifted, trying to find a comfortable spot between the two boxes that she assumed held raw ore, based on the smell. It made her head spin, or maybe the lack of air pressure and limited artificial gravity was the cause. The transport guild had mandated that all transport companies utilize a minimum set of life-preserving features within each shipping container, as they were tired of finding cold, asphyxiated bodies in their shipments. But the pressure and warmth was only enough to sustain life, not to make it comfortable. After all, they just wanted to prevent stowaway deaths, not encourage freeloaders.

Still, even with the pressure in her head and the tingling cold in her fingertips, she was warm from excitement. She was going to go "catch" Tauron today, the same way she had been catching him for years now. This game they played started when he realized Harms had given her a pirate log-in to the Universal Bank, and she was able to track him through his aliases. So he'd created a new one, and she'd found him yet again. Then he began using multiple aliases, switching back and forth. She figured out his pattern and anticipated where he'd be next. Of course, in-between these rounds, he would drag her back to the Planetary and System Science Academy and tell her to stay there. It had been a while since he begrudgingly accepted her as a pseudo member of his crew, but he still refused to make it easy for her to find him. That was how she liked it.

What she didn't like was having to get to D-882. Unsurprisingly, legal shipments to the pirate planet were quite rare, and she'd learned more than once about climbing onto a transporter and hoping it would get hijacked. Calling for help was useless. The one time she'd called Tauron to come and get her, he'd laughed in her face and told her to figure it out. That didn't mean he wasn't beaming with pride when she showed up half a day later. He told her it was character-building, tests for when she was out in the real world without him.

She checked his transaction history to see if he'd left D-882.

Ball, Tauron		
Time of Transaction	Location	Amount
UT20012-05-12-00:00	D-882	0C
-END OF HISTORY-		

Her breath caught in her throat.

Suddenly, the doors of the shipping container flew open and she was staring at the Arch of Eron in the center of Leveman's Vortex, a rope hanging from the center, and a hooded man standing on the dais.

"Tauron!" she screamed, scrambling to get to him, but her legs were lead.

She smelled sulfur. Plethegon.

Under her feet, the ground began to crumble. She was unable to breathe, a noose wrapped tight around her own neck.

The ground gave way under her…

"Yo!" Lizbeth's voice snapped her out of her dream.

Razia sat up-right and immediately regretted it, as her vision filled with black dots from moving too fast. She still felt like she was falling, but she realized they were descending onto a planet. Without the gravity stabilizers, they were forced to endure the shifting pressures—one of the unfortunate downsides of not riding in the main cabin of a ship.

"Leveman's, the things I do for this job," Lizbeth moaned, bracing herself on the boxes of raw ore. She gave Razia a curious glance. "Are you okay over there? You're pretty pale."

Razia's heart was still pounding from her dream, and her chest ached. She had forgotten for a brief moment, and was filled with such warmth and happiness. In the cold reality, however, she remembered that he was gone forever.

"Hey?" Lizbeth repeated. "Are you okay?"

"Yeah," Razia nodded. With a great thump, the transport ship landed, shifting all the boxes around them as they settled firmly back on the ground.

"So I guess we're here?" Lizbeth said, standing up slowly.

"Yeah, but where is here?" Razia wondered aloud, also coming to her feet. She pressed her ear to the container door, listening intently. When she didn't hear any voices or steps approaching, she lifted a lever to open the door.

Air rushed in as the door slid open. They were in a docking station of some kind, blackened and dirty from years of use. There weren't any other ships that she could see, but she did spy a familiar stone clocktower out a grungy window.

"We're on S-864," Razia gasped.

"The capital planet?" Lizbeth blinked. "Why would Relleck go here?"

"I don't know, but this is definitely nowhere near S-6642."

"And I don't remember there being any record of material going to S-864." Lizbeth shook her head. "Besides that, how in Leveman's Vortex did he get here so fast?"

Somewhere in the room, a large machine hummed to life.

"What's that?" Lizbeth asked.

"I—" Razia stumbled to her knees as the container lifted upwards. The door flew open as the container swung in the air, and a box tumbled out, exploding as it hit the ground. Razia's eyes nearly flew out of her head when she registered the contents sprawled out on the floor.

"Guns?" Razia gasped before the force of the container stopping in mid-air tossed her to the ground. She gripped the floor as it swung back and forth. Without the humming of the machine, she was able to hear voices.

"Did you check the cargo and make sure it was secured?" Razia didn't recognize the man's voice, but from the tone, she assumed that he was in charge.

"Listen, Sarge, my job is to drive the ship," a voice that was most assuredly Relleck responded. "If you got a problem with the way it's packed, then you gotta talk to Angelino."

"If anything else is missing or damaged, it's going to come out of your fee," the man replied. "And it's *Major*, pirate."

"Roger that, Major Pirate," Relleck said, and Razia could almost see his smirk.

If there was more conversation, she didn't hear it, as the machine hummed to life and they were swinging again, this time headed downwards. They landed with a hard thump that made all the boxes shift again, and they could hear the major screaming at the operator to be more careful.

Razia was too caught up in the bliss of standing on solid ground to realize that the door to the shipping container was wide open, nor notice the sound of footsteps approaching.

"Hide, Lyssa!" Lizbeth hissed, diving behind a stack of boxes.

"What?" Razia said, standing up just as the door fully opened and she was face-to-face with two young soldiers.

"Shit."

***

Razia took stock of her situation silently:

She was tied to a chair in a makeshift office off the side of the shipping warehouse, with one soldier and his gun standing by to guard her. She was slightly offended by their underestimation of her, but she

110

was more thankful that it would be easy enough to escape once she was untied. Lizbeth was nowhere to be found, which was either a good thing or a bad thing. She hoped that the investigator was smart enough to make herself scarce and sneak off the shipping container after Razia had made a fuss.

As Razia was dragged through the warehouse by the two guards, she noted the stacks and stacks of other shipping containers, much as she'd seen on the planet where she'd captured Cree Hardrict. But unlike on B-725425, these boxes were filled with guns, or at least some of them were—guns transferred in a faux hijacking from G-279 by Relleck, who said he had his own "special deal."

She peered around at the dusty window, spotting the clocktower next to the presidential palace. Who would want to transport guns to the capital city, especially so close to the seat of the Universal Government? The thought made her nervous. Though she couldn't care less about the UBU, complete anarchy wouldn't help anybody.

She glanced over at her guard, wondering how this military man could be mixed up in something illegal, when she realized with a jolt that his gray uniform wasn't that of a soldier. She could see a patch on his chest that she didn't recognize, clearly making out a double letter S.

But the man in charge had been called Major, which meant *he* was a soldier. So was this a commercially owned warehouse or one owned by the military? Razia peered around to the manager's desk nearby. If there were any markings or paperwork, they might be able to tell her who owned this warehouse and what it was being used for. Anything she could use to get out of this unscathed.

"Oy, quit looking," the guard growled at her.

Razia cleared her throat. "Fine then. Why don't you tell me what's going on here, junior?"

He flinched when she spoke but said nothing.

"It's rude not to answer people," Razia replied.

"And it's rude to invite yourself to places you are not wanted."

Razia sat up straight, wondering why she was surprised to see the bald man from the secret pirate meeting stroll into the office. He wore the same gray uniform as the guard, who saluted him as he would a superior officer before walking out of the room. The bald man was standing closer to her than the guard had, and she could see that the stitching under his patch said *Secure Solutions*.

"Well, it's rude to not invite people to things, too," Razia replied, wondering how much information she could suss out of him before she managed to get herself free. Secure Solutions—she'd have to remember that.

He was smiling at her amusedly. "I have to admit, I am impressed by your tenacity. But you have a habit of sticking your nose where it doesn't belong. And that has to stop."

To prove his point, he pulled a small pistol out of his pocket.

"How boring," Razia scoffed. "Do you really think that's going to scare me?"

He shrugged, but the gun remained level. "I would hope it would persuade you to tell me what I want to know."

"You know, I won't be able to tell you anything if I'm dead," she said with a smirk.

In response, he moved the gun to point at her shoulder.

"And I'm not going to *want* to tell you anything if you shoot anything less vital, either," she said. "You could, of course, try asking nicely."

After a few moments, he re-holstered his gun. "I like you, Razia. You've got spunk."

She chuckled. "That's what they tell me. So what do you want to know?"

"I want to know how you got into my shipment," he said, leaning against the desk.

"Snuck on. Wanted to know what Relleck was bragging about— and to see if I could get a cut of it."

He cursed under his breath. "That pirate has been a pain in my ass since…"

"I can take care of him for you," Razia said adding, "well, he'd be out of commission for a night."

"Yes, I hear you're quite adept at finding people," he said. "So how's about a deal? In exchange for your assistance, I may consider letting you go…without shooting anything vital."

Razia shook her head. "I never agree to a deal until I know the specifics. And it's a bit hard for me to agree to anything while tied up."

"You help me find that other woman who infiltrated our meeting, and I will let you go," he smiled. "I'll even add a sizable bonus."

Razia's heartbeat quickened, but her face remained stoic. "What do you know about her?"

"Not much, I'm afraid," he said. "But she keeps showing up in places where she's not supposed to be, and we'd like to find her and… take care of her."

"The less I know about what you're planning to do, the better," Razia said, nodding to her tied hands. "Now, if you'll untie me so I can look in my mini-computer, I should be able to find her in about five minutes."

"I'll hold you to that," he said, stepping behind her and cutting her ties with a knife.

Razia rubbed her wrists for a moment, assessing the situation in her head—how far he was from her, where his pistol was on his hip. How long it would take him to grab said pistol.

Then she shot out her leg, knocking him to the floor. On instinct, she grabbed the first thing she could get her hands on, the chair she had been just tied to, and whirled it around, knocking the bald man to the floor. He lay there, motionless, and she tossed away the remnants of the wooden chair.

The door opened just as she was running to it, and she found herself face-to-face with the barrel of a gun.

"Oh, you got free?"

Razia let out the breath she was holding when she saw the familiar friendly face of Lizbeth behind the gun.

"Well shit," Lizbeth said, dropping the gun lower. "And here I was coming to rescue you."

"Yeah, right." Razia rolled her eyes. "Let's get out of here."

***

"So they don't know anything about me?" Lizbeth smiled.

"Not even your name," Razia replied.

They were on yet another crammed shuttle on S-864, trying to lose anyone who might have followed them. Razia had to take care of two guards at a side entrance, but other than that, it was relatively easy to sneak out of the warehouse.

Almost too easy, Razia decided.

"I think it's time I go deliver a report to my superiors," Lizbeth said, looking out the window into the darkness of the underground shuttle tunnel. Yet again, General State stared down at them from his campaign posters, as if the grungy shuttle car personally affronted him. "I think we've passed the realm of simple insurance fraud."

"So *you're* bailing now?" Razia asked with a slight smile. "You're cool when we're shot at, but shipping guns is where you draw the line?"

"You would be surprised how many times I've been shot at in this line of work. People get very protective over their funding streams," Lizbeth laughed. "Besides, I'm not bailing, I'm just doing a pulse check to see if I'm still in my swim lane or if we need to start a joint task force with the Universal Police."

"Really? You want to ask for their help after what they said to you?" Razia asked, as that was the only thing she understood from that entire sentence.

"Why not? I asked for yours after what you said to me?" Lizbeth replied coolly.

"Touché," Razia conceded. "So is that where we're going? Your office?"

"Well, it's past close of business now, and everyone's gone home for the day," Lizbeth said. "So I'll have to go into the office in the morning to deliver the report."

"Yet another day of parking fees for me," Razia sighed, thinking about her ship back on D-882. She didn't even want to think about how much it was going to cost when she finally got back.

"Oh relax!" Lizbeth laughed and stood up. "I'll make sure I submit your expense report tomorrow. In the meantime, you are welcome to come crash on my couch. Free of charge."

CHAPTER NINE

Lyssa woke up the next morning with a crick in her neck from sleeping on Lizbeth's couch. She heard a faraway beeping of an alarm in the other room. She wore a large, old nightshirt of Lizbeth's, and her pirate clothes were tossed haphazardly on the other couch.

Taking advantage of the early morning sunlight, Lyssa looked around the swanky apartment. Much like Lizbeth, it was perfectly put together and just a hint of femininity. Knick-knacks and sculptures sat on wooden shelves on the walls—small details that blended into the decor seamlessly. The floors were spotless, the kitchen gleaming. The only area that seemed out of place was the dining room table, where reams of documents and an open laptop sat. She saw a cup of cold coffee next to the laptop and realized that Lizbeth must have continued working after Lyssa had gone to sleep.

Speaking of coffee…

Lyssa yawned and shuffled to the kitchen. She heard Lizbeth's alarm go off again, but didn't see the other girl stirring, so she set to making the coffee in a sleepy daze. She had half fallen asleep standing next to the coffee pot when Lizbeth's alarm went off for a third time, and she set to finding a couple of cups in the gleaming cabinets.

"Good morning, sunshine," Lyssa said, walking into Lizbeth's bedroom and placing a full cup on the nightstand.

"Go away…want thirty more minutes…" Lizbeth groaned and rolled over. Lyssa was pleased to see that at least she didn't wake up gorgeous.

Ignoring Lizbeth, Lyssa walked over to the closet and flung open the doors. The closet was jam-packed with clothes—some hung up but many others stuffed into shelves and exploding out of bins. On the floor, there were piles and piles of shoes.

"What are you doing?" Lizbeth asked.

"I need something new to wear." Lyssa dug through a pile of clothes and pulled out a black tank top. It was lower cut than she normally wore, but it would do.

"Oh, really? I thought you wore the same thing every day," Lizbeth said, curling up under her sheets.

"Do you have any cargo pants?" Lyssa asked, now sorting through the piles of jeans, slacks, and other different kinds of pants. She pulled out a pair made out of a black stretchy material and pursed her lips.

"Those would look good on you," Lizbeth commented. "You have a nice butt."

Lyssa ignored her comment and went back to searching for anything a little less…clingy, but found everything else too nice or too restricting. Even though she was accompanying Lizbeth to her office, she still needed to look something like Razia.

She took the clothes and a fresh pair of underwear to the bathroom, closing the door behind her. The bathroom was as disorganized as the closet, although the counters were covered in different colored eyeshadows, eyeliner pencils, blush, and different tinted skin cremes. There was also a faint smell of Lizbeth's perfume and shampoo, which was a mix of flowers and mint.

Lyssa hopped in the shower, the warm water washing off the remnants of the ore smell that still hung in her nose. Lizbeth had a selection of shampoos, conditioners, and body washes and Lyssa chose the one that smelled the least fruity. After leaving the shower and drying off with the fluffiest towel this side of the Manor, she pulled on the borrowed clothes and wiped the fog off of the mirror.

"Whoa," she whispered to herself. As opposed to the baggy black cargo pants and loose tank she normally wore, this tight outfit made her appear sleek and slim. She adjusted the waist of the pants to smooth out the curve on her hip, taking a moment to soak in the way she looked. She shook her head, wondering why she cared, and walked out of the bathroom.

"Hey there, hot stuff," Lizbeth grinned, sitting up in bed. Her face was pale without any makeup, and her normally perfect hair was frizzed up around her ears. "You should keep those pants. They look great on you."

"Yeah well," Lyssa said, feeling uncomfortable with the praise for her body.

"Hey…can I put a little make-up on you?" Lizbeth asked cautiously as she slipped out of the bed. "Not a lot, but just…a little bit."

"I don't wear makeup."

"I know you don't. But just…a little bit."

Lyssa hesitated, unsure what to do. She'd always been quite curious about make-up, but having grown up with her father and then Tauron, she'd never had anyone around to really show her what to do. And she often felt she'd be teased mercilessly if she tried it.

But, she was already feeling rather pretty in Lizbeth's more girly clothes. And she wasn't bound to run into any blond, asshole pirates today.

"…all right," Lyssa said after a few moments.

"Sit on the toilet," Lizbeth ordered, going through her makeup.

To Lyssa's surprise, she pulled out a pair of tweezers and began tapping them together.

"What's that for?" Lyssa asked nervously.

"Just…I kind of have this eyebrow thing," Lizbeth said, walking up to Lyssa. "I won't do much, but yours need a bit of shaping."

And without another word, she climbed on top of Lyssa and straddled her on the toilet, grabbing her forehead and tilting it back.

"*Whoa*!" Lyssa said, too shocked to push her off.

"Ssh," Lizbeth said, inches from her face. "This will only take a moment."

"I'm very uncomfortable right now," Lyssa said, her voice filled with apprehension from the intimate way this stranger was violating her personal space.

"I don't care," Lizbeth replied, holding Lyssa's skin taunt and beginning to pluck. Lyssa winced at the sharp pain of her hair being ripped from her skin.

"Ow!" she yelped when a particularly painful hair beneath her eyebrow was ripped out.

"Ssh, ssh, ssh," Lizbeth said uncaringly, placing her thumb against the skin. "You're fine."

"Do you sexually assault all your houseguests, or am I just lucky?"

"Oh stop," Lizbeth said, before looking down at Lyssa. "You aren't gay, are you?"

"No."

"Well, you know, the tough girl act, wasn't sure," Lizbeth shrugged, continuing to pluck. "I mean, it's fine if you are—"

"I'm not," Lyssa said.

"So are you seeing anyone then?" Lizbeth asked conversationally as she plucked. "I haven't seen you with anyone or calling anyone since I met you."

"I'm not *dating* anyone," Lyssa replied, wincing as another painful one came out. "I don't have time for that crap."

"Yeah, with your attitude, I'm surprised you aren't still a virgin," Lizbeth smirked, winking at her. "It's probably more secure than the Universal Bank down there."

"Can we not talk about this while your crotch is on mine?"

"Fine," Lizbeth said, sitting back and giving her a tired look. "But we're not done talking about it."

After a few more minutes of uncomfortable silence and hair plucking, Lizbeth sat back and examined her handiwork.

"Much better," she sighed, turning to grab an eyebrow pencil. "Now, hold still…"

***

It was nearly two hours later when Lizbeth and Razia left the apartment. They hopped on the underground shuttle again, which was much less crowded than the day before. As Razia hung onto the pole for balance, she caught her reflection in the window and admired for a moment. Lizbeth hadn't stopped with the eyebrows and the eyeliner, but spent some time on Razia's hair as well. Razia normally only brushed it after she got out of the shower and left the rest to fate. Thanks to Lizbeth's flat iron, today it was bouncy and full of shine.

That, plus the tight black clothes, made Razia feel gorgeous, even standing next to Lizbeth.

Lizbeth smiled when she caught Razia watching her reflection. "See how much better you feel when you put forth a little effort?"

"Too much effort," Razia said, quickly looking away.

"You're a piece of work," Lizbeth sighed, but she was smiling.

At a stop near the presidential palace, three U-POL Officers walked on, deep in conversation. Razia caught the reflection of their gold-trimmed markings before realizing one of them was the same lieutenant who had almost arrested her the year before.

And the third one was Jukin.

She was suddenly on edge. Lizbeth stood up straighter as well, especially when the lieutenant spotted them on the train.

Razia's eyes met Jukin's and she wondered whom he saw. The last person he had seen was Lyssa Peate, but today she was dressed as a pirate. Razia and Jukin had never actually had a conversation, she realized, although she was sure that he was quite familiar with her, especially after the kidnapping incident last year.

"You!" he snarled unhelpfully.

"I have a name you know," Razia replied as casually as she could. Lizbeth didn't move to say anything, continuing to glance between the two of them.

"I'd prefer not to use it, pirate," Jukin spat.

Razia smirked, but inside she was churning violently. He had seen both Lyssa and Razia but hadn't made the connection. Something about that hurt very deep inside of her, and it made her irrationally angry towards him.

And again, she was reminded that it would only take one word—one small hint that she was both Razia, the hated bounty hunter, and Lyssa, the hated sister—and his entire career, his life, in fact, would be over.

"What are you doing cavorting with criminals, Carter?" Jukin, ignorant of Razia's inner turmoil, had turned his attention to Lizbeth.

"Well, since you were *so unhelpful* when I asked you for help," Lizbeth said, relaxing a little bit with a shared look to Razia, "I opted to employ someone who would get me results."

Razia smiled and folded her arms over her chest, the inner voice increasing in volume as Jukin stood next to them. She was sure he could hear it, as loud as it was in her mind.

"You should be careful," Jukin said with an air of superiority. "Hiring a pirate is illegal under the Piracy Act."

"Then you'll be glad to know that I'm volunteering out of the kindness of my heart," Razia replied, struggling to stay present and not fall back into her churning mind. "But knowing that it pisses you off too, well…all the more reason for me to help out!"

"You had better watch your tongue, pirate," the young lieutenant replied. His name tag read Opli.

"Calm down, junior," Razia said, flashing him a grin. "I'm a card-carrying member of Dissident's web now. No need for hostage taking today."

"Don't think I've forgotten about that," Jukin snarled.

"Good to know you haven't forgotten about *that* one," Razia muttered, and the voice began roaring within her. Jukin remembered Vel being kidnapped, but couldn't seem to recall when his own sister had a gun pointed to her head. Not as if he cared then, either. "Be my guest," he had said, as if inviting Tauron to take out the garbage.

And then the son of a bitch *killed* Tauron.

The ache grew more painful and it was hard to keep her face stoic.

"Don't say I didn't warn you, Carter," Jukin said, stepping closer to them and ignorant of the war inside of Razia. "This pirate may have protections now, but we'll see how long that lasts. And when that happens, you may want to reconsider your alliances."

"Well, this is our stop," Lizbeth said, as the shuttle slowed. She grabbed onto Razia's arm tighter than was probably necessary as she dragged her off. "Pleasure, as always, Captain Peate—"

"See ya around, Jukin!" Razia said icily as the door closed and the shuttle left the station.

"Why do you have to do that?" Lizbeth asked, exasperated. "He could have recognized you!"

"Let him," Razia said, eager to talk about something else. "What did you mean back there about him not wanting to help you?"

"A few weeks ago, when you so *maturely* stormed into his office, I was there giving him all of my findings to date. Spent an hour showing concrete proof that pirates were involved in major insurance fraud, and he said he wasn't interested."

Razia stopped in her tracks, all previous thoughts about Lyssa and Razia gone from her mind. "Hang on…Jukin wasn't interested?"

"That's what he said before he threw me out of his office. I thought it was because a certain sister had just pissed him off, but he refused to see me again when I tried to schedule another meeting."

"But he's always looking for something to arrest pirates for," Razia said, watching the empty hole the shuttle disappeared through. "That's his thing?"

"That's what I thought too," Lizbeth said, stepping out into the city streets above. "So that's why I'm not willing to share any more information with anyone else until I get some top-cover."

***

"Name?"

"Razia."

She handed over her C-card with a scowl. Since the Intelligence Agency where Lizbeth worked was a secure facility, Razia had to be cleared for entry into the Investigative Division offices. This was after walking through four metal detectors, five key-carded doors. Now she had to receive approval for a visitor's badge from an annoyed, gray-uniform-clad security guard.

"That's not a name," the woman sighed, looking at the card closely. "And this isn't a valid identification. There's not even a last name on here!"

"Give her your other one," Lizbeth said impatiently. "I only have half an hour before my meeting, and I need to stop by my desk and prepare."

"Come on," Razia whined. Lizbeth elbowed her roughly, and

Razia handed over her Lyssa Peate C-card. The woman took it and began typing furiously in her computer.

"Who are you visiting?" she snapped.

"Me, Lizbeth Carter," Lizbeth replied, hopping from one foot to the other. "MC-IF-PIR."

"What in Leveman's does that mean?" Razia asked.

"Acronym for my office code," Lizbeth replied, more focused on the woman in front of them.

"And what is your purpose for visiting?"

"Meeting," Lizbeth said. "And she'll be here for just one day."

The guard handed Lizbeth a tablet which she signed and placed her thumbprint on. The tablet shone green, and she handed it back to the woman.

"You will have to leave your mini-computers here, please," the woman said to Razia.

"What?" Razia looked to Lizbeth in horror. "Why do I have to give up my mini-computer?"

"It's not a cleared device," Lizbeth said, taking the aforementioned device out of Razia's hand and giving it to the woman. Razia leaned forward with a pained look on her face, as if a piece of her soul had just been ripped away.

"But…!"

"You'll get it back," Lizbeth said, handing Razia the red visitor's badge and dragging her down the hall into a room filled with dark blue cubicles. She weaved down one aisle, then another, then took a left, then a right, until she reached a desk covered in neatly arranged stacks of papers.

"Okay, *stay here*," Lizbeth ordered. "I'm going to go pre-brief my boss before I bring you in. Isaac, if anyone comes by, just say she's with me." She nodded to the man across the cubicle hall, who turned to examine her.

"Okay?" Lizbeth pressed to the man, who seemed about sixty. He grunted in response, returning to his computer, slowly reading through the bottom lens of his thick glasses. With an exasperated noise, Lizbeth disappeared in a blaze of curls.

Razia suddenly became aware of the sterile office environment she now found herself in. All around her, the quiet click of fingers on keyboards, the soft conversations and ringing of communicators, with the occasional ding of an incoming message. There was a man on the other side of the cloth wall, as Razia could hear him coughing every few minutes, a loud, throat-clearing garble that was annoying the first time she heard it.

In other cubicles, Razia saw other government workers—including one woman who had come to work in sweatpants. Most of the workers didn't even give her a passing glance, too engrossed in working as slowly as possible. She even saw one woman working on what appeared to be a novel while her messages inbox remained empty.

Razia felt bad for Lizbeth, who was a veritable fireball of energy compared to these slowpokes. When Razia was at the Academy, she had to deal with some idiot professors and lab partners, and it was always frustrating. Lizbeth was probably bored out of her mind working here; it was no wonder she spent so much time in the field.

With nothing else to do, Razia sat down at Lizbeth's desk and began leafing through the papers piled in the corner. Every one was the same format, a Form 2875 used to report on pirate activity. These weren't related to the big case that Lizbeth and Razia were working on, but seemed to be smaller open-and-shut cases. Razia found a couple of humorous ones that reminded her of some of the jobs Tauron used to do. One featured a woman who had reported a set of her husband's expensive sculptures missing only to discover them in her lover's bedroom. Another was a case where one sibling had hired pirates to steal a family heirloom, and then the other sibling was hiring pirates to steal it back.

Another report was about a business claiming that all of their shipments had been hijacked, but it turned out the business had just encountered a bad string of luck and the case wasn't insurance fraud after all.

Razia pulled a thick folder at the bottom of the pile and found the stash of background information on the pirate meeting. She was slightly impressed with Lizbeth's formality and attention to detail. She documented detailed conversations with Sage about the upcoming secret pirate meeting and discussed a meeting on D-882 between Cree

Hardrict and a man named Alfr Jos, and another meeting between Jos and Krishna Harman.

Harman was the bald man, Razia reminded herself. The one who was guarding the shipment of guns Relleck was delivering.

The guns were more concerning to her than anything else she'd found so far. Pirates didn't use guns. It put a damper on the whole "game" aspect of piracy if there was a chance a pirate could be killed in the process (Jukin's aspirations aside).

Razia flipped through the case studies again, searching for Relleck's name on any of the reports. She paused at one from over six months ago. Relleck had commandeered a shipment from G-245, a shipment owned by Salazar Shipping. Without her mini-computer, she couldn't verify it, but she was pretty sure Salazar was the same company that owned the ship Relleck hijacked the day before. She wondered if the hijacking described in this report had been as easy as the one she saw yesterday.

Her attention was quickly diverted when she heard loud stomping coming up the cubicle aisle.

A red-faced Lizbeth came flying into the cubicle.

"This is…*Ugh*!"

"Bad meeting?" Razia asked lightly, quickly putting the manila folder down.

"*They told me to leave it alone!*" Lizbeth screamed, drawing the attention of nearly all of her cube-mates. "They said, 'Oh, if it's pirates, you should leave it alone.'"

"But…isn't that what you do?"

"*Yes*!" Lizbeth exclaimed. "I work for the *Goddamned pirate division*!"

Razia nodded and shrunk down into her seat as Lizbeth continued pacing in the small cubicle.

"They won't approve any more travel funds for this effort, they told me I have to work on some other case now," Lizbeth continued, throwing more papers into her bag. "God in Leveman's Vortex, I *hate* working for the government!"

Razia wasn't sure how to respond, so she sat in silence.

"*Leveman's*!" she cried, on the verge of tears. "I need a drink. Let's go get a drink. I can't stand to be here any longer."

"But we just got here?" Razia said, following Lizbeth out the door.

***

Lizbeth was still fuming when they stepped off the shuttle in her neighborhood, but Razia finally felt as if she'd cooled off enough to be able to speak without biting Razia's head off.

"So what happened?" Razia asked cautiously.

"So I get in there," Lizbeth said, her voice shaking, "and I tell my boss about the guns and about everything we've found out to date, about Hardrict, about the meeting, all of that. And he listened for a minute and told me to sit down, that he was pulling me off this case."

"Did he say why?"

"He gave me some bullshit excuse about needing to spread cases amongst the team, and told me that I was doing too much." Lizbeth shook her head. "You know, I should just quit. Nobody ever listens to me anyways. I get up there and I talk about these cases, and my boss just asks these inane questions that have *nothing* to do with what I just spoke about. And I put together these fifteen-page reports *every day*, and nobody ever reads them. Then they have the audacity to say, 'I have no idea what you're talking about.' Read the damn report I sent you!"

Razia nodded, unsure of what to say or how to react, but was quite sure Lizbeth needed to vent. When her father would go off on angry tirades, it was usually best to pretend like she didn't exist.

"And I feel like I'm doing all this work…and nobody's supporting me," Lizbeth finished, sounding more defeated than angry as they walked into the lift. "I know there's something going on here. I just *know* it."

Razia said nothing, still waiting for the rest of the rant to come before she tried to say anything.

"You know what?" Lizbeth snarled. "*Screw it.* I'm going to continue this investigation on my own. I'm going to find out what's really going on here and shove it in their fat faces. I don't care if they fire me, I know I'm—"

Lizbeth's breath caught in her throat as her eyes stared ahead.

"My door is open."

The hair on Razia's neck stood up, and she threw a protective arm in front of Lizbeth. She *knew* they had gotten away from the warehouse too easily. They shouldn't have come back to the apartment; they should have gone to a hotel or...

"We should call the police," Lizbeth whispered.

"Stay here," Razia whispered back, creeping up to the door and quietly pushing it open with her foot. She checked for any sign of movement or a weapon or a Dal-Jamus-sized goon, but with a flick of the light, she found the living room completely empty.

Ransacked, but empty.

"Oh Leveman's," Lizbeth said, rushing past Razia into the apartment and helplessly taking in the mess around them. "This is a mess..."

"Anything stolen?" Razia asked, peering into the bedroom to make sure no one was hiding in there. She peered into the closet as well, not completely satisfied that they were safe until she'd checked every nook and cranny.

"Lyssa..." Razia heard Lizbeth's shocked voice in the living room and came running.

"What is it?" Razia said, dashing into the living room, fists up. She saw Lizbeth staring blankly at the empty dining room table, a broken coffee cup at her feet.

"They took my laptop," Lizbeth murmured. "They took all the paperwork, my computer—all the evidence I'd been amassing....it's gone."

"Don't you have a backup?" Razia asked.

Lizbeth began to laugh frantically. "Oh sure, there's backups of my computer. But they'd need to order me a new computer, which will take up to two months. Then they'd need to submit a ticket to get the computer re-imaged, which could take another month." She gave a half-smile. "Government efficiency at its finest."

"Well, maybe—"

"Lyssa, you don't understand," Lizbeth said, looking around the house nervously. "Nobody's ever known where I lived before. This is... this is..."

"They're just trying to scare you," Razia replied, opening the kitchen pantry.

"And they're doing a good job of it!" Lizbeth exclaimed.

"Oh come on," Razia said, walking back into the living room. "I thought you said you'd been shot at before—"

"*This is my house!*" Lizbeth cried. "I'm not safe here anymore. I...no one's ever known...I don't know how I'll ever be able to sleep in here..."

To Razia's complete and utter shock, Lizbeth sank down onto the dining room chair, placed her head into her hands, and began sob. Razia watched her moan and cry into her hands and felt an odd urge to comfort this stranger. Rarely the recipient of comfort herself, she had no idea what to do.

"I can't stay here," Lizbeth moaned, shaking her head. "I can't... what if they come back for me? Oh Leveman's, what if they follow me?"

"Well look," Razia said, finally able to speak, "why don't we head back to my ship on D-882? I think I know of a place we can go where they won't be able to find us."

"Yeah?" Lizbeth sniffed. "Okay..."

"Bring your running shoes."

CHAPTER TEN

Lyssa came trotting up to the ship, panting and sweating something fierce. The fifteen miles went a bit slower than when she would run with Vel, who had a habit of goading her into running faster. But this planet was flat, the grasses low, and the temperature perfect—just as she had expected it to be. She personally felt in a much better mood than before, but she couldn't say the same for Lizbeth, who had barely said a word since they left her apartment on S-864. She just kept staring ahead in blank defeat that Lyssa knew all too well.

Lyssa knew better than to bother the girl; at least, she hated to be bothered when she was frustrated. So she'd extended her run to a couple of hours, even stopping to do a bit of excavation on a particularly interesting field with multi-colored flowers, hoping that Lizbeth would have cooled off enough to be ready to work again.

But when Lyssa saw her sullen compatriot, Lizbeth was anything but relaxed.

"Oh, so glad you decided to come back," she snapped cattily. "Thought you were going to leave me here."

"As you are sitting on my only mode of transportation off this planet, that's highly unlikely," Lyssa replied, trying not to rise to the bait.

Lizbeth angrily slapped the side of her face. "*Goddamn bugs!*"

"Oh, what's the matter?" Lyssa chuckled, walking by. "You can't handle a little camping?"

"I *hate* camping," Lizbeth seethed, slapping her arm. "I hate this planet and I *hate you!*"

Lyssa ignored her tirade and made her way onto the ship, and over to her silver cabinets. She dug around for a moment, tossing aside salves and aloe for sunburns, until she found the antihistamine and the bug spray in her first aid kid. She strolled back outside and tossed the tube to Lizbeth.

"What in Leveman's is this?" Lizbeth grumbled, carefully reading the tube.

"It'll help with the bites," Lyssa said, placing the can of bug spray next to her.

Lizbeth's face softened slightly and she carefully unscrewed the cap on the antihistamine. "Thanks…"

Lyssa sniffed in response and bent over to stretch out her sore hamstrings.

"So what in Leveman's are we even doing here anyways?" Lizbeth asked.

"I needed money," Lyssa grunted and popped back upright. "Since I'm not getting reimbursed for the enormous parking bill I racked up yesterday."

"Oh, great," Lizbeth snapped, holding her breath as she doused herself in bug spray. "So we're out in the middle of nowhere because you need money. Meanwhile, pirates are out hijacking ships filled with guns and taking them to the capital, and we have no idea why."

"Well, and I thought a run would be nice, but you didn't want to go," Lyssa said. "So I was giving you some space…"

"Yeah, space is all that I need," Lizbeth continued. "Everyone just wants me to relax and calm down and give my projects to other team members because *that's the team spirit*. I've been bringing in five times as many case reports as everyone else, but am I even seen as a team lead yet? *No!*" She had clearly begun to rant again, pacing around the small clearing in front of Lyssa's ship. "And *you*! Bringing me out to the middle of *nowhere* just so you could…could…well make money!"

"Being out here always…it always makes me feel better…clears my head…." Lyssa stammered. "I thought…"

"Just because *you* like it, doesn't mean that I…" Lizbeth trailed off, having a realization. "Is this…all of this is your way of trying to make me feel better?"

Lyssa's face reddened and she stared at the ground awkwardly. "I mean, you said that you didn't feel safe…and when I don't…I mean, no one knows we're out here…'cept for my stupid boss brother…but he's not gonna come all the way out here to…"

"God in Leveman's Vortex," Lizbeth gasped, some of the life coming back to her face. "You actually *are* trying to be nice?"

"It happens sometimes."

"Well, next time you want to be nice, you gotta let me know," Lizbeth laughed. "Because you sure confused the crap out of me."

"It's not just about you," Lyssa said defensively. "It's about…I mean, I am doing a planet excavation, because I do need money, and —"

"Say no more. I won't tell a soul that you're really a big softy at heart."

"Whatever," Lyssa sniffed angrily, marching back onto the ship to wash off the sweat and embarrassment.

***

After her shower, Lyssa wanted to take some more samples from the surrounding area, and Lizbeth decided to come along. Even though Lizbeth was no longer moping, Lyssa could tell that she was deeply preoccupied with her stolen laptop and stagnant investigation.

"So what's next?" Lyssa asked, trying to be conversational as she stuffed another leaf into her sensor and waited for the read-out. "You told your boss about the guns and he didn't care. Can you go around him?"

"Maybe," Lizbeth said. "I've done it before, but only when I had a tight case and I could definitely make an arrest."

"I mean, they're transporting guns. Is that enough?"

"We don't know what they're doing with the guns, though."

Lizbeth chewed on her lip. "For all we know, that security company could be bolstering its arsenal with shipments of stolen guns because they're a security company. That's…well, sadly, that's normal pirate business. Hijacking cargo isn't necessarily anything new, even if it is guns."

"You know that's probably not what's going on," Lyssa said dryly. "Why would they have gathered all of the pirates, all of that secrecy? Why are they hiding the hijackings altogether? Why would those two diner people shoot at us?"

"Where are those guns coming from?" Lizbeth added.

"And how is that bald guy involved?"

"Harman, yeah," Lizbeth chewed on her lip. "He works for General State."

Lyssa stuffed another leaf into her sensor. "Doesn't it seem fishy to you that General State would be working with pirates? Or that those two guys would even have connections in Llendo's administration to set something like this up?"

"Not really. Politics is shady business. And piracy's got a lot of money."

"But that's what's confusing, right? The insurance companies aren't getting notified…"

Lizbeth's head tilted up. "What's that now?"

"When a transporter is hijacked, they notify their insurance company," Lyssa said, thinking aloud as she twirled a leaf in her hand. "The insurance company then puts out an announcement about the hijacking to the U-POL which is how it ends up on the pirate intraweb."

"So?"

"So if there's nothing showing up on the pirate intraweb, then the insurance companies aren't getting notified," Lyssa said, deep in thought as she scanned another leaf. "And if they aren't getting notified, then the businesses aren't getting reimbursed for their lost cargo."

"And if they aren't getting reimbursed, then who's footing the bill?" Lizbeth finished for her. "If they're supposedly just paying the pirates to take their own cargo?"

"And we know that some of the cargo is going to S-864, and being protected by that Harman guy. He works for a company called Secure Solutions."

"Secure Solutions," Lizbeth mumbled, chewing on her lip. "Why does that name sound familiar?"

"Maybe it was something in your reports?"

Lizbeth thought for a moment and shook her head. "Can't remember. We don't all have hard drives for memories like you do."

"I don't know if a security company could afford to pay a couple hundred million credits to pirates anyways," Lyssa said. "And besides, we only saw them at that one warehouse. Maybe they were just hired to guard it. Maybe he was just wearing the uniform to fit in."

Lizbeth's face fell, the new lead suddenly evaporating under her.

"I mean, maybe not," Lyssa said quickly, trying not to deflate Lizbeth's bubble. "I mean, we're obviously onto something or else they wouldn't have taken your laptop, right?"

"That still terrifies me," Lizbeth said, and Lyssa saw her shiver a little bit. "I don't like that they know where I live now."

"You seem able to take care of yourself," Lyssa replied. "Didn't you say you knocked out three guards to come…er…rescue me?"

"I snuck up on them," Lizbeth admitted. "Knocked them out with the butt of the gun."

"Well, that makes sense," Lyssa mumbled, louder than she meant to.

Lizbeth placed her hands on her hips. "And what is *that* supposed to mean?"

"Just saying that you don't…" Lyssa trailed off, wondering if a bit of good-natured ribbing would cheer Lizbeth up. "You don't even know how to throw a punch."

"Of course I do!"

"Really, because when you tried to hit me before, you were terrible at it."

"All right, tough girl," Lizbeth said, squaring her shoulders. "Want another go at it?"

Lyssa attached her mini-computer to her belt and folded her arms across her chest. "Go for it."

With a heave, Lizbeth reached back and whirled forward, but Lyssa stepped out of the way, grabbing her arm and knocking her to the ground.

"See?" Lyssa smiled from above her. "Terrible."

"That's 'cause you knew I was coming," Lizbeth grumbled as she picked herself back up.

"No, it's because no one ever taught you how to hit. Show me your fist."

Lizbeth proffered her hand.

"See, your thumb is inside your hand there," Lyssa said. "You'll break your thumb."

Lizbeth moved her thumb to the outside.

"Don't punch with the flats of your fingers either. Hit with the knuckles and you won't hurt yourself. Aim to punch with the first two knuckles, and keep your wrist straight."

"Okay."

"Now, the other thing you're doing wrong is throwing all your weight into the punch on the first go-round. You never want to throw a heavy punch, try a one-two jab like this," Lyssa punched her right arm out, then her left. "Harder to defend in that case."

Lizbeth slowly punched the air as Lyssa had.

"Keep your arms level with your shoulders," Lyssa said, watching Lizbeth. "Keep your chin down…"

"Anything else you'd like me to remember?" Lizbeth grumbled, awkwardly trying to throw punches into mid-air.

"Don't aim for the head. Aim for the chest or the ribs. If you aim for the face you'll break something. Use your hips for power, not your upper body. Root your feet."

"Anything else?" Lizbeth huffed.

"Yeah, don't hit anyone until you've had more practice," Lyssa smirked, stepping away to test some more specimens and chuckling at Lizbeth's enraged growl of frustration.

***

Lyssa worked and Lizbeth continued to practice punching random trees until the sun began to sink low in the sky and Lyssa made the call to trudge back to the ship. Lizbeth went to take a shower, and Lyssa set to building a campfire and rehydrating some of the food. As the night descended around them, they quietly ate the bowls of noodles and vegetables, enjoying the sound of the local avian species chirping in the distance.

"I can see why you don't want to give up the whole scientist bit," Lizbeth sighed, looking up at the stars. "This is pretty amazing."

Lyssa's eyes snapped over to Lizbeth but then she turned back to watch the fire. "Well, it's good money. Untraceable. Nice to have the separate income."

"I see," Lizbeth said, sounding as if she didn't believe her. "It's been a while since I've been able to see stars on a planet. Can't ever get a glimpse on S-864, but I used to see them all the time on C-47478462."

"Is that the planet you're from?" Lyssa asked, realizing she knew absolutely nothing about this woman she'd been working with.

"Nah, I'm from S-864," Lizbeth said. "Well, I was born there anyways. Both my parents worked for the UBU. But they retired about ten years ago and bought some property on C-47478462. Spent a couple years there before I joined up with the Intelligence Agency."

"C-planet," Lyssa said, thinking. "Residential?"

"You got it. They bought about fifty square miles surrounding a giant lake. Dad always loved the water, but Mom said she wasn't going to live on an all-water planet and have to deal with taking boats to and from places. So they compromised and bought a lake."

Lyssa knitted her brows together. "Your parents sound…normal."

"My dad is a giant dork," Lizbeth laughed affectionately. "And I love my mom, but she's crazy."

"Not as crazy as mine," Lyssa murmured, but Lizbeth didn't hear it.

"Mom's always calling me to make sure I'm not dead," Lizbeth laughed. "She was worried about me going into field work, of course, but she's gotten over it mostly. The only thing she gets mad at me for now is that I don't get out to see them as often as I should."

Lyssa said nothing, an ache in her chest.

"So," Lizbeth said, completely unaware of Lyssa's pain. "Now that we've got a chance to talk…we should continue our conversation from the other day. Are you a virgin?"

"That is a completely personal and inappropriate question," Lyssa snapped, jarring from the jump from Lizbeth's parents to her sex life.

"Come *ooon*," Lizbeth said with a grin. "You're such a locked-down person. I want to know if you've ever been in love."

"I slept with someone, but I wasn't in love with him," Lyssa said. "I was sixteen, and he was a fellow student in the Academy. Everyone else was doing it, so I did it to get it over with."

Lizbeth's eyebrows bolted upwards. "…To get it over with?"

"I was tired of being a virgin so I fixed it," Lyssa said, as if it was just a normal everyday activity.

"Wow, and I bet it was just the best thing you ever had, huh?" Lizbeth drawled.

Lyssa shrugged. "It was whatever."

"Yeah, okay…" Lizbeth laughed. "You know—and I can't believe I'm having this conversation with you—sex is actually a beautiful thing, and a *lot* of fun."

"You are obviously speaking from experience," Lyssa said, with more edge than she meant to.

"Yeah, I am," Lizbeth snapped back. "Because I'm a hot-blooded female and I like to have sex. Doesn't mean there's anything wrong with me." She paused to give Lyssa a look. "And don't you dare bring up that crap with Relleck."

After a pause, Lyssa asked, "Would you have slept with him?"

"Oh I dunno, maybe," Lizbeth said, taking Lyssa off guard with her indecision about the matter. "Not for information, anyways, maybe just…you know, for fun."

"Fun?"

"Yeah, he's got a nice body."

"He's a dick."

"I didn't say I wanted to marry him." Lizbeth rolled her eyes. "You don't date someone like that. Hit it and quit it as fast as you can. Now Sage, on the other hand—I could marry that guy. Marry him and bang him like a screen door in a thunderstorm."

"Wow, this is…really uncomfortable," Lyssa said, turning to the dark forest around them. The thought of Sage having sex with anyone was enough to make her ill.

Lizbeth laughed heartily. "You are too uptight, Lyss."

"I don't understand how you can be so free with talking about that kind of stuff when everyone doesn't respect you? You said yourself that everyone's talking about sleeping with you to make you go away."

"And those people can get sucked," Lizbeth replied with a firm tone. "Who I choose to sleep with has no bearing on who I am as a government investigator, or even as a human being."

"But you're perpetuating their perceptions of you."

"Until I show up at their front door with a bunch of U-POL officers and arrest them," Lizbeth smiled. "I mean, look at you. You *act* like a man, and you're still treated like crap. So why not just do what you want to do and screw everyone else?" She paused and added, "Not literally, of course."

Lyssa was quiet for a moment and then asked, curiously, "Have you ever actually slept with someone you were investigating?"

Lizbeth opened and closed her mouth, a sly smile. "Okay, seriously you are the *only* person I have ever told this to, and don't you *ever* tell my mother but….yes."

"What?" Lyssa sat up in surprise.

"Calm down, it wasn't…totally about the case," Lizbeth said with a devilish grin. "He was this hotshot executive of this jewelry company I was investigating—one of my very first ones, to be honest…and, well…" she trailed off. "He was gorgeous, I was young and naive, and it was damned near the best sex of my life. But it was completely stupid because he ended up screwing me over in the end."

"So that's the only one?"

"I flirt a lot, and I let them think they're going to get it. And then usually they just start spilling their guts to me." She tossed a small rock over to Lyssa. "You should try being nice once in a while with these bounties you capture. It would completely throw them off."

"I'll be nice when they start respecting me," Lyssa mumbled, her thoughts drifting to her own bounty, most likely still with Pymus' credits keeping her aloft in the rankings. She hadn't checked it in a while, but she wasn't holding her breath that it had changed. Especially since she hadn't captured anyone in a few weeks.

And yet, she actually didn't mind it too much. This investigation stuff was actually kind of exciting and fun, and she didn't hate Lizbeth as much as she did at first.

"Oh boy, all this chit-chat. We need a drink," Lizbeth sighed. "You got anything alcoholic on that ship of yours?"

"You know," Lyssa said, standing up to the protestations of her tired legs. "Hang on one second."

She trotted onto her ship, grabbing onto the ladder and hoisting herself up to the top level. She made a beeline for the front of the ship, bending down to remove the panel under her dashboard. There was her father's journal, right where she had left it the year before when they returned from Leveman's Vortex. Behind it was a small wooden chest, and, tucked between some wires, a bottle. She reached in and carefully unwound it from the cables before closing the panel.

"Well, well, well!" Lizbeth grinned as Lyssa came back to the campfire. "What do we have here?"

"Bottle of top shelf whiskey," Lyssa said, taking a seat next to her. The alcohol burned as it went down and she almost gagged.

"Let me show you how it's done," Lizbeth said, taking the bottle and swallowing at least a shot.

"Damn, Lizbeth!"

"My dad taught me how to shoot my whiskey," Lizbeth winked, taking a seat and handing Lyssa back the bottle.

Lyssa took another sip and tried not to retch. "He sounds like a guy I'd like to meet."

"You know, I'll take you to meet my parents sometime. My dad would *love* you."

"Oh yeah?" Lyssa asked, swallowing another drink. "Why's that?"

"He always gets mad at me 'cause all I do when we go out on the boat is drink. You'd probably be useful to him. You'd be able to skin a fish, probably."

"Not in a few years," Lyssa laughed. "Not since my planetary survival course."

"That sounds like a riot," Lizbeth said, taking the bottle and taking another swig.

"Loads of fun. Especially since Tauron told me he was going to come get me," Lyssa grumbled, the whiskey starting to relax her shoulders and her attitude. "Three months alone on a planet, and I brought no supplies, no extra clothes, no food, nothing, because I thought I was going to be there for a day tops. But no, Tauron decided it would be funny to not come get me."

"Why?"

"Oh, he said it was 'character building,'" Lyssa scoffed. "He was always doing crap like that. Making me work to find him on D-882. That's why I became so good at bounty hunting; I had a lot of practice looking for his smug ass."

Lizbeth watched her curiously, as if she wanted to talk about something else. Instead she said, "So, you call yourself a pirate, but all you do is bounty hunt?"

"Bounty hunting *is* piracy," Lyssa replied. "It's a punishable offense under the Piracy Act."

"But I mean, can't you be *hanged* for it?"

The memory of watching Tauron on the Academy monitor came rushing back to Lyssa in her tipsy state. She did her best to shove it back down.

"Maybe now. Since, you know, I kidnapped Jukin's brother and all."

"But...you didn't kidnap him," Lizbeth said slowly. "It was your little brother, I thought?"

"Details, details."

"So why risk it? I mean, what could possibly move you to want a life where you've got the constant threat of being executed over your head?"

"I mean, I'm in the web," Lyssa said with a shrug. "So there's really no threat. Dissident's not going to kick me out any time soon."

At least, he'd better not.

"But still," Lizbeth pressed. "Why do it?"

Lyssa took another long drink and looked down at the bottle, now almost half-empty and laughed to herself. "You know, I bought this bottle of whiskey when I was thirteen to replace the one I stole from Tauron."

"Why did you steal a bottle of whiskey when you were thirteen?"

"Because Tauron had pissed me off. He was hunting a pirate that *I* had found, and he refused to take me with him," Lyssa said, realizing now that perhaps taking a thirteen-year-old to capture a pirate may not have been the best idea. She took another long sip. "So I broke into his liquor cabinet and drank half of his best whiskey. Then spent the rest of the night with my head in a toilet."

"And if you don't slow down, the same shall happen tonight," Lizbeth said, taking the bottle from her.

"Tauron wasn't even mad," Lyssa said, staring into the fire wistfully. "Said that my hangover was punishment enough, but I wanted to replace the bottle. So I bought this one as an apology, but he wouldn't take it. Told me to hang onto it and we would drink it when I...when I captured my first bounty."

The ache returned in her chest and she wished she could stop talking about this, but the alcohol was speaking for her.

"My first bounty was worth one hundred credits," she whispered, her eyes focused on the mesmerizing fire. "It took me six months to convince Dissident to let me go after anyone. And it took another year and a half before he let me go after anyone worth mentioning, and that was simply to fetch his chocolates for him.

"And even now, my bounty isn't even real. My boss at the Academy put up the money for it, hoping that someone would capture me and he could blackmail me into telling him...stuff," she said, not drunk enough to divulge *that* secret. "So...even though I'm one of the most wanted pirates in the universe, I'm still no better than when I was in the low six hundreds."

"So why do it?" Lizbeth repeated quietly.

Lyssa closed her eyes, unable to keep the truth from coming out.

"He was the first person to ever give a crap about me. And when I'm out there, when I'm hunting bounties....I feel like he's still with me."

"What about your parents?"

"My parents?" Lyssa laughed hollowly, taking the bottle back and downing another swig. "My father *left* because I'd screwed up one of his experiments, and my mother told me she wished I'd never been born."

"I'm sure that's not true."

"I heard her say it herself, in front of the entire family," Lyssa said. "Last year."

"Why would she even...I mean..." Lizbeth shook her head. "I don't even know how anyone could say that about their own child..."

"Look, I can count on one hand the number of times I saw my father call her when we were gone, and we were gone for months at a time," Lyssa said. "I don't even know how she got pregnant twenty-four times. I never saw him kiss her. I never saw him even...acknowledge her. His entire world was his research, and nobody was allowed to distract him from it. She couldn't divorce him; that would be scandalous. She couldn't change him even if she tried. So she's stuck in this loveless marriage where her husband pays more attention to his daughter,"—she burped a little, the whiskey burning her throat—"than to her. Not that he ever really gave a shit about me either. Did Jukin a *favor* by not making him his assistant."

"Does it bother you that he doesn't recognize you?" Lizbeth asked.

"No," Lyssa lied, taking another long drink.

"Slow down there, champ." Lizbeth took the half-empty bottle from her.

"Please." Lyssa tried to get to her feet, but found her balance completely off. She tumbled face-first into the ground.

"Yeah, right," Lizbeth said, grabbing her by the arm and yanking her up with some protestations. "I hope there's nothing on this planet that's going to eat us or else we're screwed."

"Nah," Lyssa slurred, steadying herself on Lizbeth's arm. "But I would need the help to walk me to the ship bed. Gotta continue the excavation in the morning."

"Yeah, that's not gonna happen."

CHAPTER ELEVEN

Some hours and a lot of painkillers later, Lyssa was leading Lizbeth through the bowels of the Planetary and System Science Academy station. She had sent a terse message to Dorst asking him to put her in the planet presentation schedule today, but hadn't bothered to check her mini-computer to see if he'd responded. She was more interested in finding her other brother and telling him about everything she'd been up to since she last saw him a few weeks ago.

Even though her head was still pounding and she was slightly nauseated, she was excited to see the little bugger. She assumed he was swamped with school work, and that was the reason why she hadn't heard from him in weeks (not that she'd noticed since she'd been so busy). Compared to Lizbeth, he was the preferable companion. As obnoxious as he could be, he was as smart as Lyssa, an invaluable second set of eyes on whatever problem she was facing. And she just liked his company, too, as he never got her drunk and asked her probing questions.

She was still slightly angry at herself for sharing such personal thoughts with Lizbeth, a veritable stranger. She'd already proven she wasn't above blackmail to get what she wanted; who knows how she'd use Lyssa's pain at missing Tauron against her?

"Where are we going anyway?" Lizbeth asked as they walked down another dormitory hallway, unaware of Lyssa's paranoid thoughts.

"Gonna go find my brother," Lyssa replied, counting the hallways as she tried to remember the path to Vel's room.

"Jukin?"

"No, the one I actually like." Lyssa smiled as she approached the door with his name on it. She turned the knob only to find it locked. Without missing a beat, she whipped out her universal key and jabbed it into the doorknob.

"Are you allowed to do that?"

"The answer to that question is normally no," Lyssa said, twisting and turning the key until the door unlocked. With a grin, she swung it open.

There was active movement coming from the bed, where a guy and a girl were tangled up in each other's arms, soft moans coming from both of them as they writhed together, half-naked in the darkness.

"Oh, sorry," Lyssa said, blinking and going to close the door.

Then she realized one half of the twisty, tangled mess was Vel.

"Lyssa!" Vel gasped, seeing the open door and nearly falling off the top bunk. The girl screamed and hid in the dark corner. He grabbed his pants from atop a nearby lamp, stammering excuses to the girl and to Lyssa.

"What in Leveman's Vortex is *this*?!" Lyssa gasped, horrified and hurt and angry all at once.

"Lyssa, I can explain," Vel said, sliding down the ladder bare chested and quickly retrieving his shirt from the floor.

"Who in Leveman's are *you*?" the girl screamed at Lyssa from her perch atop the bed. Lyssa thought she looked like a horse-faced brat.

"N-no, Isla, it's my s-sister," Vel said, slipping his shirt on and trying to calm the situation before it got worse.

"So *this* is why you couldn't come out with me?" Lyssa seethed, as Vel struggled to compose himself. "You're screwing some whore?"

"HEY!" the girl screamed.

"Can we continue this outside?" Vel pleaded, brushing his hair off of his flushed face. "*Please?*"

"You've got something, right here," Lizbeth said to Vel, putting her hand on her own neck to demonstrate as Vel pushed them out of the room and into the hallway.

"Who is that girl and how long have you been banging her?" Lyssa bellowed, sticking her finger in Vel's chest as the door shut behind them.

"Banging? Really Lyssa, she's my girlfriend," Vel said, adjusting his shirt nervously as two students walked by, giving them an odd glance. "We've been seeing each other since the start of the term."

"Y-you have?" Lyssa said, her eyes widening. "And that's why you didn't want to come hang out with me?"

"Lyssa, come on," Vel pleaded.

"You said it was because you didn't want to be a pirate!" Lyssa said, her voice rising to whining levels. "You said it was because—"

"Keep your voice down," Vel said calmly. "Yes, partially because I have a tough semester, and partially because I *do* actually see myself becoming a scientist one day, but I mean…I'm allowed to have a *girlfriend*."

"That's translation for: he wanted to get some action," Lizbeth offered, unable to keep an amused smile off of her face.

"But why did you *lie* to me?" Lyssa asked.

"I didn't want to, Lyssa, but you're always so *touchy*—"

"*I am not touchy!*" Lyssa screamed, her words echoing in the hallway.

"I was wrong to not tell you about Isla, and I'm sorry. But I didn't want you to freak out about it, and Sage said—"

Lyssa's face fell. "You've been talking to *Sage?*"

"He told me he'd keep you company," Vel said quickly, not realizing that he was making the situation worse. "I was worried about you being alone on your ship without me. You were already so upset when I went back to school."

"I was not *upset.*"

"You called me an hour after you dropped me off," Vel said gently.

Lyssa mumbled something about never having done that and that he could get sucked.

"I'm sorry I didn't tell you the truth, Lyss," Vel said, taking her hand. "I truly am. I was going to tell you the next time I came out with you, but I kept having projects assigned on the weekends, and then you didn't show up for a couple of weeks and—"

"And you were too busy screwing your whore," Lyssa grumbled.

"Seriously, she's my girlfriend, and if you call her a whore again, I will deck you," Vel smiled, but there was an edge in his voice.

"I would love to see you try, seeing as I'm the one who taught you how to throw a punch!"

"Okay, okay," Lizbeth said, stepping between them. "Lyssa, you're overreacting."

"What?!" Lyssa gasped. "He's the one who—"

"And he's right; you are touchy."

Vel smiled thankfully as Lyssa's withering glare turned on Lizbeth, who didn't seem nearly as afraid of it as Vel was.

"*Stay out of this*," Lyssa snapped.

"How about," Lizbeth said, threading her arm through Lyssa's and Vel's and turning to walk down the hall. "The three of us get a bite to eat and calm down, and we can all catch up on what or *who* we've been doing." She winked at Vel.

"I'm still angry with you," Lyssa muttered to Vel, ripping her arm out of Lizbeth's and folding it across her chest immaturely.

"He'll survive," Lizbeth retorted.

***

Vel spent the entire lunch talking about his new girlfriend, but Lyssa refused to listen, mumbling comments under her breath. Lizbeth, however, was engrossed in the conversation, and even provided some pointers on dates and things to buy her, with underhanded digs at the sullen, brooding member of the trio. After lunch, they traipsed back to her lab so Lyssa could put together her planet presentation. Naturally, the conversation turned to Lizbeth's investigation. Vel was most interested in their adventures, staying silent until the mention of Razia's outfit at the pirate meeting.

"So wait a minute, you wore a miniskirt?" Vel laughed, his eyes nearly falling out of his head.

"And she looked hot in it too," Lizbeth added.

"Get sucked," Lyssa said, as Vel cackled happily.

"So this meeting was attended by everyone—runners, top pirates," Lizbeth said, "and they basically confirmed all of my suspicions up until that point. They were paying pirates to target specific ships so the cargo could be re-sold, except none of the pirates that I was tracking were even *there*."

"The deal was only good until the election," Lyssa interrupted, typing in a comment about the water quality that may or may not have been entirely truthful. "The two guys who led the meeting were supporters of General State and said that the deal would be over once the administration changed."

"He is ahead in the polls," Vel noted casually.

"After that, we followed a lead to see if the pirates have been dropping off cargo to S-6642," Lizbeth continued. "There was a contract to deliver goods to a nearby military-owned arsenal, but one of the transporters was delivering his cargo directly to S-6642. So in a stroke of genius, your sister was able to figure out a way to get us onto the planet."

"Yeah, remember that awful woman that offered me a job last year?" Lyssa replied to Vel. "She got hired by a planetary services company that owns that planet. So I went on a job interview." She paused, frowning. "I never heard back from her either."

"The planet was completely empty," Lizbeth said. "Except for one building. So we realized that Delmur couldn't have been delivering his cargo to S-6642, but then we saw a diner nearby—"

"Who's Delmur?" Vel asked.

"The guy I was hunting when I left you on that planet," Lyssa said nonchalantly. "Remember? You only keep reminding me every second you can."

"Well, I mean, you *did* leave me without food or water, and I did have to go to the hospital," Vel said. "And me being in the hospital did result in that whole business with the U-POL..."

"Are you going to let me tell him or are you two going to keep interrupting?" Lizbeth snapped. "After the diner, we found a tall drink of water named Royden Relleck"—Lyssa snorted—"and he took us all the way to S-864. Turns out he was transporting guns."

"Guns?" Vel blinked. "But pirates don't use guns?"

"He was transporting them for somebody else," Lyssa said, "which is why I'm now even more concerned. Especially considering one of the two guys at the pirate meeting was also at the warehouse on S-864. His company was providing security, I think."

"Harman," Lizbeth said, sitting back. "But I had so much more, on my laptop that was stolen. I mean, Contestant's pirates have been hijacking government ships for months now, I had all of the case reports where pirates had specifically hit ships owned by certain companies—"

"Salazar," Lyssa said, looking back at Lizbeth suddenly. "Back in your office, I read a case report from a few months ago where Relleck hijacked a ship owned by Salazar. It was the same company that owned the ship he stole the other day." She unhooked her mini-computer and tossed it to Lizbeth. "Go look it up. Guy's name was Angelino Moses."

"Thank Leveman's Vortex for that steel-trap mind of yours," Lizbeth grinned to Vel who was shaking his head.

"So what's next for you two?"

"You're wrong, Lyss," Lizbeth said, cutting Vel off with a puzzled tone.

"What?" Lyssa said, turning around on her chair. "Wrong about what?"

"It says here the company he worked for is called Gabi—not Salazar."

"That's not right," Lyssa said, getting up and walking over to take her mini-computer.

Angelino, Moses		
Time of Transaction	Location	Amount
UT20015-04-10-90:45	Transport Station G-279	15C
UT20015-04-10-90:40	Transport Station G-279	100000C
UT20015-04-01-50:47	Universal Savings Grocery W-346267	4000C
UT20015-04-01-00:00	PAYCHECK GABI SHIPPING	10000C

"That's not the same company that I saw," Lyssa said, her brows furrowed. "I remember specifically it was Salazar, because I saw the same one on your desk."

"Can't be," Lizbeth said. "Universal Bank transactions are always right."

"No, *I'm* always right," Lyssa said, sitting back down at the computer, perplexed.

Her thoughts were interrupted by impatient rapping on her glass lab door. Dorst stood outside with his usual frown. Lyssa pushed aside her thoughts and walked over to the door, cracking it only a hair.

"Can I help you?" she drawled with an overly dramatic look on her face.

"Let him in, Lyssa," Vel snapped from behind her. "Don't be rude."

She made a huge show of rolling her eyes and opened the sliding glass door all the way, allowing Dorst to walk into the laboratory. She slumped back into her chair and made her best attempt to ignore him.

"Yes, well, thank you, Vel," Dorst said, pausing to look at Lizbeth curiously. "Who are you?"

"None of your business," Lyssa replied, adding more data points to her presentation. "Did you stick me in the planet line up today or what?"

"No, I didn't," Dorst said sternly. "You still haven't completed any of your license renewals, nor had your booster shots, and you've missed five scheduled career appointments with me."

"And I still don't care," Lyssa replied. "Put me in the line-up."

"Not until you at least get your booster shots," Dorst growled back. "You are in danger of infecting this *entire* station."

"Ew, really?" Lizbeth said, making a face.

"I'm sorry, who are you?" Dorst asked.

"Person I'm working on a side project with," Lyssa said, cutting of Lizbeth before she could say anything. "Lizbeth, this is my idiot supervisor, Dorst."

"And your older brother," Dorst insisted.

"Oh, really? Admitting that now?" Lyssa drawled sarcastically. "Here I thought I was disowned. That's what Jukin said anyways."

"When did you go see Jukin?" Dorst asked.

"When I found out he *stole* my inheritance." Lyssa was angry at

Jukin on so many levels. Stealing her inheritance was a pittance compared to the burning hatred she felt when she thought about Tauron. Even *that* paled in comparison to how she felt when Jukin didn't even recognize her. Even after seeing Lyssa in his office, and then Razia a few weeks later, he failed to make the connection.

And yet, her anger turned to curiosity as she pondered how he was uninterested in hearing Lizbeth's evidence on the conspiracy. When they saw him on S-864, he seemed almost *smug*, and he had mentioned that pirates wouldn't have their protections for much longer. Hope sprung eternal, she supposed, but it was odd how confident he felt that whatever stupid plan he was concocting was going to work.

"He...he stole your inheritance?" Dorst gaped, bringing her thoughts back into the room. "But how? That money was earmarked for you only."

"Being Captain of the Special Forces has its perks, I guess," Lyssa said, purposefully typing more in her presentation.

"I'm sorry," Dorst whispered. "Do you need money? I can transfer some of mine—"

"I wouldn't if you'd just put me in the damned planet line up today!" Lyssa scowled, completely ignoring his overture.

"Fine," Dorst said, pulling his own mini-computer own of his pocket and typing into it. "You're in for today. Now when can I expect you to complete your professional development plan?"

"When I feel like it," Lyssa said with an overabundance of sass. "I've got more important things to worry about right now."

"I'll try to convince her," Vel spoke up.

Dorst looked appreciative. "Thanks, Vel. How's your girlfriend doing?"

Lyssa's hand thunked on the desk and she spun around in her chair. "So *he* knows?"

"Well, I mean, he's here and..."

"God in Leveman's Vortex, does *everyone* know but me?"

"Well, he did bring her home last weekend to meet the family," Dorst said, ignoring Vel's frantic movements to stop talking.

"Oh," Lyssa said, looking at Vel. "You went back to the *Manor* last weekend?"

Vel sighed loudly. "*Yes*, but I promise you, I—"

"You know what? We're *fighting*," Lyssa sneered at Vel before turning back around to furiously type at her computer.

"What does that mean?" Dorst asked, glancing between Vel and Lizbeth.

"Normally it means that she's not going to talk to me for two or three days," Vel said, sounding annoyed. "Then she'll pout for a while, throwing me mean glances and finally forgive me by the fourth or fifth day. Usually by the sixth she'll have forgotten—"

He wasn't able to finish that thought as a dusty old microscope went whizzing by his head.

***

"You know, if I didn't know any better, I'd say you were a real scientist and not a spoiled three-year-old," Lizbeth said, meeting Lyssa on the side of the stage after her presentation.

"Would you like to see my degree?" Lyssa replied, giving her a look as they walked into the buyers' room together. The linoleum was peeling in the corners of the room, and there were marks where chairs had been scraped across the floor. It had that same funny musty smell of too much air conditioning in a small space.

"So this is where the magic happens, huh?" Lizbeth asked, eyeing the walls. "Geez, you'd think they would spring some money to update the decor in here."

"Why would they do that when there's pollination pattern studies to fund?" Lyssa replied as planet buyers came trickling into the room.

"So how much do you think you'll get?"

"This planet should net me enough credits to cover my expenses for a few weeks," Lyssa said, before adding with a smirk, "as long as I don't leave my ship in an expensive dock for three days again."

Lyssa intended for that barb to go to Lizbeth, but the latter had her eyes set on a prospector who had just walked into the room. The devilishly handsome planet buyer from Antica's old company took a seat in the back of the room, his dark grey suit clinging to his frame, his hair lazily falling into his eyes.

"Yummy," Lizbeth purred. "I'd go to school to study that

attractive specimen right there…"

Lyssa looked away, hoping that he wouldn't notice her fawning again. However, the handsome man was ignoring Lyssa in favor of Lizbeth, eyeing her with the same type of appraising look that Lizbeth was giving him. Lyssa shoved down the jealous feelings; who wouldn't choose Lizbeth over her anyway?

"Oh what, him?"

"Yeah him," Lizbeth said, nudging her and noticing the flush on her cheeks. "You like him, don't you?"

"I mean, he's whatever."

"Whatever to me means you are interested in getting in his pants, because that's how you described the *one* sexual encounter—"

Lyssa cut her off with a wave of her hand. "Why are you so interested in my sex life?"

"Or lack thereof?" Lizbeth taunted. "Because you need to have more fun in your life."

"I have plenty of fun," Lyssa replied. "And why do you care?"

"Excavating planets and hunting pirates? That's not fun; it's *work*. Leveman's, even when you went to Eamon's, you were working!"

"*Yes*, and that's fun enough for me."

"I think you're just lonely."

"I'm not *lonely*," Lyssa gasped and stared at Lizbeth as if she had two heads. Two of the planet prospectors looked at her curiously. "I'm happy being alone."

"If you were happy being alone, you would have been happy for Vel that he had a new girlfriend instead of being jealous," Lizbeth said. "Ergo: lonely."

"No, I'm angry because the little shit *lied* to me."

"I have a feeling that you would have reacted the same way if he'd told you the truth immediately," Lizbeth said. "He obviously cares a lot about you, and I don't think he'd ever do anything to intentionally hurt you."

"I'm not…having this conversation with you right now," Lyssa said, annoyed that the planet buyers weren't sitting down so she could start the auction.

"Seriously," Lizbeth said, leaning over her shoulder. "If you were to go over to that guy right now and tell him to take you out tonight, he would do it."

"No, he wouldn't, because he's married."

"*Aha*!" Lizbeth exclaimed loud enough for the planet buyers to glance over again. "Thank you for proving my point. You're interested."

"How does me noticing he's married prove that I'm interested?" Lyssa asked uncomfortably.

"Because if you weren't interested, you wouldn't have noticed he was married."

"I'm gonna sell this planet now," Lyssa said, standing up so she could get away from Lizbeth's prying questions.

"Suit yourself," Lizbeth winked flirtatiously at the handsome man.

Lyssa cleared her throat loudly. "Let's start the bidding at one hundred…"

"One hundred five."

"One hundred ten!"

"One hundred twenty!"

***

The planet sold for two hundred thousand credits to a young buyer who clearly had no idea what he was doing, as the planet was barely worth fifteen thousand. Still, he happily handed over his C-card to pay for his purchase, and Lyssa was happy to receive two hundred thousand credits. The handsome prospector had stopped bidding at one hundred fifty and promptly left the moment the planet was sold.

Lyssa thought about the handsome man on the way back to her ship, mulling over what Lizbeth had said about her being lonely. Sure, he was gorgeous and smelled like she wanted to go somewhere private with him, but he seemed to be a real asshole from the ten minutes they'd spent in the same room together. Besides, he was married, and he was probably too handsome for her anyway. Everyone in that company seemed to come from the same well-dressed, planet snatching stock like Antica Mikaelsson.

She thought about the stern, heel-clacking, pearl-wearing woman who had been such a formidable foe the year before. From their limited interactions, Lyssa was sure that Antica wouldn't be happy unless she were in the thick of things, barking orders at subordinates. So why would she—knowingly and seemingly happily—take a job out on a desolate planet where the only person she could bark orders to was a sweet secretary? Even if the money were good, there seemed to be no good reason why she would willingly give up such a fast-paced lifestyle.

Along that same thought, why would a company, Wedekind Planetary Services, construct only one building on a planet? Antica had said they were in contracts for fifteen more, but there were no cranes, no building materials left on the planet. It was as if they finished the one tower and decided that was enough. If they were planning to build more, wouldn't they have at least left the equipment? Moving that number of cranes, tools—it would have been less expensive to just leave it there, even if they never returned.

She slowed her walking, pondering this idea for a moment as another popped into her head.

What if the one tower was all they intended to build?

After all, Delmur had been delivering cargo to S-6642 for months when she caught up with him. She had assumed she spooked him enough to create new aliases, explaining why the four she had discovered when hunting him the first time now lay dormant. Thinking back on the actual encounter, he seemed relatively unconcerned with her, definitely not worried enough to go through the trouble of creating new aliases.

"What are you thinking about?" Lizbeth asked.

"Delmur," Lyssa said slowly. "What if he stopped delivering cargo to S-6642 because his job was done?"

"But we didn't see any cargo there?" Lizbeth replied. "It was just an empty building?"

"What if the building was it?"

"Okay, yes, but…*why*? Why go through all that trouble to build a single tower on an uninhabited planet? And if you're going to do that, why go through the trouble of hiring a new executive vice president for operations to leave her all by herself?"

"All good questions, and I think I know someone who can answer them for us."

"Who? Delmur? You said you couldn't find him again. You said all of his accounts were dormant since you captured him?"

"Yeah, but I know someone who knows *exactly* where Delmur is," Lyssa said. "Because he knows *everything*."

CHAPTER TWELVE

"Hi Harms!" Razia chirped as she and Lizbeth slid into Harms' booth.

"Leveman's Vortex, Razia, you scared me!" Harms said, one hand over his heart. He quickly turned off the tablet that he had been looking at. She thought she saw the pirate intraweb, but couldn't get a good look at it before the screen went blank.

Harms, however, had taken notice of the second woman in the booth.

"I'd heard you were running around with a new friend." Harms reached across the table to shake Lizbeth's hand. "The name's John Harms, pleasure to meet you."

"Lizbeth Carter." She shook his hand firmly.

"And you, little missy, are in a *lot* of trouble," Harms said, suddenly pointing his finger at Razia. "Dissident is not pleased that you're poking your nose into all of this stuff. Said it was much easier when you were just bounty hunting."

"Yeah, well he's never happy with me anyways, so what does it matter?" Razia shrugged.

"It matters because you've pissed off some very wealthy benefactors," Harms said, "who have threatened to cut everyone off from the millions of credits they were promised."

"What can you tell us about them?" Lizbeth asked.

"Oh no. No way. I'm not helping you dig your own grave. These men are *serious* and you could get hurt," Harms said, looking at Razia. "And by hurt, I mean *killed*."

"We know," Razia said. "Trust me, I've already been threatened with a gun more than once during this little fiasco."

"Then why are you still digging?" Harms asked incredulously.

"Because I have a job to do," Lizbeth said.

"And I can't find any pirates anyways. They've all created new aliases," Razia said. "That, or they've completely disappeared."

"What with nosy bounty hunters breaking into their supposedly secret pirate meetings, perhaps they don't want you two showing up," Harms said.

"Can you tell us what they've been contracted to do?" Lizbeth asked.

"You didn't hear in the meeting?" Harms asked, a smile twitching at his mouth. "Or did that happen after you were thrown out in your mini-skirts?"

"Oh, get sucked," Razia huffed. "We know they're hijacking government ships, we just don't know where."

"All over really," Harms said. "N-42653, S-4296, and N-38324 are the three main ones though. The guys are intercepting the cargo nearby and dropping it off on the planet. Once the insurance company completes their investigation and the company gets paid for their supposedly missing cargo, they'll pay the pirates."

"Has anyone been paid yet?" Lizbeth asked.

"Conboy Conrad said he got paid, but I think he's bluffing, I didn't see any money in his accounts," Harms said.

"Do you know of any of the aliases they're using?" Razia asked. To Harms' curious face, she replied, "I only want to talk to them."

"Unfortunately, no," Harms said. "Everybody has been so wrapped up in this thing that nobody's had time to stop by and talk to me about what's going on. So your guess is as good as mine. I can't even figure out why the runners aren't announcing the hijackings in the pirate intraweb."

"Do you think they're just pulling the records or…" Razia trailed off. "Do you think the insurance companies aren't getting notified?"

Harms cocked his head. "What makes you say that?"

"If no one's getting paid for the jobs, maybe it's because the insurance companies haven't been notified."

"I'm sure they are," Harms said. "Otherwise, why else would they have asked the pirates to go through all this trouble?"

"That's what we're trying to figure out," Lizbeth said. "Did you know about Relleck?"

"Relleck?" Harms shook his head. "What's he got to do with this?"

"He's got his own special deal," Razia said. "Transporting guns from G-279 to S-864."

"*What?*" Harms said, sounding genuinely surprised. "I haven't heard anything about anyone transporting *guns*!"

"And we saw one of the two guys from the secret pirate meeting in Relleck's gun hideout," Razia said. "Which means that the rest of the pirates might also be transporting guns."

Harms' brows furrowed. "Did Relleck know what he was transporting?"

"He didn't seem too surprised when a box of them cracked open," Razia said.

"Contestant's pirates have been hitting a specific set of government ships for months," Lizbeth said with a nod. "It's how I originally got involved. Cree Hardrict was another one acting strangely."

"Evet Delmur as well," Razia said, watching Harms' reaction.

"Oh, your old buddy Delmur?" Harms laughed. "Haven't heard his name in a few months."

"Yeah, so where is he?" Razia asked.

"He's retired—"

"Yeah that's what you told me last year, and we both know that's a lie," Razia said plainly.

Harms sighed. "Okay fine, I wasn't truthful to you last year. But now I am. Delmur *really* retired. He's out on R-3633, bought a huge house and hasn't left."

"R-3633?" Razia smiled to Lizbeth who tapped out the planet name in her mini-computer. "Thanks for that."

"God in Leveman's, I can see why you two are friends," Harms said, looking between the two of them helplessly. "I can't handle two of you. Leveman's, I can barely handle *one*."

Razia grinned and stood up behind Lizbeth.

"Razia, wait," Harms said, sliding out of the booth and grabbing Razia's hand. "If Relleck's transporting guns, that's something to be worried about."

"No kidding," Razia deadpanned. "Why do you think we're still looking?"

"Fine, well be careful," Harms pleaded. As Razia's face screwed up into what was sure to be another rant, he tugged on her hand. "Don't you dare get mad at me for worrying about you."

"Aw," Lizbeth cooed. "Don't worry, Harms, we'll be careful."

"Thanks for your help," Razia said, and followed Lizbeth out of the bar.

***

R-planets were some of the most expensive residential planets sold in the Academy. Equal parts water and ground, there was usually something unique about them that drove the price out of a general D-planet. R-3633, it turned out, had become somewhat of a retirement community. Razia was painstakingly identifying each of the inhabitants, not hard as there were only about five hundred plots of land on the entire planet. What was presently giving her trouble was most everyone on this planet had been a pirate at one point, and so they had plenty of aliases for her to sort through until she found one associated with a real person. With someone as paranoid as Delmur, she would have to definitively identify the real name of each of the inhabitants before confirming that they were not, in fact, the old pirate.

"I remember him," Razia said, finding the pirate history for Neno Hajas. "He was one of Contestant's first pirates."

"Why are they still using their aliases?" Lizbeth asked.

"A bunch of the older pirates retired after Tauron..." she trailed off. "Worried it was getting too dangerous, and they didn't want Jukin to come calling if they slipped out of the web. Most of them haven't paid dues in years, but they're still considered members. But even so, they worry that the runners don't have the kind of pull that they once did, if Jukin could do what he did and get away with it."

"I still can't figure out why Jukin would go out on a limb like that to capture Tauron. It seemed very brash, you know, especially because there are other, less deadly ways of getting stuff done in the UBU."

"He's an idiot, that's why," Razia said, hoping that would be the end of the conversation as she looked through another set of transactions.

"Did you find him yet?"

"Having a hard time," Razia said, slowly scrolling through transactions. "Half these guys get a month's worth of food shipped to their mansions, so there's not a lot of transaction history to go on."

"How are you trying to find Delmur?"

"Narrowing down the list to anyone who bought their land in the past eight months," Lyssa said, closing out another transaction history. "Checking to see if they've got any other transactions around D-882 or anything else odd. Pirates can't stay away from the city for long, even if they're retired—or any other odd transactions."

"How many do you have left?"

"Right now, about fifty unknowns," Razia said, opening the transaction history for Ahenobarbus Cruz and scrolling through the transactions. When she saw nothing out of the ordinary, she smiled. "Found him."

"What?" Lizbeth jerked upward. "How? Are you sure?"

"Evet Delmur was one of the most paranoid pirates in recent history," Razia said, standing to locate his exact location on the planet. "So he's the only one I've come across that hasn't appeared to even leave the planet since he bought it six months ago."

"He could be an invalid or—"

"No, it's him. I'm sure of it. I was right before, and I'm right now."

***

R-3633 was covered in some of the tallest trees that Razia had ever seen, thick-trunked with huge canopies. She was able to find a spot to land near a pond, hoping that the foliage would buffer the sound of her landing ship. She wasn't sure what to expect with Delmur, and she didn't want to give him an opportunity to leave the planet if he thought he had company. Lucky for her, as an Academy-sanctioned research vessel, she could turn on the engine dampeners that she was technically supposed to use on every planet she landed on.

"How far away are we from his house?" Lizbeth asked, as Razia joined her on the lower level of her ship.

"About ten miles."

"*What?*"

"Oh, what?" Razia chuckled at her panicked expression.

"You're joking."

"Nope."

"Come on, Lyss," Lizbeth whined, desperation in her voice. "I thought I was going to die when you and I were on that planet—"

"Oh, you did *fine*," Razia scoffed, strapping her utility belt around her waist and walking out the open hatch.

"I didn't. I'm not built for these long distance..." Lizbeth trailed off, following Razia off the ship and seeing the mansion rising out of the distance, less than two miles away.

Razia began to chuckle meanly.

"You are a foul creature, Lyssandra Peate."

"Couldn't resist a little fun," Razia laughed, taking two steps in front of the ship. Suddenly, something snapped around her ankle and the world turned upside-down.

As Lizbeth laughed heartily below her, Razia realized she had been caught in a trap and was dangling at least twenty feet from the ground by her ankle.

"Who's laughing now?" Lizbeth asked, standing on the open hatch. "Having a little problem hanging there, Lyss?"

"Get sucked," Razia growled. Booby-trapped front gate—she'd expect nothing less from Evet Delmur. The fence was probably electrified as well, knowing him. She reached up to her utility belt and located her knife, but then paused, realizing that she could use the rope to give herself a good vantage point.

She swung herself upright, grabbing onto the rope and pulling herself up to where it was tied around a tree branch. She hoisted herself on top of the branch, but not before realizing how far up she was.

A chill ran down her spine and she pressed her back against the trunk. Shaking slightly, she clawed at the trunk and pulled herself to a standing position, trying to overpower her fear of heights to get her bearings on Delmur's house.

Through the tree trunks, she spied it, surrounded by a high metal gate. It was decorated in the same style as the Manor, but seemed a bit too new. Whereas the Manor had been built hundreds of years before and upgraded as time and gravity took its toll, this five story monstrosity seemed to be built simply to look ornate.

"When you're quite done!" Lizbeth called up to her.

Lyssa looked down for a moment and felt a surge of panic again. She was really, really high up—higher than she felt when she'd climbed up the rope. Her mind started to sway a bit, as she struggled to get a grip on her panic until…

"Oi! I found the trap!"

Three men emerged from the thick canopy, each with a gun slung around his back. Razia crouched down on the branch, thankful that her black clothes kept her out of sight. Curiously, the men appeared to be wearing camouflage. And their guns weren't security guns, but hunting rifles. It was hard to see, but she could definitely make out that one of them was Delmur.

"Whose ship is this?"

"Looks like one of them Academy ships. Do you think they're here on a tip?"

"That stupid Van de Vliert. He wasn't careful enough. Bet he blabbed last week when he was on '882."

So now Razia was curious why three pirates were concerned about the Academy coming to…

Her thoughts trailed off, as she looked down at her foot. This snare wasn't to capture intruders; it was to capture a large animal. She unhooked her mini-computer from her belt to find the planet's information in the Academy database, scrolling through boring information about the water quality and number of different species of trees, until she happened upon the statistic that most interested her.

NAME	R-3363
GAME HUNTING	CLASS A: RESTRICTED

She stifled a happy giggle. Most planets were Hunting Class B or C planets—limited hunting was allowed by locals for food and in very limited amounts for heavily licensed sport. But a Class A planet explicitly outlawed hunting of any living creature on the planet, either due to the small number of species or because something about the species would draw an inordinate amount of hunters.

She snorted. Of course pirates would flock to a planet where there was illegal hunting.

Unlike the Universal Police, though, the Academy of Planetary and System Sciences took a very hard line on illegal hunting, as its creed was to preserve and protect all living beings, sentient or not. Based on the reactions of the three men below her, she was pretty sure that this was not the first time they'd been visited.

And that was when she was struck with a brilliant idea, but then she saw her black pants and remembered that at least one of those pirates knew her as Razia. Even though Jukin didn't recognize her, she didn't want to take the chance that Evet Delmur would. A bounty hunter wouldn't know anything about Game Class A planets or the rules of interplanetary settlement.

She chewed on her lip, wracking her brain for what to do when she heard a loud whooping.

"Well, well, well, who do we have here? A pretty girl?"

"Ain't seen one of them in a while!"

"Whatchoo come all this way out here for?"

Lizbeth stood in the middle of the three men, looking slightly nervous. Apparently, she hadn't had the sense to hide when she heard voices.

"Shit," Razia muttered, quickly slicing the rope around her ankle. She wrapped it around her hand and repelled down the tree, catching the attention of the three men on the ground.

"Oh, look there! We got another one!"

"Hello boys," Razia said confidently.

"Oi! I remember you!" Delmur locked eyes with Razia. The fresh air seemed to have done him some good, as he appeared a bit spryer than when she saw him last. The angry look on his face was enough to let her know that she'd been right to think he'd recognize her as a pirate.

Especially when he started cackling loudly.

"Oi, you here to bring me more chocolates from Dissident?" Delmur chortled. "This girl says she's a bounty hunter—"

"She *is* a bounty hunter," the man to his left muttered. "Done busted up a poker game I was playing a few months ago. Took Guido straight to the bounty office!"

"Oh yeah?" Delmur said, giving Razia an appraising look, then turning back to his friend. "What'd he do, faint? Who couldn't take on this little thing?"

"Well, you know, Guido's getting up there in age, too."

Razia cleared her throat loudly. "So we want to ask you a few questions."

"We?" Delmur said. "You mean you and your girlfriend here?"

"Yes, my name is L—"

"Lyssa Peate," Razia cut her off, adjusting her original plan to suit the present circumstances. "Dr. Lyssandra Peate, from the Planetary and System Science Academy."

"Oh yeah?" Delmur swallowed. "Say, you aren't related to that numbskull Peate are you?"

"Yeah, he's my b-brother?" Lizbeth said a mixture of confusion and amusement on her face.

"What was that you were saying about illegal hunting you saw here?" Razia said, hoping Lizbeth would pick up the ruse. "What was it, a Class A restricted planet for game hunting?"

"Y-yeah," Lizbeth said with a sly and almost proud grin. "Class A."

"Boy, and look at all these animal traps around here," Razia said, tossing a stick over into a pile of leaves. The trap clamped shut, metal teeth slicing through the thin leaves that had been covering it.

"Totally illegal?" Lizbeth said, watching Razia's slight nod. "Yes, totally illegal. I am here to…report you to…my brother?"

"Well, and it's a good thing here," Razia said, walking up to the three, now petrified, old pirates, "that Lyssa and I happened to have struck up a conversation. Because I am wondering about your little business dealings over the past eight months."

"I am *retired*," Delmur repeated, but more nervously. "I ain't got —"

"You weren't when I caught up with you eight months ago," Razia said without qualifying. "And you know how old 'numbskull Peate' can be—once a pirate, always a pirate…"

"So what are you saying here?" Delmur said nervously.

"You come with me, and answer some questions about your little trips to S-6642, and Dr. Peate and her big bad brother will leave you alone."

***

The inside of Delmur's mansion rivaled anything Mrs. Dr. Sostas Peate had in the Manor, although it still had that air of nouveau riche. In the Manor, the fixtures had been attached to the walls for so long they seemed to have grown into them. Here, everything was purposely placed to look old and refined. The most out of place was Delmur himself, as he settled into an exquisite chair still wearing his camouflaged hunting clothes.

"So, what do you want?" he grunted.

"So, we—I," Razia said, clearing her throat, "I have been working on a project."

"Oh yeah?" Delmur chuckled. "Dissident not giving you any more jobs, huh?"

"Side project," Razia said, needing to get off the background quickly. "Your name came up as Benson Zephyr. You've got a company, yes? Contracted with the government?"

"I don't know nothin'."

"Lyssa," Razia said, feeling rather odd calling out her own name.

"One phone call to brother dearest," Lizbeth taunted. Razia tried not to look annoyed by the brother dearest comment and turned back to Delmur, who was sufficiently compliant.

"I meant"—he cleared his throat—"I didn't know it was with the government. Was doing some sub-contracting work with a company called Salazar."

Both Razia's and Lizbeth's eyebrows went up, but Razia recovered faster.

"Go on," Razia nodded.

"I was on contract to pick up a shipment from G-245 and deliver it to J-646 for the military. But I got orders to just deliver it to a little diner near S-6642 and leave it. Return back to G-245 and go back again."

"Was anyone else coming there as well?" Razia asked.

"I suppose so, yeah," Delmur said. "Somebody was moving the cargo from the diner to the planet, I suppose."

"What kind of cargo was it?" Lizbeth asked, and Razia elbowed her. "I mean, I'm curious to know if you were…transporting…animals or something…"

"No animals," Delmur said, giving Lizbeth an odd look.

"Do you know why they only built one building?" Razia said.

"One?" Delmur guffawed. "With the amount of material I delivered there, there'd probably be a hundred buildings there!"

"Was there anything different about what you picked up?" Razia pressed. "Was it all building materials, or was it something else?"

"Honey, I never knew what was in my shipping boxes," Delmur laughed. "That's why they chose me, right? Got that pirate mentality."

"I bet," Lizbeth said. "And you never peeked inside?"

"I will thank you, *Dr. Peate*, to leave the *questioning* to me," Razia growled before turning back to Delmur. "So why'd you stop? Seems like you were making a lot of money."

"They told me the job was done," Delmur shrugged. "Said they had all they needed for now, and they'd give me a plenty nice bonus for, uh…for keeping my mouth shut." He looked around with a satisfied smirk. "All bought and paid for anyways."

"Pirates are still moving stuff though," Razia said. "Know anything about that?"

"No, I—" Delmur started, but stopped when Lizbeth raised her mini-computer to her ear. "On second thought…well, you know, he asked me if I could put him in touch with some other pirates."

"Which pirates?" Razia asked. "Dissident's?"

"To be perfectly frank, I wasn't too pleased about his little bounty hunter joke," Delmur snorted. "So I sent him over to Contestant."

"And so Contestant's pirates picked up where you left off then?" Lizbeth asked.

"You working with your brother then?" Delmur asked. "Got a lot of questions—"

"Oh you know those scientists," Razia said, giving Lizbeth another silencing glare. "Always curious about things they don't need to be."

"Yeah…" Delmur said.

"So back to S-6642," Razia said, feeling like she should wrap up the interview quickly, before their threats wore off. "Did you ever find out what you were delivering materials for?"

Delmur glanced at Lizbeth and cleared his throat. "Now, I don't know if this is true or not, so don't be coming back here if it's wrong, but I overheard my guy saying they's gonna build a new military base on that planet."

Razia and Lizbeth exchanged glances.

"It's a commercially owned planet," Razia said. "Why would they build a military base on a commercially owned planet?"

"Like I said, I ain't sure. I just know they talked an awful lot about a bunch of contracts with the military, and all that stuff I was bringing to them was gonna be put to use when they got it. So I only assumed they's building a base with all the materials they assembled."

"But you already had a contract to ship the materials," Lizbeth said.

"Wasn't about my contract," Delmur said, shaking his head. "One they hadn't gotten yet. Jos said—"

"Jos!" Lizbeth gasped, looking to Razia.

"Old boyfriend." Razia cut her off with another glare. "What else can you tell us about—"

"I think that's quite enough," Delmur said, giving them the eye. "I'm starting to think that this girl ain't really related to Jukin Peate after all."

"You're right, I lied," Razia said, standing up, and yanking Lizbeth up with her. "But thanks for the information anyways!"

Before Delmur could say anything, they bolted out of the house, filled with more questions than answers.

CHAPTER THIRTEEN

"Alfr Jos was the other man in the pirate meeting," Lizbeth said, pointing to the account history displayed on Lyssa's dashboard. Unsurprisingly, it was sparse, as was the history of Krishna Harman next to it. "He's been giving marching orders to pirates for months."

"Jos told Delmur to take the cargo to a diner near S-6642," Lyssa said. "The planet where our friend Antica and her secretary are sitting in a single office building."

"So where'd the rest of the cargo go?" Lizbeth asked.

Lyssa chewed on her lip, deep in thought, and wondered about the supposed boss of Jos and Harman. "Do you think General State knows what's going on?"

"If it were Llendo, I'd say no way in Leveman's." Lizbeth shook her head. "But General State runs a tight ship from what I hear. I'd be surprised if too much goes on without him knowing about it."

"Why is he doing this though? If this kind of deal were to get out, people would be *pissed*," Lyssa said. "He's already going to win the election."

"That's what concerns me the most," Lizbeth muttered darkly.

"Especially considering Delmur mentioned those contracts that Wedekind was hoping to get. There's already an arsenal planet nearby."

"Wait a minute," Lyssa said. "That's where they store—"

"Guns..." Lizbeth trailed off, catching onto Lyssa's train of thought.

"How much do you want to bet that Delmur was transporting guns instead of building material?" Lyssa said with a knowing smile. "That was a big tower on S-6642, you could store a lot of weapons there."

Lizbeth didn't share her excitement. "That doesn't make me feel any better."

"But that's two places where pirates are involved in the *same* activity," Lyssa said, ignoring the implications of pirates covertly transporting guns. "Not only that, but Delmur said he was working for Salazar. That's the same company that Relleck hijacked from—twice."

Lizbeth shook her head. "No, remember, it *wasn't* Salazar, it was a different company."

"I'm telling you that I remember Salazar."

"So you're saying the Universal Bank is wrong?" Lizbeth asked.

"No," Lyssa mumbled, sitting back in her chair, mulling over what Delmur had said, trying to fit all of the misshapen puzzle pieces together.

She was right that he had stopped transporting cargo because his job was completed, but that wasn't the end of it, was it? He had sent them over to Contestant.

"What about Cree Hardrict," Lyssa said suddenly.

"What about him?"

"Remember that Delmur said he sent Jos to Contestant to continue moving stuff," Lyssa said, typing in her dashboard. "And you said that Hardrict had been on your radar for months, right?"

"Yeah," Lizbeth said, unable to resist a small smile. "I would have been able to question him if somebody wouldn't have interfered."

"But he wasn't anywhere near S-6642 nor the capital," Lyssa said before snapping her fingers. "But he was moving cargo from a military planet."

Her fingers flew over her dashboard as she located her previous search history for Cree Hardrict. She drew up his bank account information:

Kayden, Bobby		
Time of Transaction	Location	Amount
UT20015-04-06-23:98	Belvoir Supplies and Sundries A-539	30C
UT20015-04-06-15:76	McNair Diner B-725425	30C
UT20015-04-06-04:25	Belvoir Supplies and Sundries A-539	50C
UT20015-04-05-90:15	Transport Station G-279	20,000C

"See, he's barely even on G-279—" Lyssa did a double take to the transport station. "Hang on a second, that's the same transport station Relleck picked up *his* cargo up from!"

"Oh Leveman's, you're right!" Lizbeth gasped.

"Hardrict was moving something from A-539 to B-725425," Lyssa thought aloud. "And that planet was *filled* with boxes, just like that warehouse in the capital."

"A-539 isn't on my master planet list," Lizbeth said, flipping through the original government contract that started the investigation. "And neither is G-249."

"Hm…" Lyssa said, searching the internet for information on the military planet. She clicked on the first news report that appeared in the search results.

A-539 Exercise Bravo Considered a Success

200015-01-05 / A-539 | General Charles State announced the completion of a three month long military exercise on A-539. Members from the Universal Aquatics Elite Squad completed several live fire simulations resulting in…

"Live fire means…?" Lyssa said, knowing the answer.

"Real guns," Lizbeth said, chewing on her lip. "You know, military exercises are huge things—lots of cargo coming in, lots of cargo going out. The Universal Military is notoriously terrible at keeping track of equipment. Wouldn't surprise me if they had a couple thousand guns missing and they didn't know about it."

"So someone is amassing weapons on S-6642 and B-725425, as well as the capital planet," Lyssa thought aloud. "What's the connection? Both B-725425 and the capital are highly populated areas, but S-6642 is newly settled in the middle of nowhere."

"They're all near military planets," Lizbeth offered. "Maybe General State is funding his campaign with the illegal sale of weapons."

"Yeah, but to whom?" Lyssa asked. "Pirates don't use weapons."

They sat in silence, and Lyssa's mind began to spin out of control with wild conspiracy theories of why the highest ranking general and a presidential candidate would be secretly transporting guns—especially to the capital.

"Maybe there's something else," Lizbeth said, sounding as if she was on the same train of thought as Lyssa. "Can you check to see who owns the B-7 planet?"

Lyssa switched applications to the Academy planet database and searched for the purchase history of B-725425.

NAME	B-725425
DISCOVERED	19978-06-10
DISCOVERED BY	B. ABELLO DSE854794
SOLD	19978-06-12-03:27
SOLD TO	COBB PLANETARY SERVICES
AMOUNT	5,000C
SOLD	200012-90-98-89:45
SOLD TO	WEDEKIND PLANETARY SERVICES
AMOUNT	2,500C

"Wedekind Planetary Services owns both planets," Lizbeth said, sounding a little less nervous than before. "Maybe *they're* behind all of this."

"So safe to say that we should probably look into them next..." Lyssa smirked. She searched the internet for Wedekind, unsure of what she was searching for. She scanned their webpage, but nothing of interest caught her attention. Until she moved to the "about" section:

Wedekind Planetary Services (Est. 20012) includes subsidiaries Salazar Shipping, Mason Dining Services, and Secure Solutions.

"Secure Solutions!" They exclaimed at once, sharing a look of surprise.

"Wedekind owns the company guarding Relleck's guns!" Lizbeth said.

"And the company that hired Delmur!" Lyssa replied, blinking and narrowing her eyes at the date of establishment. "And how in Leveman's Great Vortex does a planetary services company have three subsidiaries when they're only a few years old?"

"I don't follow," Lizbeth said.

"Most planetary services companies are formed from existing companies, because it takes a *lot* of capital to buy and colonize planets," Lyssa said. "So for this company to be only three years old, to own all of these planets, to have purchased all of this material, and to also have three subsidiaries? That seems off to me."

"And they're offering the pirates fifty million credits for hijacking ships," Lizbeth said. "And they've *been* paying at least some of it; you remember the size of Delmur's mansion."

"So it sounds like they got a windfall of credits from somewhere," Lyssa said, turning to the Universal Bank to search for the company's financial history.

But nothing could have prepared her for what she found.

WEDEKIND PLANETARY SERVICES		
Time of Transaction	Location	Amount
NO RESULTS		
-END OF HISTORY-		

"That's odd," Lizbeth remarked. "Maybe…maybe it's just a different name in the Universal Bank? Does that happen?"

"Not usually," Lyssa said, chewing on her lip. "But let me try looking for the subsidiaries."

SALAZAR SHIPPING		
Time of Transaction	Location	Amount
NO RESULTS		
-END OF HISTORY-		

SECURE SOLUTIONS		
Time of Transaction	Location	Amount
NO RESULTS		
-END OF HISTORY-		

"Ok, that is *definitely* unusual," Lyssa said. "Because I know that Salazar and Secure Solutions are paying people."

"How difficult is it to remove transactions from the Universal Bank?" Lizbeth asked in a quiet voice.

"Impossible unless you're…well…Jukin," Lyssa said.

Lizbeth nodded, absorbing this information.

"I don't want to jump to that conclusion," Lyssa said quickly. The idea that someone could be removing transactions out of some nefarious intent, and not simply because they were an immature little…that was almost as concerning as the guns. "Maybe you're right. Maybe they were bought out or renamed. Maybe, if I can find the original purchase receipt for S-6642 in Dorst's transactions…"

She opened the planet database and searched for the purchase history of S-6642 again.

NAME	S-6642
DISCOVERED	20012-08-03
DISCOVERED BY	D. PEATE DSE2474786
SOLD	20012-08-27-10:50
SOLD TO	WEDEKIND PLANETARY SERVICES
AMOUNT	45,000C

"Look, see," Lyssa said, pointing to the timestamp. "I bet we can find it."

She left that window open and searched for Dorst's account in the Universal Bank. Lizbeth said nothing as Lyssa flitted backwards in the transaction history, until she reached the time frame when the transaction would have occurred.

PEATE, DORST		
Time of Transaction	Location	Amount
UT20012-08-27-23:98	ODYSSEUS STATION CAFETERIA S-864	150C
UT20012-08-27-10:76	ODYSSEUS STATION CAFETERIA S-864	150C
UT20012-08-27-10:10	ODYSSEUS STATION COFFEE SHOP 54 S-864	25C
UT20012-08-27-09:85	ODYSSEUS STATION CAFETERIA S-864	150C

"Where is it?" Lyssa gasped, standing up. She compared the time on the planet sales receipt and the time stamp on Dorst's transactions. The Wedekind planet purchase should have been right between the cup of coffee and dinner at the Academy cafeteria.

"So, about that removing transactions theory…" Lizbeth sounded as if she already thought it a foregone conclusion.

"That's…that means that whatever is going on, someone very high up must be involved," Lyssa said, remembering what the bank manager said about her inheritance. "There's no way Wedekind could have removed their own transactions without help."

"I think we've already come to that conclusion," Lizbeth nodded, looking as nervous as before. "But we need to find out where the money from Wedekind is coming from, or what the name of the company really is. We need to find that missing transaction."

"Leveman's Vortex," Lyssa sighed, sinking into her chair. "Short of marching into General State's office, I don't know how we can get it. When I asked about my missing inheritance, the manager said that I needed approval from the officer leading the investigation. And *then* it would be another ten to twelve weeks before they could retrieve it from the archive."

"So a manager can expunge the data," Lizbeth said thoughtfully. "Or at least, we know of *one* manager who has that ability."

"What are you thinking?"

"I think we need to head back to S-864," Lizbeth said. "Only this time, let's take your ship instead of hiding on a transporter."

***

"Dr. Peate!" The bank manager looked awfully nervous to see Lyssa in his doorway.

"Hello again," Lyssa smiled, helping herself to a seat in the man's office, Lizbeth following on her heels and taking the other seat. Lizbeth made a point to close the door, which seemed to make the manager even more nervous.

"Who's this?" the man asked, nervously.

"L—"

"Our family accountant," Lyssa smiled. Lizbeth muttered something about being able to make up her own alias, but Lyssa stared firmly ahead at the nervous man in front of them.

"O-oh?" the manager stammered. "Well, what can I do for you?"

"I'm actually here on behalf of my brother," Lyssa said.

"Captain Peate?"

"No, one of the other ones," Lyssa said. "Dr. Dorst Peate. He's a fellow DSE with me at the Academy and he's asked me to help him prepare for an Academy audit."

"I'm sorry, a what?"

"Every five years, the Academy selects a subset of scientists and asks them to provide a full audit listing of their planet excavation history," Lyssa said, lying through her teeth. There was no way the Academy could manage something like that. But this bank manager didn't know that. "It's incredibly arduous and difficult, lots of paperwork, very expensive…"

"I bet," the manager said, obviously waiting to see how this would impact him.

"It also includes a full listing of receipts for planet sales," Lyssa said. "And, it would seem as though the Universal Bank has failed again to live up to its sterling reputation."

"O-oh?" he stammered, and Lyssa saw the sweat appear on his forehead.

"Yes, a planet sold by Dr. Peate to a company called Wedekind Planetary Services seems to have just…disappeared from the Universal Bank records, even though there's clearly a record of the sale in the Planetary and System Science Academy."

"Oh, well of course we would be happy to look into it," he said, but Lyssa could see something behind his eyes. "As I mentioned before, it will take some time to retrieve the file in question from our Universal Bank archive, and we will need to ensure that the transactions were not removed for an investigation."

"Yes, of course," Lyssa said, leaning forward. "You know, I'm curious about this archive. Can you tell me more about it?"

"I'm sorry, Dr. Peate," the manager tutted. "Unfortunately, the location of our archive is secret. We would not want to compromise the integrity of our accounts."

"I think it's a little late for that," Lizbeth interrupted, pulling out her badge and placing it on the table. "Sorry, girl. Got tired of him stalling."

"And who are you?" the manager said.

"Agent Lizbeth Carter with the Universal Beings Union Intelligence Agency, Major Crimes Directorate, Insurance Fraud Division, Piracy Branch," Lizbeth said without missing a beat.

"You need a shorter name," Lyssa muttered.

"And what does the Intelligence Agency have to do with Dr. Peate's accounts?" the manager said, sitting back and no longer looking as nervous as he did before.

"It fits a pattern of systematic removal of transactions in the Universal Bank," Lizbeth replied. "Many of which happen to be in accounts owned by known pirates."

"My dear Agent Carter, pirates have ways of getting around our system," the manager said. "Multiple aliases, that sort of thing."

"What about whole companies?" Lizbeth pressed, looking as on top of her game as Lyssa had ever seen her. "Wedekind Planetary Services, to be exact. Appears as though there aren't any transactions at all. But as my associate said here, there's obviously a record of the company in *her* databases."

"Then the company simply does not exist," the manager said.

"Why would a company exist in the Planetary and System Science Academy and not in the Universal Bank?" Lizbeth smiled, clearly enjoying this back and forth.

"Because the Academy obviously keeps shoddy records," the manager said, his voice raising a bit.

"That or you're removing transactions," Lizbeth said.

"I do not have the *authority* to remove records," he sniffed, but his voice was unsure.

"You removed mine," Lyssa reminded him.

He gritted his teeth. "When the Universal Bank is told to isolate accounts by the Universal Police, we must comply—"

"Who within the Universal Police has the authority to make that call?" Lizbeth asked.

"Captain Peate," he replied haughtily.

"Seems odd for such a lowly *captain* to have such power over the stability of the Universal Government," Lizbeth said with a knowing smirk. She reminded Lyssa of a cat about to pounce. "In fact, I looked it up. Only a high ranking official in the Universal Government can make that call, not Captain Peate."

"I don't know what you are insinuating!" the manager exclaimed.

"I'm insinuating that you're lying," Lizbeth said simply. "Covering up for Captain Peate, or even his boss General State. And believe me," she leaned in closer, and Lyssa was impressed by her threatening face, "if I find out that you're doing either, you will *fry*."

"I will submit your paperwork to locate this missing transaction," he huffed, angrily typing on his keyboard. "And then I want you two *out* of my office. And if you don't leave, I *will* call security!"

True to his word, once the manager returned with a printed sheet of paper, he was accompanied by two security guards who escorted Lyssa and Lizbeth promptly off the bank premises.

They sat down at one of the tables in the presidential square, surrounded by the tall stone walls of the castle. They sat in silence and watched the glass and stone bank across the street, as if it would give up its secrets to them if they sat here long enough. The square was a bit busier than the last time Lyssa had been here, as the excitement of the upcoming election permeated the seat of the Universal Government.

Lyssa picked up a leaflet for General State's campaign that had been left on their table. General State stared back at her, nary a smile on his face nor any warmth in his eyes.

"How in Leveman's Vortex is this guy ahead in the polls?" she asked, showing Lizbeth the picture.

"People think Llendo is a moron," Lizbeth shrugged. "I'm inclined to believe them, to be honest. If I didn't suspect State was involved in some massive gun-running conspiracy, I'd vote for him."

Lyssa nodded, her eyes drawn to a security guard walking the length of the wall surrounding the square. He was joined by three more, who nodded and continued walking. They looked formidable, even from down here.

"Extra security for the election and inauguration," Lizbeth said, following her gaze.

"I think they should be paying attention to the warehouse five blocks from here," Lyssa snorted.

"It's funny, I remember coming to the presidential palace every year on field trips when I was a kid," Lizbeth said, taking in the giant stone castle on the other side of them. "See that clock tower up there?" She pointed to the now familiar stone clock tower with the sixty-twelve time system. "Shirou Mantovani bet me a hundred credits that I couldn't run all the way up to the top and back down in ten minutes. It's all ramps, you know," Lizbeth motioned to it. "Nearly twenty of them to get to the top. Needless to say, I lost that bet."

"You'd think they'd put in an elevator or something…"

"Nah, the building is too old, and the political firestorm that would come from any modification to the building would be crazy. The castle is one of the last remaining structures on this planet from the original inhabitants, and the tower used to be a place where they would call to prayers, if I remember correctly."

Lyssa made a face, thinking about the Temple at the Manor.

"I mean, it's a pretty cool place," Lizbeth said. "The palace has all these underground jails from way back in the day. Vitor Coiro tried to lock me in one year because I wouldn't go on a date with him." She pointed to the upper floors. "Second and third floors are all presidential staff. The rest is a museum, I think. We should go sometime."

"Sure, because that's about as likely to happen as our getting a copy of my brother's missing transaction records," Lyssa sighed, pulling out the print-out they received from the bank manager.

"Yeah, I'm s—hang on a second," Lizbeth said, pulling the paper over to her. "How many planets have that many numbers, Dr. Peate?"

Lyssa pulled the paper back to her and noticed the scribbled numbers at the top of the page.

"B-583-78-2-7-52-9-1," Lyssa said, reading the top line. "What the…"

"B-583, that must be the planet," Lizbeth said. "Seventy eight, two…do you think these are coordinates?"

"He wouldn't—"

"Maybe he thought if he helped us, I'd grant him immunity," Lizbeth said, looking back at the bank. She looked as if she were considering it.

"Or maybe he realized that he could give us the coordinates, and there's no way in Leveman's Great Vortex that we could ever get the file."

"Why?" Lizbeth said, snapping back to her.

"This is the *Universal Bank Archives* we are talking about," Lyssa exclaimed. "The backbone of our entire system of government."

"Yes and?"

"And if you think security was tight in *that* building,"—Lyssa pointed across the street—"you have no idea how secure the archives must be. You probably can't get into the star system without them knowing." She wished she could wipe the determined smile off of Lizbeth's face. It was odd being on this side of a stubborn person. "Besides that, we already know what it's going to say anyways. We know that Wedekind bought the planet."

"That's not the point," Lizbeth said. "I *need* proof, definitive proof from an official source that they are involved. If I can show my bosses that Wedekind bought *this* planet, and that someone's trying to hide Wedekind's activities, I'll have enough to get a warrant and really go after these guys!"

"There's just one problem with that," Lyssa said, giving her a knowing look. "This plan hinges on whether or not we can actually *get* that proof."

"So?" Lizbeth's smile grew wider. "That's why I have a pirate."

"Yeah, and in case you didn't notice, breaking into things is not *exactly* my area of expertise," Lyssa said. "I'm the money-tracking girl, not the security-disabling girl."

"Well, do you know anyone as good at breaking into places as you are at bounty hunting?"

"I…no."

"You were about to say something," Lizbeth said, picking up on her hesitation.

"No, I wasn't."

"Yes, you were."

Lyssa tried to growl, but it came out more like a whine. "I'm not asking for *his* help!"

"Then *you* get to break into the archives," Lizbeth said, using a tone of voice that meant arguing was useless. "Or, you get to go ask *him* for help."

The pit of her stomach dropped as the full realization washed over her.

"This is going to be *painful*."

CHAPTER FOURTEEN

"What do I call you two, Razbeth? Lizzia?" Sage chuckled. "You're quite a duo."

It wasn't hard to find Sage. A quick call to Harms to get his latest "secret" alias, and Razia found him lounging at a cigar bar on D-882. The smoke was thick in the air, but Sage didn't seem bothered by it as much as Lyssa was. Or maybe she was just sick with what she was here to ask him.

She checked off all of his crew in the bar: Ganon, the pilot; Sobal, the young computer hacker; Keal, his ship's mechanic. His three thick body-men were even playing cards in the corner, turning to full attention when Razia and Lyssa walked in the front door, ready for whatever fireworks were about to blow up.

"So, I know you didn't come all the way out here to have a smoke with me," Sage grinned, taking a long puff of the cigar. "By the way, in case you were wondering what I did to deserve this—"

"We need your help," Lizbeth said, cutting him off immediately.

Sage glanced between the two of them, a devilish grin growing on his face. "We need your help," he said, tossing a look to Ganon, who began snickering. "We need *your* help. *We* need your help. We need your *help*. We *need* your help."

Razia rolled her eyes, knowing exactly where he was going.

"We need your help," he said, turning his eyes to Razia. "You need my help."

"Yes, I think you've pretty much covered it," Lizbeth said dryly.

"I thought," Sage drawled slowly as if savoring this moment, "you didn't need my help...Razia?"

Lizbeth shot her a look, but Razia's face didn't move.

"You *yelled* at me, too. Didn't she, Ganon?" Sage chuckled.

Beside him, Ganon emphatically nodded. "I remember, multiple occasions."

"And now you stand here—"

"I swear to God in Leveman's Vortex, Sage," Razia grumbled. "Just let it go."

"Not until you say it."

Razia pressed her lips into a thin line and clenched her jaw.

"Say it."

"Come on," Lizbeth muttered quietly. "Just say it already so we can get a move on."

"No," Razia growled.

"Do it," Lizbeth said, giving her a look that could kill.

"Whew, I like your friend," Ganon said with a wink at her.

"Go on," Lizbeth said, ignoring him.

"I..." Razia swallowed, feeling rather green, "ineedyourhelp."

"What was that now, darling?" Sage cooed, lifting a hand to his ear.

"I said," she felt as if the very words inflicted pain, "I need your help, Sage."

"Excellent!" Sage clapped his hands together and leaned forward. "So, dearest Razia"—his eyes glittered as her alias rolled off his tongue—"what can I help you with?"

"We need to break into the Universal Bank Archives," Lizbeth said.

Silence filled the room—even those not involved in the conversation stopped to look at the two young women. Razia tossed a mind-your-own-business look to two older men in the corner.

"Whoa, whoa, whoa," Sage said, his cocky demeanor slipping. "You can't do that."

"Why not?" Lizbeth asked.

Sage laughed, tossing a look to Ganon. "It's illegal."

"Yeah, and you're a pirate," Lizbeth replied.

"No, I mean, that's way outside the limits of piracy protection," Sage said, leaning forward. "You can't tamper with bank records."

"They've already been tampered with," Razia snapped. "Which is why we have to break into the archive to go find the original records. The ones online are wrong!"

"What?" Sage blinked, before shaking his head. "No, that's impossible, no one can—"

"Somebody did," Lizbeth replied. "So we need to get on the planet to see what the original transaction records say."

Sage paused, looking between the two of them before settling on Razia. "You know you would be out of the web if Dissident found out."

"He won't find out, unless you or your crew open your big fat mouths," Razia said warningly. "This…well, I'm not helping Lizbeth because it has anything to do with piracy."

"So you're willing to risk your tenuous membership of the pirate web to help someone else?" Sage asked, genuinely shocked.

"Well, when you put it like that…" Razia said, throwing Lizbeth a look.

"You know I'm worth it," Lizbeth said.

"All right then," Sage said suddenly, "we'll help you."

"What?" Lizbeth blinked. "Why the sudden change?"

"Because this one"—he jutted his thumb out at Razia—"only thinks about bounty hunting. So if you've got her thinking about something else, it must be important. And it's good for her to consider someone else's needs above her own, for once."

"Oh, get sucked."

***

Sage was able to procure the plans to the Universal Bank archive on B-583 relatively quickly. Or rather Sobal, the young computer whiz

181

who sweated nervously around her. In almost no time, Sage and Ganon were pouring over the printouts, arguing over the best way in. Lizbeth had been right that the bank manager provided coordinates to the planet; the file in question was located on the seventh floor of building two in section seventy-eight. But that was never the difficult part.

Razia sat in the corner, and for once, had no idea what the best course of action was. Sage, however, was in his element. All of his cocky swagger had disappeared, and in its place was a calm focus. His eyes were glued to the plans in front of him, his brow furrowed in concentration.

He reminded her of Tauron. Which made sense, she supposed, since he grew up on that pirate ship. He'd been there years before even she had showed up.

"Yeah, because if we go in underground, these vibration sensors they have in place won't pick it up," Sage snapped, giving Ganon a dry look. The pilot was used to it and ignored him, pointing out other options.

As much as she hated to admit it, it was probably the right call to ask Sage for his help. Bounties and transactions she could handle, but when it came to this kind of stuff, Sage...well, he was just *better* at it than she was.

But she'd rather die than tell him.

"Like anything you see?" Lizbeth came to sit next to her with an amused smile on her face.

"Get sucked."

"So why hasn't anything happened between you two?" she asked, her voice low enough that none of the others would hear. "I can tell he's crazy about you."

"He's not...that's not what it is," Razia stammered uncomfortably. "We just grew up together. Tauron told him to look out for me."

"So, you're the reason you two aren't together?" Lizbeth observed, chuckling as Razia's face contorted into a deep scowl. "Look, you can try to tell me you aren't lonely, but we both know that's a lie."

"Why do you care?"

"Because I'm your friend, and I see more than you know."

The word hung in the air and Razia forgot about Sage. Friends. Razia didn't have friends. Pirates could barely even stand her, let alone want to be her best buddy. Harms was less a friend than a kindly uncle and Sage, well…maybe she'd consider being his friend if he weren't such an insufferable dickhead all the time.

Lyssa didn't have friends either. Most of her brothers made sure that she was reviled as much at the Academy as she was at home. Vel was…well, she didn't really consider Vel a friend. He almost *had* to like her, as they'd been through so much together.

But Lizbeth had just said it like it was a foregone conclusion. They were *friends*.

"So, I got some bad news," Sage said, walking over to the two of them. "Or good news, depending on your perspective."

"We can't get in?" Lizbeth asked, deflating.

"No, we can. It's just..." Sage turned his eyes to Razia. "We're going to have to do a space jump."

Razia's face paled considerably and she hated herself for it.

"I think I get the core concept, but what does it entail?" Lizbeth asked.

"Basically, this planet has tightly controlled access in or out," Sage said. "Because it's not an active archive; not a lot of ships come in. So ours would definitely raise some eyebrows if we broached the atmosphere. So we'll skim the highest levels of the atmosphere, just out of their radar and then just parachute in."

"How do you parachute from space?" Lizbeth asked. "Won't you float away into space or burn up?"

Razia's heart leapt into her throat and she began to smell sulfur.

"No," Ganon said, "you're technically in the stratosphere. So we'll be pulled down at a high rate of speed. It's three and a half minutes from the ship until we pull parachutes, then another four to six until we land." He gave Sage a cocky look. "Think we can break the sound barrier again?"

"Sounds like fun," Lizbeth grinned giving Ganon a once-over before turning to Razia. "You said you've done this before, right?"

"Yep," Razia nodded, her voice strained. Sure, she'd fallen out of the ship, in her dreams, straight into Plethegon. Breathing was now incredibly difficult as she tried to get a grip on her spiraling terror.

"Razia," Sage said, concern evident in his voice. "Are you—"

"No, I love space jumps," she said, wondering why her voice sounded small and weak. "They're my favorite thing to do in life."

Before he could say another word, she walked out of the room so she wouldn't be sick in front of them.

***

Razia stood in the bay, nervously adjusting the too-big gloves over her fingers. The ship was hovering at just about twenty-five miles above the surface of the planet. In order to make it all the way down to the ground, they needed to wear special suits to protect them from the icy chill and the low oxygen. The suit was four sizes too big for her, made for one of Sage's crew, and the helmet was moving oddly on top of the extra fabric.

On the other side of the room, she spotted the other two. Lizbeth looking like she was swimming in her suit as well. Sage, the taller of the two figures, gave Razia a thumbs up and she nodded, hoping that the helmet was enough to hide her queasiness.

It returned ten-fold as the hatch on the end of the room slid open with a loud groan, revealing the planet beneath her feet.

It was a long way down to the ground below.

She could see the curvature of the planet, the blue tint of the atmosphere clashing against the blackness of space. Lights dotted the surface, although they were almost inseparable from up here, she knew from the plans that they sat atop giant buildings that towered at least a mile into the sky.

She forced herself to look away from the hatch, and tightened the straps on her parachute. That was when she noticed a fourth person standing with a protective suit on—Ganon.

"Why is he coming?" Razia asked, tugging at Sage's suit.

Sage tapped the side of his helmet.

"I said, *why is he*—" Razia stopped mid-sentence when Sage flipped a switch on the side of her helmet. Suddenly, she heard Sage's crew doing status checks, of Ganon telling Lizbeth what was going to happen, and Sage's voice, a few nanoseconds after his lips moved.

"What'd you say?" Sage said.

"I said," Razia snapped. "Why is *he* coming? The more people we have with us, the more chance we'll be seen."

"Ganon is going to jump with Lizbeth," Sage said, as Lizbeth happily slipped her arms through two straps on the front of Ganon's suit. Razia could see him grinning handsomely as he looped another set of straps through her legs and around her waist. Razia resisted an eye roll at their already too-familiar flirtation.

"Okay, so why can't she jump with you?" Razia said.

Sage raised his eyebrows and pointed to the same harness on the front of his suit.

"…No way."

"C'mon," Sage said, ignoring her. "If we don't jump soon we're going to miss the spot."

"I don't need you to jump with me," Razia insisted, her stubborn ego winning over her paralyzing fear of heights. As *if* she were going to get strapped onto Sage like some damsel in distress. "I've done this before."

"The only way you're jumping off this ship is strapped to me, so you'd better get used to it," Sage stated.

"Get sucked, Teon."

"Yeah, let her jump if she wants to jump," Lizbeth offered. "She said she's done this before—"

"And she nearly got herself killed then, too!" Sage snapped at Lizbeth. "She's petrified of heights!"

"*Teon!*" Razia snapped, but it was too late.

The snorts and cackles filled her helmet, as the crew—having been running status checks until this point, began laughing from the bridge.

"Afraid of heights?"

"Well, that *is* surprising!"

"Oh, no, she's going to fall outta da ship and break her nail!"

Razia's eyes narrowed into an icy glare directed at Sage, who didn't even flinch. Tossing him a rude gesture, she marched over to the open hatch.

"Razia, I mean it," Sage warned, nerves in his voice as she moved closer to the edge of the ship. "Get over here."

"Yeah, go get strapped in," Ganon smirked at her. "You don't wanna *fall*."

Razia narrowed her eyes.

"Lyssa," Sage said warningly. "Don't you *dare*—"

She didn't hear the rest of what he said, as she flipped off her helmet microphone effectively silencing him. He let loose a silent diatribe that she was sure was full of colorful curses, his breath fogging the front of his helmet.

She smirked at him, then leaned backwards and fell out of the ship...

...immediately regretting her decision.

Everything was quiet as she floated for a moment, except for her own panicked breathing and the similarly panicked voice in her head. As the seconds ticked by, she was speeding up, based on the way the sky and the ship were spinning, and sickness rose in her throat from fear and dizziness. As she spun faster, black dots speckled her vision, and her panicked internal voice began to worry that her helmet wasn't completely attached, that maybe she was suffocating. She wanted to rip off her helmet so she could take a deep breath.

How long had she been falling at this point?

Was she coming in too fast?

If she pulled her parachute, would she snap her neck?

The black dots turned into a tunnel vision as everything grew hazy...

She was back in Leveman's Vortex, standing in front of the Arch as the ground disintegrated beneath her feet. This was what it felt like. She may already be dead and falling to Plethegon.

Funny, she thought it would be warmer to be burned alive—

She came back to herself as a hand grabbed her arm, and a firm body pressed against her back. A hand roughly threaded her arm into a strap, and then another hand did the same to her other arm. Then, more gently, the hand gently intertwined with her fingers, pulling her hands outward and upward. The air was growing thicker around her and her legs hitched upwards, aligning to his legs as the extra fabric pooled out around them, slowing them down further. She could feel the steady rise and fall of his chest as she pressed against him and her panic quieted enough for her to crack open her eyes.

It was absolutely beautiful.

She felt open and exposed as they floated but was completely unafraid. She leaned back into him, comforted by his presence behind her.

His arms left their spot behind hers and one arm snaked around her waist, holding her tight to him. She saw the parachute deploy behind them, and they slowed down even further. She leaned into his arm around her waist. His other arm came to join it, securing her tight to him.

The world was closer now, and she could see the buildings, although she realized she had no idea which building they were targeting. Shame began to flood her cheeks, and she was grateful that he couldn't see. She couldn't believe she'd gone off on that kind of panic-induced crazy, one that quite possibly could have gotten her killed.

To think she'd worried that she was already dead, going to Plethegon. She'd already dealt with that, hadn't she? She was a good soul…wasn't she?

She became acutely aware that the two arms around her were uncomfortably tight, pressing her against a taught chest that was heaving heavily. She could feel the vibrations through the thin fabric of the suits, and was glad her microphone was switched off. She really didn't want to hear what he had to say.

Unfortunately, he realized she couldn't hear him, and he flipped the switch on her helmet.

"*Can you hear me now, you stupid idiot?*" He screamed through the speaker in her ear. "*What is wrong with you?*"

"What's wrong with you?" she mumbled, grateful that he was behind her and couldn't see the embarrassment on her face. It was bad enough that Sage thought she needed to jump with him, but the fact that he just *saved* her—it was mortifying.

"I mean, I can't even, you are—the *depths* of your *idiocy!*" he continued, so angry that he was unable to form coherent sentences. He continued yelling at her as they landed atop one of the tall buildings that had once been a small dot but was now a behemoth of a tower.

He angrily unhooked her from him and she stumbled forward,

unable to keep her balance on the gravel rooftop. He ripped off his helmet, his eyes wild with fury and his face bright red.

"Don't you ever, *ever* do that again," he bellowed, his voice echoing off of the rooftops.

"I think I handled it fine," she replied, meek compared to him.

"Fine. *Fine?*" he exclaimed. "*Fine?*"

Ganon and Lizbeth landed on the roof next to them, and Ganon pulled off his helmet. "Okay, guys, keep it down. We don't want to —"

"I don't recall telling you to help me," Razia snapped, becoming more confident in the presence of others.

"Oh, here we go!" Sage threw up his hands. "I save your life and —"

"You didn't save my life," Razia spat back. "I would have—"

"Splattered on the ground like a damned bug," Sage growled, getting in her face.

"Not to break up this little—" Ganon started.

"Shut up!" they hissed at him in unison.

"Your ego is going to get you killed one day!"

"Get sucked, asshole!"

"*Seriously*," Lizbeth said, stepping between Razia and Sage before they came to blows. "We just jumped out of space and made a spectacular landing on top of this building. Everybody's okay and in one piece. So how's about we not blow this entire operation because you two need to just screw already?"

Razia's eyes grew to the size of saucers and Sage turned five shades of red.

"I would never—"

"S-screw?"

"That's what I thought," Lizbeth said, walking back over to Ganon, who was watching in gleeful humor. "Lead the way."

***

There were over a hundred floors in this archive skyscraper, the same as the rest of the buildings in this sector. Ganon had stayed behind on the top floor to keep a look-out for the inevitable security detail that was going to arrive, while Sage and the two girls took the lift (after he had deactivated the security sensors on the elevator). The journey was silent—Sage refusing to even look at Razia, and she him. Lizbeth seemed to be the only one actually enjoying herself.

Once they got onto the seventh floor, Sage disarmed the cameras using a robotic spider-like jammer that attached itself to the four cameras in the hallway. Razia and Lizbeth crept behind him, as he coordinated with Sobal on the other end of his mini-computer.

"Well I don't know, Sobal. That's your job, isn't it?" Sage snapped. Razia heard a muffled response on the other end and then the sound of electricity shutting off. The vast room in front of them went completely dark.

"All right. We've got about an hour until company shows up," Sage said, handing the two of them flashlights. "So hurry it up."

"You start on that side; I'll start over here," Lizbeth said, opening a nearby filing cabinet. "Start looking for row fifty-two."

Razia began walking down the aisles of filing cabinets, her eyes drifting over the numbers on the front as her flashlight drifted over them.

598-78-2-7-1-9-1	190518011414100504040409040918
583-78-2-7-1-9-2	190518011414100505040518 0108
583-78-2-7-1-9-3	190518011414100513130 1011414

She paused at a filing cabinet and opened it up, shocked to see it only half-full. She reached in and pulled out the first hanging folder, reading the first page:

SERANN, JEDDIDIAH	190518011414100504040409040918	
TIME OF TRANSACTION	LOCATION	AMOUNT
UT20015-03-99-90:45	Brandon Supplies C-2779	5000C
UT20015-03-99-70:60	Jules Cafe D-378469	50C
UT20015-03-99-65:12	Junior's Finery M-424235	60C

The name wasn't familiar, but the surname was. She opened the file cabinet above and found Serann, Jemma-Anne, probably another cousin she never heard of. Below, Serann, Morgan.

"*Over here!*" Lizbeth called. "Found them!"

Razia jogged over to where Lizbeth was counting through the cabinets in row fifty-two. Sage was standing over her with the flashlight as she quickly opened the top cabinet.

"Like I said," Lizbeth grinned, flipping through the cabinets, "the bank manager gave us the exact coordinates."

"Hmm," Lyssa said, opening the cabinet closest to her and pulling out the first folder.

PEATE, JINJINA	16050120051009141019140100000	
TIME OF TRANSACTION	LOCATION	AMOUNT
UT20015-03-95-15:98	Ellie's Hair Extensions D-2669	4000C
UT20015-03-85-36:02	Courtney Beauty Products C-4747	750C
UT20015-03-60-74:51	Natalie's Workout Wear K-3846	9000C

```
Razia hated her sister Jinjina—nothing but a bimbo baby-maker.
She put the file back and opened the cabinet directly below,
pulling out the first file again. Immediately, she saw a familiar
name.
```

PEATE, LYSSANDRA	16050120051225191901140418O1	
TIME OF TRANSACTION	LOCATION	AMOUNT
UT20015-03-99-10:90	Mintxo Docking D-882	20000C
UT20015-03-95-42:61	Bulgogov Diner F-835	50C
UT20015-03-95-42:40	Refueling Station F-835	100000C

She stared at her own transactions for a moment, trying to remember what she had been doing at the time. She might have been hunting Guido Tedesco or some other pirate. But seeing her name next to D-882 was a little concerning. It would be so easy to track her if some pirate knew to look at Lyssa Peate's transactions. It was one thing to simply slide her C-card; it was quite another to see it in black and white like this.

"What'd you find?" Sage asked, still holding the flashlight for Lizbeth.

"Found mine," Razia said.

She went to close the drawer and stopped. Since she was here, maybe she could solve a little mystery. She wasn't even sure that she'd find her inheritance—it may have been a separate account—but she had to try.

Thumbing through the files, she pulled out a folder every few pages to see what year she had landed on. There were at least three years' worth of transactions here; at least, that's how long she'd been using her own C-card account. Before she graduated from the Academy, she was using a minor card and funds from her family's account.

Pushing all of the files to the end of the cabinet, she pulled out the very first folder in her file and opened it up.

"All right, jackass, where's my money?" Razia said, flipping to the very last page, the first set of account activity after she received full control of her bank account.

PEATE, LYSSANDRA	1605012005122519190114041801	
TIME OF TRANSACTION	LOCATION	AMOUNT
UT20012-05-12-45:12	TRANSFER TO // MCDOUGALL, JOHN	5,000,000,000C
UT20012-05-01-00:00	TRANSFER FROM // PEATE, ELEONORA SERANN	5,000,000,000C

"What in Leveman's?" Razia wondered aloud. "Who in Leveman's Vortex is John McDougall?"

"The Congressional Minister?" Sage said, looking up at her.

"Who's that?" Razia blinked.

"He's the leader of Congress," Lizbeth said. "Part of the President's cabinet. Why do you ask?"

"So why was my inheritance transferred to…." Her heart stopped beating in her chest as she looked down at the paper in front of her. Or more specifically, the date.

She'd never forget that date.

"Lyss?" Sage said, watching the color drain from her face. "What is it?"

"Jukin…he…" she whispered, the file dropping from her hands.

"Lyssa," Sage hurried over to her, "what is it?"

"He stole my inheritance," she stammered, suddenly unable to breathe. "Jukin…he stole it…and he…paid the Congressional Minister off to…"

"To what?"

"Kill Tauron."

CHAPTER FIFTEEN

The words echoed in the quiet room and in her mind.

She'd always known Jukin had paid off some high ranking official, but she always assumed it was *his* own money or that maybe he borrowed it from their mother. She never in a million years thought that it would be *her* money.

But of course it was *her* money.

She took a step back, and her chest constricted as breathing became difficult. She felt the coolness of the metal filing cabinet against her back, and it felt like her entire body had slipped into an ice bath.

Tauron's death was paid for with her money.

She was responsible.

If she'd just *known* about her inheritance, maybe she could have kept him from taking it.

But she didn't, and Tauron was dead, and it was her fault.

Everything was always her fault.

"You were born."

That's what her mother had said, wasn't it?

Maybe if she hadn't been born, Tauron would still be alive.

After all, if she never existed, there never would have been an inheritance available for Jukin to steal.

Sostas would have picked Jukin to be his assistant, and Jukin never would have decided to become a U-POL officer.

Fever rushed to her cheeks as the room heated up around her and she felt a rumble beneath her feet. She breathed in the pungent odor of sulfur, so familiar at this point, so *warranted.* Maybe the Great Creator was here to take her back to Leveman's Vortex.

She deserved to burn in Plethegon, after all.

Someone had grabbed her by the arms and yanked her hard to the floor as lights danced in front of her face. She could see Sage talking to her, but she was unable to hear anything but muffled words. Something about the bank's security arriving faster than he anticipated.

He was looking at her. How could he look at her?

Tauron raised him. The crew was his family.

She was the reason why all of that was taken from him.

Sage was pulling her across the room, she guessed, but her whole body was numb. He was talking, but all she could hear was the terrible voice in her head—the one which had been quiet for so long, the hateful voice that was telling her that she was a bad, evil soul damned to burn in Plethegon, no matter what Vel might think.

The sulfur smell was so strong that she began coughing. Her eyes widened as the ground rumbled beneath her, and she knew she was going to see cracks soon. Her eyes began to water either out of fear or pain or because of the thick smoke that was filling her lungs. The ground rumbled again, and someone had pressed her against a cold metal cabinet.

She could hear yelling, something about coming out with their hands up.

She should just go turn herself in and let them shoot her.

She could feel a tug on her shirt and saw a pair of wide, green, almond-shaped eyes, filled with fear and worry. Lizbeth was talking to her, but she couldn't process the words. Ganon had rejoined them as well, his dark skin even darker from soot and ash. He was talking to someone behind her.

A flash of light filled her vision and someone grabbed her and pushed her downwards. She banged her head on the floor, and her mind snapped back into full speed.

They had been caught by the Universal Bank security forces, who had swarmed on the roof and in the stairways, effectively blocking their exit. The security forces were lobbing flash bombs and gas canisters into the room to try and smoke them out—or worse.

"Shit, these dicks don't play around!" Ganon said as another flash bomb went off over their heads. "We need to bail now."

"How are we going to get out of here?" Lizbeth said. "They've got us surrounded!"

"We've gotten out of worse scrapes than this." Razia finally registered that the weight she had been feeling on her back was not psychological, but Sage, who had thrown a protective arm around her shoulders.

"Get off," she mumbled, shoving him off.

"Fifteen armed guards with more on their way," Sage said, pulling out his mini-computer. "Hey, you bastards, when are you planning to get us out of here?"

"Working on it, boss!" came the voice on the other end.

"You still got that extraction magnet?" Sage asked, tugging at her utility belt until his fingers clasped around the magnet. He tugged at it several times to make sure it was secure around her waist.

"Oh Leveman's, not again." Her words were drowned out by the sound of a huge, building-rocking explosion. When the smoke cleared, there was a giant hole in the outer wall, gaping to the outside.

"*Go!*" Ganon cried, half-dragging Lizbeth towards the hole.

Razia let out a cry of despair as Sage pulled her by her arm towards the hole. And as much as she didn't want to, she followed him past the ledge, dropping like a stone.

Before she even had time to think, she heard the click of the magnet against the line that had fallen from Sage's ship, hovering above.

"I thought you said you couldn't get the ship through the radars," Lizbeth cried, clinging with both arms and legs to Ganon, who didn't look too upset to be in that position.

"Oh, we don't care when we're leaving," Ganon said, as they were pulled upwards. "Let 'em know we were here. Give the boss a bounty boost!"

Razia felt Sage's eyes on her, waiting for her trademark scoff about his own bounty standing. But Razia's eyes were on the ground disappearing beneath them, her thoughts wondering why the Great Creator continued to torture her.

***

"Did you kids have a fun time!" Sobal cheered as Razia hoisted herself onto the open hatch that she had leapt from just under an hour before. It seemed like an eternity ago. She had been so angry at herself for thinking she was going to burn in Plethegon, and now it seemed as though it was just foreboding.

One of the three huge men that Sage employed as his bodyguards was helping Lizbeth back onto the ship, while another extended a hand to Ganon, who brushed it away and pulled himself up. Sage was the last one to climb aboard, ordering one of the beefy men to tell Keal, who was piloting the ship in Ganon's absence, to get them as far away from this planet as fast as they could.

"You okay?" Sage said to Razia.

"Fine," she muttered. "I've done magnetic pullbacks—"

"No, I mean…about finding out about Tauron," Sage said more gently.

She felt eyes on her and did her best to shake it off.

"It's fine," Razia lied, standing up. "Don't want to talk about it."

"You looked pretty shocked," Sage said, reaching a hand out to her.

She batted it away with gusto. "I said I don't want to talk about it."

"Well, I do," Lizbeth said, checking her appearance in a reflective cabinet. "Jukin paid five billion credits to Congressional Minister McDougall? What in Leveman's is *that* about?"

"Tauron's…" Razia trailed off.

"Yeah, but besides that," Lizbeth said, waving Razia off. "That's a lot of money just to kill one man—"

"Lizbeth, don't," Sage said warningly.

"Oh, so you think this is just another break in the case?" Razia whispered, anger punctuating every word. "Yet another *twist* in your little investigation?"

"Yes, I..." Lizbeth trailed off when she finally sensed Razia's anger.

"He *stole* from me to *pay* off..." Razia couldn't even finish the thought. She could feel the lump growing in her throat and was dangerously close to breaking down in tears. But she would be *damned* if she cried in front of Sage's crew.

"But why the Congressional Minister?" Lizbeth asked. "Don't you think it's odd—"

"*Who cares!*" Razia roared, taking everyone by surprise. "Who cares? Tauron is *dead* and....God in Leveman's...it was *my* money."

"So?" Lizbeth replied.

"So?" Razia stammered. "So?"

"So he *stole* your money, but that doesn't mean you had anything to do with it!" Lizbeth said. "If anything, wouldn't he have paid off General State?"

"*He killed Tauron!*" Razia screamed, her words bouncing off the walls in the room.

"And that had nothing to do with you," Lizbeth replied. "God in Leveman's Vortex, quit playing the *victim*!"

"V-victim?" Razia sputtered.

"Lizbeth, seriously, just leave it alone," Sage warned, interjecting before the situation got even more out of hand. "You don't understand."

"No, she needs to hear this," Lizbeth snapped. "Everyone walks on eggshells around you because they're afraid of sending you off the edge of some abyss. Leveman's, even *Harms* is afraid of pissing you off!"

"Excuse *me*?"

"Seriously, that is *enough*." Sage growled.

"No," Lizbeth snarled at him. "Enough is when she quits acting like a damned child. What she needs is a swift kick in the ass."

Razia smiled icily. "How's this for a kick in the ass: you're on your own from now on."

"Oh am I?" Lizbeth laughed.

"Yeah, I'm done," Razia growled. "I'm done digging into whatever in Leveman's is going on. I'm done sneaking around with you and getting *shot* at. I'm done doing things that could very well get me *kicked* out of the web! Or *worse*."

"Because you're doing so well as the laughing stock of the pirate web," Lizbeth retorted.

"At least my only move isn't to *sleep* with pirates in order to get them to talk with me."

"*Enough!*" Sage bellowed, stepping between the two before they came to blows. "Everyone just needs to take a five minute break and *calm down*."

"Get sucked," Razia hissed at him. "And take me back to my ship. *Now*."

"Yes, Sage," Lizbeth said, "take her back to her ship. Keep coddling her like she's a priceless doll that will break if you let her make a mistake."

"He doesn't *coddle* me!" Razia seethed.

"He jumped out of a damned ship for you after you threw a temper tantrum!" Lizbeth replied.

"I didn't ask for him—"

"You're a piece of work, you know that?" Lizbeth shook her head. "Everyone comes to your rescue and you just act like you have your shit together. Well, you know, you don't fool me, *Lyssa Peate*!"

Razia was about to fire back when she heard Ganon speak.

"P…Peate? As in…Jukin Peate?"

Razia became acutely aware that the small room they were standing in was filled with the entirety of Sage's crew; all of whom were staring at her with their mouths open.

"Shit," Lizbeth whispered, her hand over her mouth. "Oh, Lyss, I'm so…I didn't mean…"

Razia stared at her, unable to speak. She felt exposed again, the same way she'd felt jumping out of this ship not even an hour ago.

But this time there was no one to lean back into.

"Okay, yes," Sage said with authority. "She's Jukin's sister. But if any of you tell a soul, you will *piss blood for a month*." His eyes alit with fury as he dared them to contradict him. "Trust me, he didn't do her any favors."

Razia suddenly felt a surge of anger towards everyone and everything. She just wanted to *hurt* something, to make something else feel the pain and the hurt that she felt.

So she turned to the only thing within reach.

"You…stupid…*bitch*!" Razia growled, lunging towards Lizbeth. She might've killed the other woman had Sage not yanked her back, a firm grip on her flailing arms, her hands so eager to wrap around Lizbeth's neck.

"Ganon, get her out of here!" Sage said, struggling to keep Razia away from Lizbeth as she kicked and clawed and struggled against his grasp on her. "Lock her in a room somewhere and get us back to D-882 so we can put a few systems between these two!"

"*I hope you burn in Plethegon*!" Razia screamed as Lizbeth tore out of the room with Ganon and the door slammed shut behind them.

She took a few deep angry breaths as she stared at the closed door. Her whole body was shaking.

"Lyss," Sage whispered. "I know she didn't mean it."

She clenched her teeth together and stared stonily ahead, unwilling to show any more weakness than she had already displayed. Her head began to thud with a dull ache as the weight of everything settled on her shoulders.

"My crew won't tell a soul, I promise," Sage continued behind her. "I trust these guys with my life, and they'd never…they know better. I promise you, they won't."

She took another deep breath and closed her eyes, focusing all of her energy on trying to keep the tears from leaking down her face. She wouldn't cry, not over this.

Not in front of Sage.

Not again.

"Just get me back to my ship," Razia whispered.

***

She had just finished her last exam, and she was feeling lighter than air. Her things were packed and she had shuttle ticket to the nearest transport station, where she'd hop another and then another until she reached D-882. Tauron would be there eventually; he always was. He liked to make her work to find him, but she welcomed the challenge. And this time—the very last time she would be leaving the Academy for D-882—well, she had hoped he would make it really difficult to find him, as a "welcome to the pirate web" sort of present.

She remembered wondering if Tauron had already called Dissident to tell him to put her in the web. He'd promised her he'd toss in a few credits and his name, but she'd have to make her own way, just like Sage when he finally decided to break out on his own.

She remembered the way she had her entire life planned out at that moment.

Then she saw the news, playing a live feed from the half-finished prison on D-882.

Jukin Peate had captured Tauron Ball and his crew.

And they were to be executed.

There was no jury, no trial. Simply capture and kill.

It was going to send a message.

She knew she needed to tear her eyes away, to get out of the Academy and get to him, to figure out some way to break him out of that prison on D-882. She had to go help him. After everything he had done for her, she had to.

But all she could do was stand in the middle of the hallway, staring at the too-small screen, watching the execution of the only man who'd ever really loved her.

The rope went around his neck.

The hood covered his face.

The floor gave way.

He was gone.

And it was her fault.

She swallowed the tears, opening her eyes to the residential planet. The sounds of birds and idle chatter on the patio of this coffee shop replaced the sickening sounds in her head. She had no idea what the name of this planet was or how she even got here, but she had been here so long that the waitress had stopped coming by to ask if she wanted a refill on her cold coffee. She would have preferred something stronger but couldn't gather the strength to get up from the table.

She wanted to forget everything that she now knew about herself.

Every time she closed her eyes, she saw his resolute face on that pixelated screen, the last time she would ever lay eyes on him. She heard the sickening sound of the floor giving out from under him.

The spectacle of it all.

Paid for with *her* credits.

She'd often wondered if Tauron's soul had made it past the Arch, or if his soul had been damned to burn in Plethegon. He was a pirate, but he was so...good. And kind to her. He gave her a home when no one else wanted her. That had to be worth something to the Great Creator.

Even if she wasn't worth anything to Him or to anyone else.

Her mother hated her.

Her father had abandoned her.

And the one person—the only person in the universe to ever care whether she lived or died...paid for with *her credits*...

She lay her head on her arms, staring through the small holes in the wrought iron table. She couldn't close her eyes, or they would fill with visions of pixelated faces. So she stared through the hole, opening and closing one eye and then the other, mesmerized by the way the holes seemed to shift. It was a simple effort, and nobody would be killed when she did it.

She heard the chair in front of her scraping away and she didn't have to even lift her head to know who had come.

"Break up with your girlfriend?" she asked, her voice sounding odd as she tried to pretend she wasn't a mess.

"Are you okay?" Vel placed his hand on top of hers.

"No," she whispered, opening both eyes to look through the slits in the table.

"Want to talk about it?"

"No."

"Lyssa, come on," Vel said, not letting go of her hand. "Just because that money was earmarked for you doesn't mean it's your fault it was stolen. If anything, he would have stolen the money from one of our other brothers."

"No, he stole it from me because Sostas chose me instead of him," Lyssa rasped, not lifting her head. "Jukin left the Academy because

Sostas chose *me* instead of him. Jukin wanted to make a name as a great crusader for justice because of..." she trailed off. "Mother was right. I never should have been born...I just screw everything up by existing."

"Lyss," Vel said, squeezing her hand. "I thought we were past all this nonsense?"

She didn't respond.

"Remember?" Vel said, shaking her hand a bit. "You led us to the Arch. You never would have been able to do that if the Great Creator —"

"Then why did He take away the only thing in this entire universe that ever made me happy?" Lyssa barked, snapping her head up to look at him for the first time. She was sickened by the way he watched her lovingly. "Why me? Why does everyone else get to be happy and...and I don't."

"Because you don't let yourself be happy," Vel replied gently but with edge in his voice. "You obviously cared a lot about him; you trusted him. And you haven't trusted another person since, me included!"

"I trust you," Lyssa mumbled, unable to meet his eyes.

"No you don't. Because if you did, you wouldn't have been jealous that I had a new girlfriend. If you trusted me, you wouldn't be sitting here telling me that you still think you're a bad person, and that you're damned to Plethegon even though I told you otherwise. If you trusted me,"—he reached across the table and took her hand—"you would tell me what you saw last year."

"I can't," she whispered, anxious at the thought of sharing something so personal.

"Well, you can't go through life pushing people away and expect to find the same kind of safe haven you found in Tauron," Vel said, releasing her hand and sitting back. "To get that kind of connection again, you're going to have to trust that maybe not everyone is the enemy. Maybe you'll lose someone again, but that's no excuse to shut everyone out completely, especially the people who obviously care about you."

They sat in silence as the minutes dragged on.

"I saw myself," Lyssa whispered, barely audible.

"What?"

"At Leveman's Vortex, I saw myself," she said, barely moving her lips. "I saw this girl who everyone had abandoned, everyone had kicked around. And I realized that...I'd done it too. I-I abandoned myself.

"And I spent all this time trying to create this person—Razia." She looked down at her hands, feeling quite silly vocalizing all of this. "I thought Lyssa was...weak. Damaged. But, she, Razia, she wouldn't be anything without...without..."

"Without Lyssa," Vel finished for her.

Lyssa finally looked up at Vel, who was watching her comfortingly.

"And you know what?" she laughed. "I...I actually like being Lyssa. I like excavating planets, and I like...I like being me. But I can't stop...I can't stop thinking that being Lyssa is...bad...that I ruin everything..." She softened. "I made Sostas leave and I... Tauron..."

"First of all, you did not make Father leave," Vel snapped, the harshness in his voice shocking to Lyssa. "If you ask me, maybe he finally saw what his actions were doing to you, and decided that it was time to pull his head out of his ass."

"What?"

"Leaving an eight year old girl on a planet alone? Dragging her through Leveman's Vortex?" Vel snapped, sounding angrier than she'd ever heard him when it came to Sostas. "You saw what happened when you left me alone for three days!"

"He didn't care about me, Vel."

"From what you and Dorst have told me about him, he was *obsessed*. Oblivious to how his actions damaged other people, including you. Maybe when the Great Creator showed him what was headed his way when he died, he finally decided to quit tormenting you."

"Maybe," Lyssa whispered, having never considered that option before. She was sure nothing could have wrenched Sostas from his studies, but maybe seeing his mortal fate could have shocked him enough to change his perspective.

"And as for Jukin," Vel sighed, "from what I can tell, he's the exact same way. He took your money because he saw a means to an end, not because he was intentionally trying to hurt you."

"What makes you say that?"

"Because you would have found out about it when it happened," Vel said. "Believe me, in our family, if he had wanted you to know, you would have known."

Lyssa nodded, knowing the way her elder sisters gossiped.

"You've made so much progress, Lyss," he said. "Don't abandon yourself again."

"Nope," Lyssa said, on her feet in a second and walking away out of sheer annoyance and panic. It was a mistake to tell him. He now knew her deepest fears and it was…Oh, it made her skin crawl to think—

She didn't get too far before Vel caught her, yanking her into a firm hug. She couldn't believe that he was so much taller than she was now. She felt like resisting, like running away, but she found herself tired of running from him. After all this time, he had finally worn her down.

With a great sigh, she laid her head on his shoulder, defeated. He wrapped his arms tighter around her, as if he were trying to make up for months of lost time. She didn't resist or fight him, and she even quietly admitted to herself that it was nice to not have to pretend to be so strong all the time.

"Thank you for telling me," Vel said, his head on her shoulder. "I know it's hard to change old habits."

She sniffed.

"Also, I think you need to apologize to Lizbeth," Vel said, releasing her.

"What?" Lyssa snapped, stepping back from him. "She needs to apologize to me! She's the one who told everyone about…well… my *thing*."

"She was trying to help and things got *way* out of hand, from what I hear."

"Yeah, and she should apologize first."

"Or, you could be the bigger person and just get it over with. Besides, I can't say I don't agree with her about you playing the victim."

"I do *not* play the victim," she said, but the protestation died with Vel's skeptical face. "I don't *want* to play the victim."

"Then you need to trust us," Vel said, taking her hands. "And we'll be able to trust you with handling the truth and not throwing a temper tantrum when we do."

"What else have you not told me?" Lyssa asked, scrutinizing him.

"I've been going to the Manor on weekends at Dorst's request," Vel said. As Lyssa puffed up in indignation, he gave her another knowing look and she deflated. "And," he continued, chuckling. "I've been doing my level best to grease the wheels for that time when you feel able to come home and have a proper conversation with the family. Dorst as well."

Lyssa scoffed. "Don't bring *him* into this."

"One of these days, maybe you'll be able to see that he's changed. He's really looking out for your best interest these days."

"Whatever."

"Good God in Leveman's, you hold a grudge," Vel laughed good-naturedly. "Do you not even realize how much flack he's been getting for you missing all of your license renewals?"

"So do I have to take you back to the Academy or is Sage still hanging out nearby?" Lyssa asked, changing the subject to avoid thinking about Dorst doing anything nice for her.

"Oh, no, Sage is..." Vel trailed off and glared at her affectionately. "Very clever. That's another one you need to—"

"Look, I just made a huge leap of progress, let's not get too hasty," Lyssa snapped.

CHAPTER SIXTEEN

"I'm sorry, but I am *not* going to give you a visitor's badge until your escort gets here," the angry gray-uniformed security guard snarled at Lyssa. The latter had been able to slide in behind others who assumed that because the stranger was wearing a button-up and nice pants that she must work there as well. But she had hit a brick wall at her nemesis, the annoyed security guard who refused to let her in without an escort.

"Just *call* her," Lyssa snarled back. "Lizbeth Carter."

"I did call her. She ain't answering."

Lyssa let out a grunt of frustration and was wondering how far she'd get if she attacked the security guard when a voice called her name.

"Lyssa?"

Lyssa spun around, her breath catching in her throat as she spotted Lizbeth holding a paper cup of coffee and a muffin. They stared at each other for a moment, unsure of what to say. Then they spoke in unison:

"Sorry, I—"

"Lyss, I—"

They stopped, embarrassed.

Lizbeth spoke first, taking a few steps forward with a pained expression. "I'm…oh God in Leveman's Vortex, Lyssa, I'm so sorry I told them your secret. I swear, if I could take it back I would."

"To be honest," Lyssa said with a small smile, "I was surprised Sage hadn't told them already…"

"I told you he's crazy about you." Lizbeth laughed a little before growing more serious. "I'm sorry that you had to find out about Tauron like that. I'm sure it wasn't an easy discovery to make."

"No, it wasn't," Lyssa replied quietly. "But I shouldn't have…what I said was…well, it was really shitty of me to say it. And I'm…" She took a deep breath and steeled herself. "I'm sorry."

"Wow," Lizbeth said quietly. "That must have been hard for you."

"Oh get *sucked*," Lyssa snarled.

"No, no," Lizbeth said, stepping forward. "No, I know…I mean, I know that…well…I know that wasn't easy for you…to apologize…"

She trailed off and they stood in awkward silence.

"Got a muffin there?" Lyssa said, after a few moments.

"What?" Lizbeth said, looking down at her hands. "Yeah…from the cafeteria."

"I'm kind of hungry."

"Oh, well…oh right!" Lizbeth said, understanding her meaning. She turned to walk back the way she came from with Lyssa walking quietly beside her. They passed by a muted television station where Jukin was talking.

"That dick," Lizbeth growled. "How could he steal from you?"

Lyssa thought about what Vel had said, about being a means to an end, and said nothing.

"But you know what pisses me off even more?" Lizbeth said, stopping in the middle of the hallway. "He doesn't recognize you. What kind of an asshole brother is he, anyways? It's one thing that he stole your money, but to not even know his own sister?"

Lyssa couldn't help but smile at Lizbeth's indignation and they began walking towards the cafeteria again.

"It's not right, and it's not fair to you. And whatever reason he had for taking your money, that is really unforgivable," Lizbeth finished before grinning wryly. "And you say the word, I'll beat the shit out of him for you."

"I think you'd get arrested."

"You're worth it," Lizbeth said as they walked into the cafeteria. "That's what friends are for, right?"

"Yeah," Lyssa chuckled, more focused on the word. Lizbeth had said it again, so casually, so easily. Lyssa supposed they were friends after all, especially now. "Anybody that you want me to beat up for you?"

"My boss?" Lizbeth muttered hopefully. "Got my ass chewed out this morning when I got back. But I really feel like we are on the brink of cracking it."

"Did you end up finding the name of the company Dorst sold the company to?" Lyssa asked, keeping her voice down.

"Wedekind, but…I can't continue this investigation. I'm in enough trouble as it is, and unlike some people, I don't have a secondary career I can moonlight in…"

Lyssa smiled, but her eyes were drawn to the television screen hanging above them in the cafeteria. It was replaying the same story, but what caught Lyssa's attention was Alfr Jos and Krishna Harman being led away by Jukin's Special Forces.

"Leveman's Vortex," Lyssa mumbled, tugging at Lizbeth's shoulder. "Look!"

Lizbeth swiveled her head and her eyes nearly bugged out of her head.

"What in…?" Lizbeth gasped, running up to the screen and feeling around for the volume button.

"…Alfr Jos of S-864 was arrested near N-42653, whereas retired Major Krishna Harman was picked up en route to S-4296. Both men surrendered to Captain Peate without incident."

"Captured by…Jukin?" Lyssa said.

"Oh, look, they're replaying it," Lizbeth said, turning up the volume.

"Breaking news from S-864. Two officials associated with General Charles State's presidential campaign have been arrested on charges of conspiracy to commit insurance fraud."

"*What?*" Lizbeth exclaimed, her coffee falling out of her hand.

"*The two men are accused of hiring pirates to hijack cargo bound for S-4296 and filing insurance claims for almost four hundred million credits, while delivering the cargo as 'new' to the government. The money is unaccounted for, but police suspect that it has been funneled to General State's presidential campaign, which has been running in the red for the final three months of the campaign.*"

Jukin's smug face then filled the screen.

"*I credit the hard work of my Special Forces with tracking down those responsible, and hope that this will send a message to our elected leadership that piracy will not be tolerated.*"

"Get sucked, you son of a bitch," Lyssa snarled as the newscast played on to the point when they had first seen it.

"I don't understand," Lizbeth said sitting down. "How in Leveman's did they know?" She closed her eyes, and her face contorted into a snarl. "Those assholes *were* reading my reports! And funneling them over to Jukin!"

"You know, I don't think—"

"Of course!" Lizbeth seethed. "Of course they'd want to pass on the buck to someone else. They never give me credit for anything. Jealous of me, I suspect. Sons of bitches."

"Lizbeth."

"Maybe I'll just stop working so hard, you know?" Lizbeth continued unabated. "Maybe I'll just be like the rest of them, come to work and just sit there like a lump and pretend to work. You know, half of them just play card games on their computers. I know Wendy, she's even writing a damn *novel* while—"

"*Lizbeth!*" Lyssa said, finally getting the girl's attention.

"What?"

"They only mentioned the three planets Harms told us the other pirates were focusing on," Lyssa said. "Not on S-6642, not on Hardrict, and not on Relleck."

"Yeah, because I stopped submitting my daily status reports. So they missed that integral piece—"

"No," Lyssa said, eyeing a rather large portrait of President Llendo in the cafeteria. "Don't you think it's odd that two of General State's men were captured two days before the election?"

"What?"

"General State was a shoe-in," Lyssa said, her eyes not wavering from the presidential portrait. Llendo was staring back at her with a smile of someone with a low IQ. "Up twenty points the last time I checked. I would guess, not anymore."

"You don't think it was some kind of political conspiracy to ensure Llendo got re-elected?" Lizbeth said dubiously. "That's silly."

"I've seen a lot of silly lately," Lyssa said. She glanced up when a security guard on break walked into the cafeteria, walking over to the coffee machine and pouring a cup. When the guard turned around, Lyssa's eyes nearly fell out of her head when she saw the uniform.

Or rather, the very familiar patch on her chest.

"Lizbeth, were you aware that Secure Solutions provides the security for your building?"

Lizbeth's eyes followed hers and she gasped, "*That's* where I've heard that name before!"

Lyssa's mind began spinning. "Who else do they provide security services for?"

"Leveman's…everybody. Consolidated under a giant contract a few years ago." Lizbeth seemed to be thinking the same thing as well.

"And the warehouse where Relleck is delivering guns," Lyssa said. "And they're a subsidiary of the company where other pirates have been amassing cargo. And, oh by the way, that company doesn't actually exist in the Universal Bank."

"What are you saying, Lyssa?"

"I'm saying that if you get fired for this, I may allow you to join Dissident's web as a fellow female pirate," Lyssa smiled. "You know, moonlight a second job."

Lizbeth seemed genuinely touched.

***

"Lizbeth, you need to see this," Lyssa said. They were huddled at the Lizbeth's dining room table with a bunch of papers scribbled with thoughts splayed out. They had spent the past two hours trying to piece together what they knew and what they didn't know.

Lyssa pushed her mini-computer over to her partner and smiled.

"What in...?" Lizbeth gasped.

Wedekind Planetary Services		
Time of Transaction	Location	Amount
UT20015-04-01-00:00	DISBURSEMENT // Salazar Shipping, INC	700,000C
UT20015-04-01-00:00	PAYCHECK // Antica Mikaelsson	105,000C
UT20015-04-01-00:00	PAYCHECK // Lorelle Pearson	50,000C

"Looks like our bank manager got scared and put all of the missing transactions back," Lyssa said, glancing up from her mini-computer. "Do you think your threat spooked him?"

"That, or he heard about the break-in at the archive," Lizbeth said, moving the scrap of paper marked "bank manager" to a pile with other papers called, "Harman" and "Relleck." "He probably figured that whatever he was being paid to remove them wasn't enough to get him tossed in jail."

"This is good, then," Lyssa smiled. "Now we can find proof. Let's see where Jos and Harman have been going."

With that, she searched on the first man's transaction history, scrolling quickly through his account history.

"Yes, look at this. All of his transactions are...hang on a second," Lyssa stopped when she noticed the date. "What day is it?"

"Nineteenth" Lizbeh replied. "Election Day."

"Then how in Leveman's Vortex is Alfr Jos on D-882?" Lyssa asked.

"Pirate prison?"

"I don't think they have whores in the pirate prison," Lyssa said, shoving the mini-computer back over to Lizbeth.

Jos, Alfr		
Time of Transaction	Location	Amount
UT20015-04-19-32:89	Madame Guerri D-882	8500C
UT20015-04-19-32:75	Madame Guerri D-882	25C
UT20015-04-19-32:61	Madame Guerri D-882	50C

UT20015-04-19-32:89	Madame Guerri D-882	25C

"You have *got* to be kidding me," Lizbeth shook her head. With a sigh, she picked up the piece of paper with "Jukin" on it and put it in a pile with Jos and Harman. "So what does that tell us?"

Lyssa saw a payment from Jos to a "Mason Dining" account and searched the Universal Bank for their account.

Mason Dining Services		
Time of Transaction	Account	Amount
UT20015-04-01-00:00	TRANSFER TO // JOE'S DINER S-6642	10,000C
UT20015-03-01-15:46	TRANSFER TO // JOE'S DINER S-6642	10,000C

She narrowed her eyes, and sat back, "And another piece of the puzzle falls into place. Wedekind owns that diner."

"Shocker," Lizbeth said.

Lyssa searched on the name of the diner and was surprised to see a list of names.

Joe's Diner - S-6642		
Time of Transaction	Account	Amount
UT20015-04-16-54:84	King, Owen	100C
UT20015-04-15-15:46	Marleu, Brody	125C
UT20015-04-14-67:89	Jack, Tobin	100C
UT20015-04-14-46:69	Craddock, Riley	75C

"That's interesting," she mumbled. "How are all of these transactions here if they didn't even have a C-card machine?"

"Maybe they had it in the back somewhere?" Lizbeth shrugged, moving a piece of paper that said "Hardrict" to a different pile.

"King...that's...that's Relleck!" Lyssa said, doing a double-take on the list. "And that one is Silas Brendler. Costa Enoch, Max Fried, Conboy Conrad...These are all pirate transactions!"

"Why were they all out there?" Lizbeth asked, confused. "Harms said they were out near N-42653, I thought."

Lyssa opened the transaction history of the alias of Max Fried.

Jack, Tobin		
Time of Transaction	Location	Amount
UT20015-04-18-32:89	Apollonia's S-4296	110C
UT20015-04-17-32:75	Magda's Sundries N-42653	25C
UT20015-04-16-32:61	Dinah Diner B-725425	50C
UT20015-04-15-67:89	Joe's Dinner S-6642	100C

"Holy shit," Lyssa said. "All of these planets...there's no way that Fried has been hanging around all these planets. It's completely... infeasible."

Lyssa sat back and thought for a moment, running through several scenarios. Even though she could see a smattering of transactions from near N-42653, it was infeasible for pirates to be criss-crossing the universe the way their transaction histories were suggesting. She knew for a *fact* that no pirates except for Hardrict and Relleck were anywhere near B-725425, and definitely not near S-6642. Neither planet was mentioned in any of the news briefs they'd seen about the arrests of Jos and Harman.

"Why only tell half the story?" Lyssa asked aloud. "Why didn't any of the news reports mention S-6642 or B-725425?"

"Maybe because the other planets were just a distraction?"

"A distraction from what though?" Lyssa said, chewing on her lip deep in thought. The breaking news had resulted in the almost inevitable re-election of President Llendo, but that didn't account for the amassing of guns in that warehouse five blocks away. And it also didn't account for why half of the transactions from these pirates were showing in places they had never actually been. It was almost as if someone were trying to frame the pirates for something.

The only person who would ever want to frame the pirates for *anything* was Jukin, who also happened to be the only person she knew that had successfully modified transactions. But that was only to hide the fact that he'd transferred five billion dollars to the Congressional Minister…

Her eyes opened as big as saucers.

"The Congressional Minister," Lyssa gasped. "What would have happened if State had won the presidency?"

"He would have been able to nominate his own minister, confirmed by the…" Lizbeth trailed off, her mouth dropping. "Do you think?"

"Do I think that the five billion credits transferred by Jukin three years ago to the Congressional Minister was used to set up a planetary services company? Do I think it's no longer a coincidence that Wedekind was established three years ago and that's when all of this shady business started?" Lyssa said. She typed into her mini-computer, searching for definitive proof. It took her a few minutes, but she found the account in question, for once, not tampered with:

McDougall, John		
Time of Transaction	Location	Amount
UT20012-05-12-45:13	TRANSFER TO // WEDEKIND PLANETARY SERVICES	5,000,000,000 C
UT20012-05-12-45:12	TRANSFER FROM // PEATE, LYSSANDRA	5,000,000,000 C

"Wow," Lizbeth said, sitting back. "So your inheritance was transferred to Minister McDougall, who then used it to set up Wedekind. Leveman's, this just gets more twisted the more we dig."

"You were right. Five billion was an awful lot of money to pay for someone's life, even if it was Tauron's. I think it was a down payment for something bigger. Something that would allow Jukin to finally arrest every single pirate out there without anyone getting in his way."

"But it would have to be *big*." Lizbeth said. "Just because the pirates were seen near S-6642, and just because a pirate was hijacking cargo…well, that's not enough to get Llendo or even the Congressional Minister to let Jukin just go round up all the pirates."

"Jukin's got something up his sleeve," Lyssa said, pacing nervously. She remembered the glint in his eye when she saw him on the transit station and, now it scared her more than before.

"Then what do we do?" Lizbeth said quietly.

"We put a *stop* to it," Lyssa snarled. "I am not letting him get away with destroying another life—or lives—because he's got some warped sense of justice."

"How are we going to stop it if we don't know what *it* is?"

Lyssa snatched up her mini-computer and typed angrily into the keyboard.

"Who are you looking up now?" Lizbeth asked.

"Besides Jukin, there's one other person who seemed to know a lot more than he should about this," Lyssa said, tossing Lizbeth a confident smile. "And he just bought a coffee on G-279."

***

"There's security guards crawling all over this place," Lizbeth whispered as they crouched in an alleyway near the warehouse they had escaped from only a few weeks before. Razia hadn't had a chance to really survey the place when they were running for their lives, but now saw it was an older warehouse, the paint of multiple owners peeling off the side.

"Two out front," Razia said, spying the guards, "and a security camera. No wonder they let us go so easy. Probably just followed us home."

"We need Sage here," Lizbeth said.

Razia glared at her with pursed lips. "Now why in Leveman's Vortex would you say that?"

"Because *you* said you're the money girl, not the breaking-into-places girl," Lizbeth pointed out. "And we could probably use some of those camera scramblers again."

"Fair point," Razia admitted, rolling her eyes.

As luck would have it, they didn't need to worry about getting inside because Relleck came swaggering through the doors, pausing to chat with the guards for a moment. The two guards laughed at whatever he said, and he gave them a flourished bow before putting his hands in his pockets and strolling down the street.

"That'll work." Razia grinned at Lizbeth. "Stay here and watch for anyone coming."

"Wait, I thought you said not to take Relleck alone?" Lizbeth said, grabbing her arm. "You said he doesn't play fair?"

"Yeah, and in this case, it's going to work to our advantage," Razia said. "Yet again, he's neglected to inform his crew of his whereabouts because he doesn't want to split the payout with them."

"Be careful, please," Lizbeth pleaded as Razia turned to jogged after Relleck.

She wasn't trying to be quiet, so it wasn't very long before he heard the footfalls behind him. He paused in the middle of a deserted street and turned around, and his trademark smirk flashed across his face as he stared down at her.

"You really don't quit, do you?" Relleck shook his head. She saw his eyes roam up and down her body before settling on her face.

"And you," Razia said, putting her hands on her hips. "All this money you're getting from Wedekind and you aren't even bothering to split it with your crew."

His eyes flashed and he chuckled. "How'd you find out about Wedekind?"

"Relleck, come on." Razia rolled her eyes. "This is me we're talking about."

"Dissident's little gnat, always buzzing around, annoying everyone."

"Yeah, well, this little gnat is going to save your ass," Razia said seriously. "I just need you to tell me everything you know about what Jos and Harman were planning."

Relleck laughed. "Really? Do you think it's that easy?"

"You know what's going to happen if you don't. Don't make me repeat your embarrassing performance from last year."

"As I recall, you're the one who let me go. Why was that guy *so* interested in catching you?"

Razia shifted and narrowed her eyes. "Don't be difficult. I can make you talk."

"I would love to see you try," Relleck said, walking up to stand mere inches from her. She tilted her head upwards as he sneered down at her with his signature cocky smirk.

He was so cocky that he left his left side open, she thought, amusingly. She could drop down, knock him off his feet, and tie him up before he even knew what hit him. She could pummel him until next week, until he was black and blue and begging for mercy.

But as he stood just inches from her, she thought of trying a different tactic.

"That's right." His voice was low and gravely. "You don't have the —"

Gently, awkwardly, she slid her hands over his chest, trying not to focus on how solid he was under his thin shirt. Her mind drifted to that state-of-the-art gym on his ship, and realized he must use it often. His chest shuddered under her fingertips and she finally lifted her eyes to lock eyes with him.

He was watching her like a scared little boy, her gentle touch both shocking and disarming. She realized suddenly that Lizbeth had been right—it didn't take much.

"They had me transporting guns and other weapons from B-725425," Relleck stammered, his words coming faster than his mouth was moving.

"Tell me—" She couldn't finish that thought before Relleck had leaned forward, his lips pressed against hers. She leaned into it, momentarily forgetting that she was supposed to be interrogating him. Her only thought was it had been ages since she'd been kissed, and Relleck was definitely much more experienced in this field than she was. She knew she had to stay in control, but she had to admit, it did feel kind of nice, the way his lips moved over hers and—Oh Leveman's, was that his *tongue*? That sure felt nice. His hand was clutching at the back of her head, and his other was being rather gentlemanly on her hip.

She stepped back, trying not to pant. He leaned forward to kiss her again and she stepped back, shaking her head.

"Why are they amassing guns here?" she asked.

"They said it was for some big military contract they were going to win," Relleck whispered. "Jos said something about the government suddenly needing more security right after the election."

"More security after the election?" Razia thought to herself as Relleck pulled her close and tried to kiss her again. She shook her head, brows furrowed in thought, and he began kissing down the side of her neck, his arms coming to gently wrap around her. "Why in

Leveman's Vortex would the government need more security after the election?"

"Never asked," he muttered. "You smell *amazing—*"

"There was talk on S-6642 for a big military contract, too," Razia said, pausing only for a moment when he began sucking on a particularly tender part of her neck. "And the only thing I found there was…a bunch of pirate transactions….wait a minute," she stood up a little straighter. "Security, pirates…pirates and…ooh," she closed her eyes and moaned when he began nipping at her neck.

"Leveman's Vortex, just kiss me again," he whispered, his lips crushing hers again.

Security and pirates…

Why would an empty planet need security contracts?

Why would someone want to make it look like S-6642 was a pirate hotspot?

Unless someone was planning to make it look like pirates were some kind of danger to the military and to the government?

She lifted her lips from his again and watched him intently, hoping something in his countenance would deliver her to the deep dark secret.

"Tell me again what you know," she said.

"I was to transport guns so that when a contract was let in a week or so, Wedekind would be ready to assist with increased security. Something to do with the election. Changing administration."

"How in Leveman's Vortex would the administration change if Llendo was a shoe-in to be reelected?"

And suddenly, just like puzzle pieces falling into place, everything suddenly made sense.

Wedekind was moving guns, not to take over the military, but to *protect* military installations as Secure Solutions, using nearby planets as a base of operations.

Which meant that there would suddenly be a greater need for security on these military planets.

And all of the phantom pirate transactions made it seem like there had been a spate of pirate activity near these planets.

Jukin would stop at *nothing* to round up every last pirate.

The only way he'd be able to round up pirates would be if they did something big—something so shocking that no one would begrudge him for arresting every last one, and hanging a few of them, to boot. Something that no amount of pirate money could change.

All this talk about the administration change.

"God in Leveman's Vortex, they're gonna kill him," Razia whispered, breaking free from Relleck as if he was on fire.

"What?" Relleck said. "Kill who?"

"Gotta go," Razia muttered, dashing away from him.

"Wait!" Relleck called after her. "Can I…I mean…do you want to get a drink sometime?"

She stopped mid-stride and turned around.

"What?"

"A drink," he said, uncharacteristically nervous. "Like…coffee or something. With me."

"Like… a date?" Razia stammered, her face growing hot.

"Sure, why not?"

She looked around the alley and then remembered she had to go save the government and piracy as she knew it.

"Uh…maybe later," she said, sprinting away.

CHAPTER SEVENTEEN

"The Congressional Minister is planning to assassinate the president," Razia gasped more out of panic than out of exertion. "The administration change, Wedekind, the guns—it all makes sense!"

"Wait, wait, slow down," Lizbeth said, yanking Razia to a halt. "I need you to explain to me clearly what you *think* is going on. Because you just said something *insane*."

"Wedekind is going to manufacture a security crisis, and McDougall is going to reap the rewards," Razia said breathlessly. "They're going to assassinate, or attempt to assassinate, the president."

"Why would the *Congressional Minister* want the president dead? For crying out loud, they're in the same party!"

"It's not about wanting him dead, Lizbeth, it's about *money*!"

"He got money, remember? Five billion from your brother."

"What's the first thing that would happen if there was an attack on the president?"

"I don't know—"

"*Think!*"

"They would...." Realization dawned on Lizbeth. "Oh Leveman's, they would *throw* money at any security company that came knocking!"

"And who do we know already has contracts with nearly every single military and government office?" Razia continued emphatically. "*Wedekind.* Both Delmur and Relleck talked about how they were preparing to win contracts. Well, *these* are the contracts they were waiting for!"

"But what about S-6642?"

"All of those pirate transactions out there? They're going to make it look like it's a pirate hotspot. I would wager that every single planet that Wedekind purchased in the past three years magically has *some* kind of pirate activity nearby, and also probably has a government or military-owned planet nearby."

"But wait, who cares if pirates are nearby?" Lizbeth said. "Why would they need security from pirates?"

"Who do you think they're going to frame for the assassination?"

"Oh, Leveman's," Lizbeth whispered. "Of course, and if everyone thinks pirates are suddenly a threat to the Universal government—"

"They'll be more than happy to let Jukin pick up every last one of us, or just shoot us on the spot."

"The five billion was just a down payment," Lizbeth said slowly. "It would fund the entire operation, pay off pirates, buy planets, just so they could get an even bigger payday after…" She closed her eyes and shook her head.

"We have to stop this," Razia said. "Seriously, we *have* to stop this."

"Lyssa!" Lizbeth said, grabbing her arm suddenly. "The election is *today.*"

"Yes, hence my concern."

"Llendo is going to give a speech from the presidential palace balcony," Lizbeth hissed. "After the election is called, his victory speech!"

"Shit, shit, shit, shit," Razia said, pulling Lizbeth down the street towards the nearest shuttle station. "And all that security, it's Wedekind's security. He's a sitting duck!"

"Really, Lyssa," Lizbeth said, stopping in the middle of the street.

"Do you really think your brother would go so far as to kill an innocent man just to finally be able to conquer piracy once and for all?"

Razia stopped in her tracks, realizing that she didn't know the answer. "We need to get downtown."

***

Night had descended on the presidential square, crammed with people buzzing with excitement at the unforeseen turn of events. Many of the partygoers were wearing Llendo's party colors and various silly hats and glasses in celebration of the president's re-election. The presidential square was even more crammed with people.

Razia wove through the crowd, ignoring the angry looks of people she pushed aside. Her eyes frantically scanned the crowd for something, *anything*, that seemed suspicious or out of place. All around her, smiles, laughter, no one who seemed like they were about to murder someone.

"They've already called it for Llendo!" Lizbeth yelled, her hand latched onto the back of Razia's shirt as they moved. "He's going to give a speech in half an hour!"

"Shit." Razia doubled her efforts to scan the crowds. "We don't have long to find our assassin."

Movement caught Razia's eye, drawing her gaze upward, to the stone wall that surrounded them. Guard patrolled the wall, black guns hanging by their sides. Even from this distance, she could see the telltale uniform of Secure Solutions.

"There's tons of them up there. Which is our guy?" Lizbeth asked.

"The one who's pointing the gun at the president," Razia growled out of frustration. "How in Leveman's do we get up there?"

"The clock tower!" Lizbeth said, grabbing her arm. "C'mon!"

As fast as the thick crowd would allow, they pushed and shoved their way towards the foot of the giant stone clock tower. When they approached the doors, Razia cursed again when she saw two of Secure Solutions' finest standing in front of the tall wooden doors leading to the stairs.

"Your way or my way," Lizbeth whispered over Razia's shoulder.

"Joint," Razia smiled. "You distract them, I'll knock them out."

"Love the way you think, baby," Lizbeth said, adjusting her shirt lower over her chest. Razia slipped around the other side, watching as Lizbeth stumbled up to the two guards like a drunk bimbo. When Razia saw them crack a smile, she knew she was in.

In the loudness of the crowd, nobody noticed when the two security guards fell down, knocked out by a brunette in a black tank top. Razia jammed her universal key into the door, unlocking it with a mighty heave. The door opened a crack and they slipped inside, the shut doors muffling the sounds of the crowd and the excitement. It was pitch black, save for the small light from above.

Razia waited for a moment, listening for footfalls. When she heard nothing but silence, she put her finger to her lips and began slowly climbing with Lizbeth in tow. Lizbeth wasn't kidding about the ramps—up half an incline, then turn a corner, up another incline, turn a corner, up an incline.

"How much longer until we reach the top?" Razia whispered.

"I don't know, I haven't been here since I was a kid," Lizbeth whispered back.

They turned a corner and saw an opening out to the palace walls. Shadows crossed in front of the light, signs of guards patrolling just beyond.

"We're going to have to go out there," Razia said, looking back to Lizbeth.

"Wait a minute," Lizbeth said, grabbing Razia's arm. "I don't think the guy is out there. The ramps keeps going to the clock tower." She pointed up. "If someone was going to shoot the president, they'd probably do it where no one could see them."

Razia hesitated, looking back out at the wall. "We only get one crack at this."

"Trust me," Lizbeth said, tugging her. They passed the doorway quickly before anyone saw them, but Razia got a dizzying view of the square and the crowd below before following Lizbeth higher into the top of the clock tower.

They stopped dead as a voice boomed over the loudspeakers.

"*Welcome supporters!*" The roar of the crowd swelled up in the tower and through the doorway beneath them.

"Oh shit, it's starting," Lizbeth hissed. "We have to *move!*"

Razia muttered something and began shuffling louder up the ramp, her footsteps hidden by the cheering sounds. She was sure they were nearing the top, but every corner she turned was just another ramp.

Suddenly, they turned the corner into a giant room, the light streaming through the clock face. For a brief, terrifying moment, Razia thought that Lizbeth was wrong, that the would-be assassin wasn't here, he was somewhere along the wall taking his aim.

And then she saw him, crouched against the clock-face, pointing one of Secure Solutions' guns through a hole in the clock. He was wearing the same gray suit, and once he let off his kill shot, he'd be able to just walk back down and blend into the crowd.

"Oi!" Razia bellowed, her voice echoing across the empty room. The man moved quickly, pulling a pistol out of his pants pocket and shooting. Lizbeth screamed and they dove in different directions. Razia crouched behind one of the dusty cogs, ducking as another volley of bullets came flying her way.

"Come on out, sweetie," he said, aiming the pistol. "They told me you might show up."

"Oh, good," Lizbeth called, ducking as more bullets came her way.

Razia looked to Lizbeth and motioned for her to keep talking.

"So, how much money is Harman paying you?" Lizbeth asked.

"More than you can even guess," he said.

Razia leapt to another protective cover as he shot at her again.

"I hope you already got your payment," Lizbeth said, smiling, "because you aren't going to get money. We've got enough proof to shut this whole thing down."

Razia dove behind a musty box, but this time the bullets didn't follow.

"Yeah, you're gonna have a hard time doing that when you're dead," he said.

"Honey, do you think we would be up here if we didn't have a ten-page report sitting in the director's office?" Lizbeth taunted.

"Really?" Razia said popping her head up. She ducked again as more bullets came whizzing by her head.

"Dammit, Razia!" Lizbeth hissed as the man laughed again.

"*Welcome and thank you! I just heard from General State, who very graciously conceded—*" A roar of cheers drowned out the rest of Llendo's words.

The man pointed the pistol at Lizbeth and pulled the trigger, but nothing came out but clicks. He was out of bullets. Razia burst out from her hiding spot and tackled him to the ground. She kicked and punched, but the man was solid, a former soldier.

His elbow connected with Razia's jaw and she went flying, seeing stars for a moment as she lay splayed on the ground.

"*Lyssa!*" Lizbeth screamed.

"'m fine," Razia grumbled, her head spinning. She saw the man crouch down against his other gun against the window, and tried to move her legs to get to him. But her head was spinning too much and she couldn't—

Out of the corner of her eyes, she saw Lizbeth running towards the man.

There was a crack of the gun, and a scream. More screams from the crowd below and for a brief, terrifying moment, Razia worried that they had failed. But then—

"*Hah!*" Lizbeth cried. "You missed!"

Razia, eyes watered from the pain in her head, jumped to her feet. To their surprise, the would-be assassin began laughing.

"Well that's just fine, ladies," he chuckled, wiping blood off his lip. "Dead or not, the effect is still the same. Because from what I can see, I got a pirate up here and a rogue agent. Looks like we won't need to frame nobody after all."

And with that, he took off running down the ramp.

"Aw...*shit!*" Razia screamed, taking off after the man.

"Wait, *Lyssa!*" Lizbeth cried.

Razia, still starry-eyed from the elbow to the head, slammed into the bottom of the ramp, sliding on the stones. The gray uniform disappeared around the corner and she pushed herself off the wall, grabbing the corner of the ramp to help her make the turns at quick speed. He slipped through the open door, and she put on a burst of speed, the full sound of the crowd and the height of the building crashing on top of her.

She swooned for a moment when she saw the distance to the ground, but her attention snapped to the one security guard running down the length of the wall. She narrowed her eyes and took off, flying as fast as her legs could carry her. The man was fast, but she wasn't a Deep Space Exploration scientist for nothing. She dug deep and pushed her legs harder, gaining speed until she was close enough to grab the back of his uniform.

He tried to deck her again, but she ducked, and punched him in the gut. He let out a loud breath of air, and she pivoted around, her knee connecting with his side. She whirled around again, but felt his hand clamp around her leg and flip.

She landed on the ground, and he leered over her. She froze, unsure of how she was going to get out of this one.

Lizbeth appeared out of nowhere, planted her feet, then punched the man in the gut, then slammed her elbow into the back of his head, effectively knocking him out.

"*I did it!*" she grinned, rubbing the back of her elbow gingerly.

"We're not out of the woods yet," Razia said, quickly getting to her feet. Just as the words left her mouth, she heard the telltale sounds of footfalls on the stone coming from both sides.

"*Hands up!*" Jukin's faithful lieutenant Opli was the closest, the gold flecks on his uniform gleaming angrily.

"Perfect." Razia sighed, putting her hands in the air.

***

"So, this could be worse…" Razia offered, leaning against the dank stone wall. They were in the basement of the presidential palace, presumably while chaos reigned upstairs. No one had questioned them, or even come down to talk with them, regardless of how much Lizbeth waved her shiny badge around.

"I am telling you, Lieutenant Opli, I am Lizbeth Carter," Lizbeth tried again with the obstinate young police officer. "I met with your boss over a month ago. Look, I have a badge and identification."

"And I also see you hanging around with a known pirate," Opli sneered with a nasty glance to Razia.

"Oh, get off your damned high horse," Lizbeth muttered. "You know I wasn't the one who fired the gun!"

"We found a rifle in the clock tower," Opli said, "and I'm sure it will have your fingerprints on it."

"Because I would be so stupid." Razia rolled her eyes. "If I was gonna shoot Llendo, I am damn well gonna wear gloves."

"*You aren't helping!*" Lizbeth hissed.

Opli smirked and sat back.

The door to the jail opened, and in walked the very last person either of them expected to see.

"*General State*!" Lizbeth cried against the jell cell.

Up close the General was formidable, but had a sort of grandfatherly feel to him. His uniform was a dark blue military dress uniform with an array of different colors on his chest. The moment he walked into the room, Opli was on his feet, staring sternly ahead with an almost over-enthusiastic stoicism. But his eyes weren't on State; they were on the other man who followed.

Jukin.

"Agent Carter," State said, looking at Lizbeth. "You have thirty seconds to convince me to let you out of this jail cell."

"McDougall was planning to use the assassination to generate trillions of credits in security contracts that he was going to steer to his company, Wedekind Planetary Services," Lizbeth recited, sounding as if she'd rehearsed that line for days.

General State's face was unreadable. "And you have proof?"

"Yes sir," Lizbeth nodded. "Razia and I do."

"Who is Razia?" State asked, turning his gaze to Razia. "You?"

"Yes sir," Lizbeth said when Razia didn't speak up. "She's been assisting me in the investigation all this time."

"You look familiar." Razia withered slightly under State's intense stare.

"Sir, she's...well, she's a bounty hunter," Lizbeth admitted. "You've probably seen her on wanted posters."

Jukin sniffed.

"Something to add, Peate?" State asked, his voice firm but not menacing.

"Just that if this agent hired a pirate, she's already in violation of the Piracy Act," Jukin said.

"What, do you want to hang her too without a trial, too?" State asked.

Razia wasn't sure if she wanted to glare at Jukin or kiss State.

"As for me, I still believe in the theory that all people are innocent until proven otherwise," State said. "So, Agent Carter, please explain."

"Thank you, sir," Lizbeth nodded. Jukin looked about ready to spit fire. "Six months ago, I began investigating a series of similar pirate hijackings. They were centered around the same area, and with the same company. My branch handles piracy-based insurance fraud," she added nervously.

State nodded.

"S-So…" Lizbeth swallowed and then pushed her shoulders back, as if it would give her some confidence. "After a few months of digging and trailing pirates, I centered the source of the conspiracy on two men—Alfr Jos and Krishna Harman."

"I know them well," State nodded with the smallest hint of a smile on his stoic face.

"Yes, well, maybe not as well as you think," Lizbeth said nervously. "They had called all of the most wanted pirates and the runners to a meeting, and told them to target government shipments near N-42653, N-38324, and S-4296."

"And I arrested them," Jukin interjected, "not three days ago, for that very same crime."

"Hah!" Razia barked, unable to resist a jab at him. "Did a bang up job, Jukin, as usual."

"Explain," State ordered.

"Based on their accounts in the Universal Bank," Razia said, more serious under State's piercing stare, "they're out on D-882…and not in the pirate jail."

"Oh sir, she's *lying*," Jukin growled.

"I can prove it, if you'd return my mini-computer to me," Razia said, holding out her hand.

"Lieutenant," State ordered simply.

"But sir," Opli stammered. "She's dangerous—"

"If she tosses it at my head, I'll be sure to duck," he said humorlessly.

Opli, still unsure, thrust the mini-computer into Razia's hand. She quickly searched the Universal Bank, praying to the Great Creator that Harman and Jos hadn't had their bank manager friend remove all the transactions.

Jos, Alfr		
Time of Transaction	Location	Amount
UT20015-04-19-32:89	Madame Guerri D-882	8,500C
UT20015-04-19-32:75	Madame Guerri D-882	25C
UT20015-04-19-32:61	Madame Guerri D-882	50C
UT20015-04-19-32:89	Madame Guerri D-882	25C

"See, look," Razia said, offering the mini-computer to the general. He took out a pair of reading glasses and scanned the screen.

"Appears as though your prisoners have escaped, Captain Peate," State replied, with a casual glance to Jukin. "Perhaps you accidentally incarcerated them in the wrong jail."

Jukin said nothing, but Razia saw a muscle twitch in his jaw.

"Please continue, Agent Carter," State said, sitting back down in the chair. "We know that the pirates were targeting those planets on orders from Jos and Harman."

"Yes," Lizbeth said, "but those weren't the only planets, and, if I were to make an educated guess, the others were just distracting from the real cargo movement."

"What cargo movement?" State asked.

"A company called Wedekind Planetary Services has purchased several planets near military bases," Lizbeth said, "including the planets that I've already mentioned, but also a few more. They purchased S-6642, which is near to one of the military's new arsenal hold on J-636.

"J-636 was one of the many planets included as part of a big contract," Lizbeth continued. "What I—we discovered, was that Wedekind was purchasing planets near military installations to re-route guns and other weapons to store until they were needed."

"Needed for what?"

Lizbeth swallowed. "After the president was assassinated, Wedekind would be first in line to get more of those security contracts that would presumably be offered in the aftermath."

"Sir, you don't believe them, do you?" Jukin spat. Razia noticed the panic behind his eyes; he knew just how deep their investigation had gone.

"Agent Carter, if you please," State said, holding up his hand to silence Jukin. "What does this have to do with Minister McDougall?"

"McDougall owns Wedekind," Lizbeth said, "or at least put up the original money to fund it. Five billion credits."

Razia's eyes swept over to Jukin as he turned a particularly nasty shade of green.

"And where did he come up with this huge sum of money?" State asked.

"Jukin," Lizbeth said quietly.

It was the first time that General State was surprised as he looked to his captain. Jukin's jaw was set in stone.

"And where did Jukin get this money?" State said, talking to Lizbeth but his attention on Jukin.

"He stole it from his sister," Lizbeth replied.

Razia's breath caught in her throat as she waited for Jukin's eyes to sweep over to her. But they didn't. In fact, they didn't seem to be even in the room anymore. He was staring at the ground, as if preparing himself for the inevitable, and Razia saw something familiar in him.

"Why would my very best police captain want to pay Minister McDougall five billion credits?" State asked.

"Because he needed someone to cover his ass when he killed Tauron Ball," Lizbeth said. "And the minister agreed to do it."

Razia thought she would feel a surge of hatred towards Jukin, but she found herself watching Jukin with a numb sort of observation. He looked like he knew everything he had worked so hard to attain was about to disappear. Once she and Lizbeth told State that Jukin was in on the assassination attempt, he would most assuredly be arrested, his career destroyed.

This was the moment she had been waiting for, wasn't it? From back in his office, to the train when he didn't recognize her. And for as much as she dreamed about it, somehow, it didn't feel half as good as she wanted it to.

Something about him, the defeated and familiar stare, it made her feel almost *sorry* for him.

"Ah," State nodded. "I wondered why John took such an interest in your young career, Captain."

"We believe that the deal extended farther than that," Lizbeth continued. "As part of the conspiracy—"

"Jukin didn't know about the assassination attempt," Razia said, cutting Lizbeth off. The latter shot the former a look of stunned surprise. And Jukin's eyes grew so large that they might fall out of his head.

"Oh?" State asked curiously.

"Jukin paid off the minister," Razia continued, and a part of her wondered what in Leveman's Vortex she was doing, "because he thought that if he could catch one pirate, the money and support would follow."

"I see," State nodded.

"We believe the minister acted on his own accord after he received the money," Razia finished.

State studied so intensely Razia that she was sure he knew her name was really Lyssandra Peate.

"Very well," State said, standing up. "Lieutenant, please release them."

Opli looked nervous about opening the cell doors, but was probably more nervous about defying a direct order from the highest commander. The cell doors swung open and Lizbeth bolted out as if she thought State would change his mind.

"Now, there's also the matter of Minister McDougall," State said. "Lieutenant, I would like to have a chat with him, please bring him down here to me."

"Y-yes sir." Opli nodded before sprinting out the door.

"Captain, you had better go with him, in case there is any trouble," State said.

"S-Sir," Jukin stepped forward, unsure of what to say.

"Is there a problem, Captain?" State asked.

"Are you sure that you...I mean, I..." Jukin stammered very uncharacteristically.

"I don't see any reason to throw you in here along with the minister," State said. "Unless you think the pirate is lying about your innocence."

Jukin's eyes met Razia's for brief moment and she found herself searching them for any sign of recognition. Nothing stared back at her but shock and confusion.

"No sir," he whispered, turning on his heel and disappearing out the door.

"Agent Carter, I would like a full debrief on my desk first thing in the morning," State said.

"Sir," Lizbeth said hesitantly. "Might I have an extension. My apartment was broken into and the majority of my information was stolen, it may take me—"

"Tomorrow morning," State said firmly.

"Y-yes sir," Lizbeth said. "Come on, Razia, we have a long night ahead of us."

"I would like a word with the pirate," State said, causing Razia to shrink down a little.

"Yes sir," Lizbeth nodded supportively to Razia and then disappeared out the door without another word.

Razia stood in the room alone with the old general, wondering how a seventy-year-old man was more intimidating than any pirate she'd ever faced. State continued his penetrating stare and she moved nervously from one foot to the other, uncomfortable to be the subject of his intensity.

Finally, he spoke. "I want to know why you lied about Jukin's involvement."

"I...I didn't lie," Razia stammered unconvincingly.

"You were on Tauron Ball's crew, were you not?"

Razia's eyes grew wide; nobody, save Sage and Harms, seemed to remember that about her.

"How did you...?"

"My dear, you are the only woman in the pirate web," State said.

"I would think it would be an insult to my intelligence to not recall your involvement, especially after you kidnapped the brother of one of my captains." He paused, tilting his head at her. "And yet, you just saved his career. A career, I might add, built on the idea that you and all of your fellow pirates deserve to swing from a noose."

"You don't agree?"

"I do not approve of his methods nor his results," State said with a disgusted look on his withered face. "In fact, if it wasn't for the political headwinds being so indecisive about piracy, I would have had him tried for murder three years ago."

Razia's heart jumped to her throat.

"I, personally, have never felt piracy to be anything other than a nuisance to multi-trillion dollar corporations," State said. "But Jukin, it seems, has a one-track mind. He seems to believe that the very existence of the pirate webs is an affront to his sense of righteousness. He is, obviously, willing to put his career on the line in the hope to completely eradicate it."

"I know," Razia replied quietly.

"Indeed, and you had the power to stop him completely. Yet, you chose to let him continue his vendetta," State replied, reflecting the same stern, piercing expression she'd seen on all his campaign posters. "I can't help but wonder why?"

Razia didn't answer him, because she was wondering the same thing.

CHAPTER EIGHTEEN

"Well, if it isn't the Universal Beings Union's favorite pirate!"

Razia grinned as she walked into Harms' bar, glowing his praise. Until she saw the shaggy blonde head sitting across from him.

"Yes, it's a wonder you have time for us little people, when you're being showered with adoration and media requests." Sage grinned as she slid into the booth next to him. "Your buddy's been all over the news lately."

"That's her job." Razia shrugged, sitting back. "I was simply helping out—you know, putting my extensive bounty hunting skills to use, uncovering one of the biggest government conspiracies in over three hundred years."

"And also cutting all twenty of the top pirates and their runners out of close to a billion credits," Harms interrupted, unable to keep the amused smile off of his face.

Razia's face fell; she'd completely forgotten that Jos and Harman had only paid a fraction of the money out to the pirates. Not only that, but because Jukin's part of the conspiracy remained under wraps, nobody knew how close they had all come to the brink of pirate extinction.

"How bad is it?" Razia winced.

"I'd go off and disappear to that place you tend to disappear to," Harms said. "Dissident, in fact, is nothing short of livid."

"Fantastic," Razia huffed, sitting back. She just couldn't win, could she?

"And you should be thanking Sage here," Harms said, tossing the other man a look. "From what I can tell, he saved your ass."

"Oh *God* in Leveman's Vortex, Teon," Razia bellowed, turning on him. "Just because I had a *little* freak-out during the space jump *doesn't* mean you had to tell *everyone* that—"

"He means about the Universal Bank thing," Sage interrupted her with a knowing grin. "You know, how we broke about a hundred pirate web rules?"

"But do tell about this space jump thing?" Harms cooed. "Did he jump out and *save* you?"

"What are you talking about?" Razia said to Sage, ignoring Harms.

"Dissident was *pissed* when he read you had broken into the archives," Sage said. "But I told him it was my idea, my plan, and he let it go."

"Of course, he let it go for *you*," Razia grumbled.

"Which is why I told him it was *my* idea," Sage said, "because he would have kicked your ass out otherwise."

Razia's face heated up and she tossed him a meek look.

"I'll take that as a thank you. Besides, if you're out of the web, who am I going to compete with?" Sage winked mischievously to Harms who was watching their interaction amusedly. "Whatdya say? I'll go hijack a ship worth four million credits, and you can go find the fourth most wanted pirate in the universe."

"Fine," Razia snapped back, whipping out her mini-computer to see who it was.

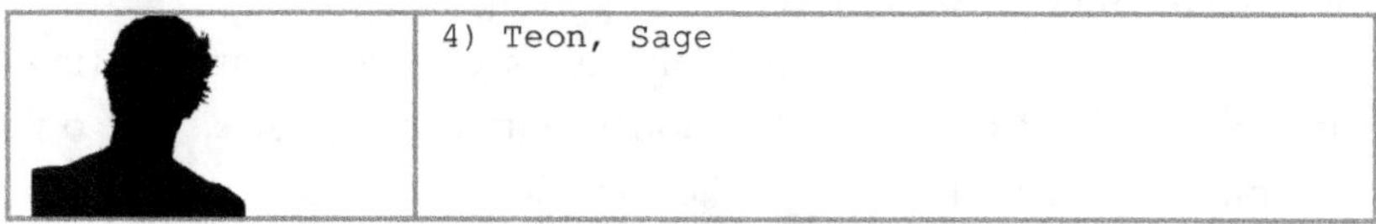

Wanted for	Engagement in piracy, grand theft larceny, bounty hunting, illegal sale of stolen goods, trespassing in the Universal Bank Archives
Reward	45,875,985C
Known Alias	Jamison Leon, Alfie Barney, Willem Gibson, Bennet James
Known Accomplices	Tauron Ball, Ganon Perter, Nalton Shone, Keal Wynn, Paren King, Jorwen Warren, Sobal Rider
Pirate Web Affiliation	Dissident

"Oh get *sucked*," Razia growled as he cackled happily beside her. "How in *Leveman's Vortex* are you number *four*?"

"What can I say?" Sage laughed, sitting back. "Breaking into the Universal Bank? Got everyone's attention—"

"*What in Leveman's?*" Razia screeched. "What, so you break a bunch of rules and they love you for it, but I save the entire damned system of government and everybody's *pissed* at me?"

"It was a lot of money," Harms said placatingly.

"It was *my* damned—*oof!*" Razia's rant was interrupted by an elbow to the side from Sage. She rubbed the spot gingerly, muttering her thanks to Sage, who shook his head at her.

"What?" Harms said, sensing that he had missed something.

"Nothing," Razia grumbled.

"That's two you owe me," Sage whispered, as he stood. "Well, I'd best be outta here. Being the fourth most wanted pirate in the universe…lots of pressure you know. Better go hide out until the attention dies down."

Razia glared at him as he strolled away whistling.

"It's a fake bounty, you know," Harms said, once he was out of earshot. "It'll be gone in a month probably."

"Bastard," Razia sniffed, sliding down lower. "Why's he gotta rile me up like that?"

"Really?" Harms raised his eyebrow at her. "You don't know?"

"Know what?" Razia mumbled, glaring after the direction Sage left.

"Speaking of lovers, what in Leveman's is going on with you and Relleck?" Harms asked.

Razia's face turned five shades of purple and her eyes widened to the size of saucers. What had that son of a bitch *told* everyone?!

"I..what…I mean… I don't know…" she stammered.

"It's funny, because *he* had the same reaction when I mentioned *your* name," Harms chuckled. "Fine, if you want to keep your illicit love affair a secret—"

"It wasn't—" Razia exclaimed before she clamped down on her mouth. After a few moments, she continued, "It wasn't anything. I was just…well…"—she blushed even redder—"I needed to get some information out of him and he wasn't cooperating. So I tried a different tactic."

She peeked up at Harms, anxious for his reaction. He rubbed his graying beard curiously and asked, "Did you get the information you wanted?"

"Basically, yeah."

"Then no harm, no foul," Harms said with a reassuring wink. "I just…you know, wouldn't go around using that tactic on everyone."

"No way," Razia blanched. After a second, she asked curiously, "So…he seemed…?"

"Seemed like I don't want to know anything about your dating life," Harms shook his head, and held up his hands. "I'm your pirate informer, you've got to go somewhere else for love advice."

A smile blossomed on Razia's face. "Yeah, I got that covered."

***

S-864, it turned out, was not all government buildings and skyscrapers. There was a small enclave of older buildings filled with trendy shops and cafes, and trendy-looking young men and women. But there was one trendy woman that Lyssa was searching for amongst the coffee shop tables.

She spotted the familiar mop of light brown curls and jogged over.

"Hey!" Lizbeth grinned, hopping to her feet and wrapping her arms around Lyssa. The latter had now become accustomed to this type of greeting, but still awkwardly returned the hug.

"You look good," Lyssa said. "Did you finally get a good night's sleep?"

Lizbeth didn't answer, but was intently studying Lyssa's face.

"What?" Lyssa said nervously.

"Checking your eyebrows." After a tense moment, she sat back, Lyssa's brows passing inspection. She finally got around to examining the rest of Lyssa and gave an appreciative nod. "Look at you, wearing actual clothes for once. Jeans and a cute shirt?"

"You told me I had to wear these," Lyssa replied, but with a hidden smile.

"And wearing some eyeliner to boot!" Lizbeth grinned before sitting back. "Speaking of drastic changes, thanks for the alternate identity."

"Are you getting rid of your apartment?"

"I'm not sure. With McDougall gone and all of his cronies getting swept up in the investigation, I'm hoping maybe I'll move back in once everything dies down. The commute from here sucks."

"So, are you in a hotel or something?"

"Nah, I'm staying with one of my girlfriends."

Lyssa stiffened, trying not to let the jealousy rise within her.

"Stop it," Lizbeth chided. "Merja's just an old friend from college. Don't be jealous."

Lyssa mumbled she wasn't jealous.

"Speaking of jealousy," Lizbeth asked. "Have you told Sage about Relleck?"

"I am not *seeing* him," Lyssa spat, turning purple.

"Good, because I don't approve of him for you."

"I don't know what in Leveman's it is," Lyssa admitted with a heavy sigh. "I don't want anyone to know that I'm even…interested in him. Bad enough that Dissident's angry at me for busting up his payday, but if he thought I was fraternizing with the enemy…" She shuddered at the thought.

"And that, my dear, is still a mystery to me," Lizbeth said. "Why didn't you tell State the truth about Jukin?"

Lyssa's mouth shut quickly.

"You could have not only put the man who killed Tauron in jail, but you would have been hailed a hero of the pirates."

"Yep," Lyssa nodded, having told herself the very same thing every single day since the election.

"But instead, Jukin's exonerated completely, although State's got a closer eye on him, and all the pirates are pissed at you."

"Because I just wanted something over him," Lyssa shrugged.

"Don't lie to me, Lyss."

"I'm not lying."

"*When* are you going to trust me?"

"Quit talking to Vel!" Lyssa barked.

"I didn't talk to Vel," Lizbeth replied sweetly. Lyssa gave her a doubtful look. "Okay, so we chatted at the Academy a few weeks back about you, and he told me about your trust issues."

"I'm going to *kill* that little asshole."

"Do you even know how many people care about you?" Lizbeth asked, smiling. "Me, Sage, Vel, Harms…yet you continue to push us away." She sighed and sat back. "Did you push Tauron away?"

Lyssa swallowed and remembered Vel's warning. "No."

"So why isn't your brother sitting in a jail cell right now?"

"Because…" Lyssa trailed off, staring at a leaf on the ground intensely. The truth had been staring at her in the face, ever since she laid eyes on Jukin back in his office, before he even said a word to her. "Because he reminded me of my father."

That was not what Lizbeth had been expecting. "How so?"

"My father was *obsessed* with Leveman's Vortex," Lyssa said, continuing to stare at the leaf. She closed her eyes and felt as if she were falling out of the ship again. "Because he discovered how to get past it without being pulverized. All the way to the Arch of Eron."

Lizbeth's eyes bugged out of her head. "*What?*"

"Yeah, it's all real, by the way, so, you know," Lyssa smirked, still not taking her eyes away from the leaf, "adjust accordingly. My father was trying to figure out how it all worked. He would bring all of his DSE equipment with him to take samples, but there's a strong magnetic field that would scramble everything five minutes after he'd turn it on. He would prepare for weeks, trying everything from encasing his tools in iron to using another magnet to reverse the polarity. Nothing he tried ever worked, and he would get so *frustrated*." She paused, taking a deep intake of breath. "And normally he would take his frustrations out on me."

"Did he hit you?" Lizbeth asked quietly.

"No, never physically." Lyssa shook her head. "But he did know how to cut me down."

Lizbeth nodded, but remained silent for Lyssa to continue.

"And when I saw Jukin," Lyssa said, her eyes still on that leaf on the ground, "when I saw that same frustration, the same *defeated* look on his face, he just reminded me so much of my father…

"I want to hate my father for what he did to me. I want to hate him for the way he spoke to me, for the way he left me on planets for days. I want to hate him for leaving me when I was eleven to fend for myself with my shitty siblings. But, I…well, I can't. And for whatever reason, I can't hate Jukin either." She paused, closing her eyes and chuckling at herself. "Good God in Leveman's Vortex, you must think I'm insane."

"No," Lizbeth said, reaching across the table to take her hand, "I think it proves to me that you're human."

Lyssa finally lifted her eyes to meet Lizbeth's and was surprised to find her warmly returning her gaze.

"Which is a good thing," Lizbeth said with a smirk. "Because I was actually kind of afraid you were a cyborg."

Laughter, real, honest laughter, erupted from Lyssa's chest. It felt like eons since she'd had a good laugh.

"You just wanted to protect him," Lizbeth said. "The same way Vel wants to protect you. The same way Sage jumped after you when he knew you were in trouble. No matter what you say, deep down, you still love your big brother."

Lyssa gave Lizbeth the most dubious look she could muster.

"Don't look at me like that," Lizbeth laughed. "I'm serious. And the fact that you put saving his ass above your own reputation…well." She reached across the table and grabbed Lyssa's hand. "I'm proud of you."

"Oh get sucked," Lyssa snapped. "I was just giving him a chance to do the right thing." General State's words about justice and unintended consequences came to mind again, and she did her best to shove them back down. She had hoped, perhaps that just as her father had, Jukin might see the error of his ways before he caused any serious damage.

And no sooner did she have that thought than two universal policemen appeared at their table.

Her heart leapt to her throat and she cast a nervous glance to Lizbeth. "Can I help you?" Lyssa asked, trying to sound normal.

"Your brother has ordered us to bring you in," the one on the left said.

"Oh?" Lyssa said, sizing Lizbeth up for a hostage.

"You've been on our radar for some time, but it's been hard to track you down," the one on the right said.

This was it. They'd finally caught her.

"And really, what has she done?" Lizbeth snapped at the officers.

She hoped Lizbeth would be able to read her mind and sense the desperation that was there. They would have to escape, Lyssa would become synonymous with Razia, and she'd have to come up with a new identity. Forget planet excavations, forget running around with Vel, it was a new life.

"From what we hear, she's significantly overdue on her annual physical."

And she'd have to come up with—

"Wait, what?" Lyssa gaped. "*Dorst* sent you?!"

"He put in a call to Captain Peate and asked us to specifically bring you in." The officer on the right grinned meanly and stopped forward to take her by the arm. "Captain Peate authorized us to use force if necessary. Recommended it, in fact."

"Oh, son of a… *Unhand me!*" she screamed as she was carted off between two Universal Police Special Forces Officers.

Lyssa's story continues in

CØNVICTIØN

Available Now

ALSØ BY THE AUTHØR

The Lexie Carrigan Chronicles

Lexie Carrigan thought she was weird enough until her family drops a bomb on her—she's magical. Now the girl who's never made waves is blowing up her nightstand and no one seems to want to help her. That is, until a kind gentleman shows up with all the answers. But Lexie finds out being magical is the least weird thing about her.

Spells and Sorcery is the first book in the Lexie Carrigan Chronicles, and is available now in eBook, Paperback, Audiobook, and Hardcover.

DEMON SPRING TRILOGY

Three years ago, Jack Grenard's wife was brutally murdered by demons. Now, along with his partner Cam Macarro, he's trying to rebuild his life in Atlanta. But on a routine investigation, they find a demon who saves instead of kills. They must discover who she is before Demon Spring, the quadrennial breach between the human world and demon realm, when all hell—literally—breaks loose.

The Demon Spring Trilogy is the first urban fantasy from S. Usher Evans and will be released in 2018 in eBook, Paperback, and Hardcover.

ALSØ BY THE AUTHØR

empath

Lauren Dailey is in break-up hell, but if you ask her she's doing just great. She hears a mysterious voice promising an easy escape from her problems and finds herself in a brand new world where she has the power to feel what others are feeling. Just one problem—there's a dragon in the mountains that happens to eat Empaths. And it might be the source of the mysterious voice tempting her deeper into her own darkness.

Empath is a stand-alone fantasy that is available now in eBook, Paperback, and Hardcover.

THE MADION WAR TRILOGY

He's a prince, she's a pilot, they're at war. But when they are marooned on a deserted island hundreds of miles from either nation, they must set aside their differences and work together if they want to survive.

The Madion War Trilogy is available in eBook, paperback, and hardcover. Download the first book, The Island, for free on all eBookstores.

ACKNØWLEDGEMENTS

As always, thank you, dear reader, for going with me on this adventure. As an indie author, I rely on my awesome folks like yourselves to help share the word about my work. Please consider leaving a review on Amazon, Goodreads, or any other fine book retailer. I am so excited to hear what you think—even if it's a short review. And don't forget to check out my other work below and subscribe to my newsletter to get all the latest info from yours truly.

This book would not be where it is today if it weren't for a couple key people:

To my B-39837, Bexter, you will always be the Dorcas to my Remus, and I am so incredibly thankful to have you in my life and your unwavering support to my writing.

To my B-583-78-2-7, Kristin, my very first reviewer and beta-reader extraordinaire: your help, support, and guidance mean the world to me, and I count myself blessed to call you my friend.

Thanks also go to Renee, my new author BFF, my baby cousin Alex, and my Momma for helping me get this book to where I want it and pointing out where I was making zero sense.

Extra special *major* thanks to Gina, my copy editor, for helping catch all of my stupid typos, and my not-so-stupid ones.

There's a million other people who conspired to give me the courage, confidence, and support to continue writing, but I don't have enough space in this book to name them all. Just know that I am humbled by the outpouring of support and love from all corners of this big world. I can only bow my head in gratitude, as there's no way I could ever repay it.

ABOUT THE AUTHOR

S. Usher Evans was born and raised in Pensacola, Florida. After a decade of fighting bureaucratic battles as an IT consultant in Washington, DC, she suffered a massive quarter-life-crisis. She decided fighting dragons was more fun than writing policy, so she moved back to Pensacola to write books full-time. She currently resides with her two dogs, Zoe and Mr. Biscuit, and frequently can be found plotting on the beach.

Visit S. Usher Evans online at:
http://www.susherevans.com/

Twitter: www.twitter.com/susherevans
Facebook: www.facebook.com/susherevans
Instagram: www.instagram.com/susherevans